THE PRICE

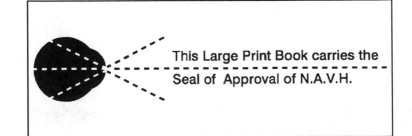

This Large Print Book carries the
Seal of Approval of N.A.V.H.

THE PRICE

KATHI MILLS-MACIAS

THORNDIKE PRESS

An imprint of Thomson Gale, a part of The Thomson Corporation

THOMSON

™

GALE

Detroit • New York • San Francisco • New Haven, Conn. • Waterville, Maine • London

THOMSON

GALE ™

LIBRARY OF CONGRESS CATALOGING-IN-PUBLICATION DATA

Mills-Macias, Kathi, 1948–
    The price / by Kathi Mills-Macias.
      p. cm. — (Thorndike press large print christian mystery)
    A Matthews and Matthews mystery, #2.
    ISBN-13: 978-0-7862-9520-3 (alk. paper)
    ISBN-10: 0-7862-9520-1 (alk. paper)
    1. Young women — Fiction. 2. School shootings — Fiction. 3. Large type books. I. Title.
    PS3563.I42319P75 2007
    813'.54—dc22
                                          2007002526

Published in 2007 by arrangement with Broadman & Holman Publishers.

Printed in the United States of America on permanent paper
10 9 8 7 6 5 4 3 2 1

To Yeshua, my faithful Lord and Savior;
To Al, my loving husband and
very best friend;
To Uncle Arnold and Aunt Carmen,
whose steadfast love and support
continue to be an example and
inspiration to us all;
And to all the students and families
whose lives have been forever changed
by school shootings.

ACKNOWLEDGMENTS

Many thanks and blessings to those whose faithful proofreading kept me on track:

Detective Doug Lane
Laurel West
Jane Hall
Shelly Macias
Mary Gramckow
Kacy Gramckow

And, of course, my husband, Al Macias, who was the first to read every word as it came "hot off the press" and to "speak the truth in love" to make this the best book possible.

CHAPTER 1

The cracking sound of gunfire exploded behind them, continuing for several seconds before Melissa and Carrie, en route to the auditorium with dozens of other students, realized there was a problem. As scattered screams joined the staccato barrage, Melissa stopped in her tracks and turned back toward the sound. Her wide green eyes took in the surrealistic scene even as its reality began to register in her brain. Teenagers — some of them her friends, others known only by sight — stood, for the most part frozen in fear and disbelief, while a few others bolted for the nearest exits. Then she saw him — the vaguely familiar face, terrifying in its calm resolve, the gloved hands holding the assault rifle in front of him as he fired into the crowd.

Suddenly, amid the escalating screams and gunfire, Melissa heard a moan. Willing herself to turn away from the horrifying drama unfolding in front of her, she looked down. There, lying at her feet, was Carrie, her skin so white it seemed grayish-green against the crimson pool spreading from beneath her twisted young body. It was then that Melissa's screams escaped from somewhere deep within as she fell to the floor beside the seemingly lifeless girl who had been her closest friend for as long as she could remember.

Less than one week before, as an early snowfall dusted the streets of their small town of River View in southwest Washington, Melissa had spent the Thanksgiving holiday — the first since her father's death — helping her older sister, Toni, prepare the sumptuous feast. The two sisters, along with Toni's romantic interest, police detective Abe Matthews, and an elderly friend named April Lippincott, who was visiting from Colorado, had joked and laughed and eaten until they swore they'd never eat again. Safe in her own home, Melissa had felt peaceful and secure and very, very loved, despite the recent traumas and tragedies of her young life. That her feelings of love and security could so abruptly be shattered in a matter of days never even entered her mind. She had, in fact, never felt more confident of

God's care and ultimate plan for her life.

The day had begun serenely enough, with both Toni and Melissa rising early to begin preparations for the meal. Melissa, peeking out the living room window to greet the day, had been the one to discover the unexpected snowfall, and she was thrilled.

"Toni," she called, clasping her soft flannel robe tightly to her chest as if to keep out the cold, "come look. It's snowing!"

Her older sister stepped up behind her, peering over her shoulder at the fat white flakes drifting down from the sky. "It sure is," she agreed, her enthusiasm only slightly more subdued than Melissa's. "Doesn't look like it'll stick, but how perfect to have our first snowfall of the season on Thanksgiving. Who knows? Maybe we'll get an inch or two on the ground before it's over."

Melissa nodded, fighting the urge to slip into a deep melancholy as she recalled the countless times she'd spent frolicking in the snow with her father. How she missed him! But she would not allow that sense of loss to ruin her day. She and Toni had a lot of work to do, and Mrs. Lippincott would undoubtedly be up and around any moment. Their dear friend was spending Thanksgiving away from her family, and she had suffered such a deep loss of her own

11

that Melissa felt it was up to her — and Toni, of course — to make this day a happy one for the elderly lady. On top of that, Abe Matthews was coming for dinner, and Melissa was sure that he and Toni would have an announcement to make very soon — at least she hoped they would.

Just a few months earlier, Melissa would have been devastated to think that Toni would marry anyone other than her high school sweetheart, Brad Anderson, but so much had happened since that time, and so much had changed. Now Melissa knew it was right for Toni and Abe to be together, and she was anxious for them to finalize their plans. Just last weekend she'd heard Abe teasing Toni and telling her that she might as well plan on marrying him someday so she wouldn't have to change the last name on her driver's license. Melissa smiled to herself. It was ironic that Abe and Toni already had the same last name and were both involved — to one extent or another — in detective work, Abe as a police detective, and Toni, the daughter of a private investigator. Although Toni had obtained her private investigator's license, she swore that was only to please her father. She claimed to have no intention of following in Paul Matthews's footsteps, wanting only to pursue a teaching career and maybe write a book or two someday. These were her self-proclaimed goals throughout her many years of schooling, right up until obtaining her master's degree the previous year. Then, of course, their father had died, and every-thing had changed. In an effort to get to the bottom of Paul Matthews's sudden death, Toni had instigated the investigation that had led to his murderers, as well as uncover-ing an international baby-selling ring. Since then, Toni had struggled with her decision about whether or not to sell the agency and had opted to limit her teaching to oc-casional substitute jobs for the time being, living on the money their father had left them. Secretly, Melissa hoped Toni and Abe might decide to team up professionally as well as personally and keep the agency go-ing.

Melissa turned to her sister. "What time do you expect Abe?" she asked, studying Toni's early morning face — the sky-blue eyes; the short, tousled, curly blonde hair, the naturally rosy complexion. Even without makeup, she was beautiful — for someone who was almost twenty-seven, that is. Melissa smiled to herself. She supposed that someday twenty-seven wouldn't seem so old to her, but right now — having just turned fifteen — it seemed ancient.

"He should be here by early afternoon," Toni answered, turning from the window. "I don't know about his Aunt Sophie though. Did I tell you we invited her? Abe even offered to drive to Centralia to pick her up, but she insisted she could drive herself, even though she said she had no intention of coming at all." Toni sighed. "I was hoping she would, but . . . well, you know how she feels about Abe right now. I just wish she'd reconsider. After all, he's all the family she's got left since Sol . . ." She caught herself and looked at Melissa, her eyes registering her regret. "Sorry. I shouldn't have brought that up. I know it's still pretty fresh for you."

Melissa shook her head. "It's OK, Sis. Really. I'm getting over it, slowly but surely."

Toni smiled and reached out to touch Melissa's cheek. "I know you are. It's just that . . . we've been through so much — so much loss, so much pain, so much change. Who ever would have thought we'd be spending this Thanksgiving without Dad, or that I'd be waiting for Abe to come to dinner instead of Brad? And a year ago we didn't even know April Lippincott. Now she's practically part of the family."

"Oh my, I did come in at the right time, didn't I?" Melissa and Toni jumped at the sound of April's voice. "I'm sorry, my dears. I didn't mean to startle you, but I knew you'd be up and around and beginning dinner preparations, so I thought I'd see what I could do to help. And now that I know I'm practically part of the family, I don't see how you can possibly turn down my offer."

The elderly lady's pale blue eyes sparkled with mischief as a gentle smile played on her lips. Unlike Toni and Melissa, who were still in their robes and pajamas, April was fully dressed, her silver hair swept softly up off her neck. Melissa thought she must be the most perfect grandmotherly type she'd ever seen. If only April hadn't lost her granddaughter in such a horrible way. . . .

Melissa closed her eyes as if to rid herself of any and all depressing thoughts or memories. This was a day of thanksgiving and celebration, and she was determined to enjoy it regardless of what had transpired in the last several months. She smiled as she remembered that even in the midst of the recent tragedy and turmoil God had lovingly revealed himself to her. Never again would she doubt his faithfulness or care. Things, after all, were looking up. The worst was behind them. From here on out, life would be positive and good.

The kitchen was warm and full of delicious smells as the three women bustled about, joking and laughing with one another. Toni, however, kept an anxious ear open for the doorbell, more excited than she would let on about Abe's imminent arrival. Only the night before, as they talked on the phone, Abe had hinted that he had something very special he wanted to ask her today. Her heart raced as she wondered what it might be. Dare she hope that this handsome detective was as serious about their relationship as she? Was it possible that he was going to propose to her before the day was over? If so, what would she say? In her heart she knew what her answer would be. She loved Abe Matthews with an all-consuming passion she'd never before imagined possible. But her logical, analytical, "detective's daughter" side warned her that it was much too soon to make such a serious commitment. After all, what was the rush? Wouldn't it be prudent to wait a few months, to see how the legal and moral ramifications of their recent personal lives were finalized? But even as she argued with herself in an effort to hold back the ever-growing flood of emotion she felt for this man, the doorbell rang. Her resolve melted as she forced herself to walk calmly toward the living room and entryway, only steps behind her younger sister, who raced for the door without any such thoughts of restraint or composure.

A gust of cold air assaulted them as Melissa yanked the door open, but Toni scarcely noticed. Her blue eyes were fixed on the tall, dark-haired man framed in the doorway, a few scattered snowflakes melting on the broad shoulders of his navy parka. His deep brown eyes seemed to dance with joy as he removed his gloves and put them in his pocket, then handed a bouquet of flowers to Melissa and dropped a kiss on the top of her head. "Happy Thanksgiving," he said, returning her hug with one arm, while balancing two remaining bouquets in the other. "Don't squash the flowers," he admonished her. "They're the only things your sister would allow me to bring to this event, even though I offered to do some of the cooking."

Toni laughed as he shifted his attention to her. "You call sticking a frozen pie in the oven cooking?" she asked. "I'm afraid that would never fly around here, detective."

Abe handed Toni a bouquet and grinned,

then slipped his free arm around her shoulders and pulled her close. "You mean, not all pies come out of the frozen-food section at the grocery store?" He kissed her lips lightly as she cradled her flowers and smiled up at him.

"Not hardly," she laughed, "especially not with April in charge of the baking."

"You're absolutely right about that," April announced, wiping her hands on a dish-towel as she walked in to join them.

"Ah, there she is," Abe said, releasing Toni and presenting April with the remaining bouquet. "Happy Thanksgiving. You know, April, I've already been greeted by two very attractive young ladies since I arrived, but I think you must be the most beautiful woman in this house — and that's really saying something!"

April's eyes sparkled as she received Abe's flowers and a friendly kiss on her cheek. "You're quite the charmer, Abe Matthews, but at my age I'll take any compliment I can get, so thank you. And I suppose if wrinkles are what you're looking for in a woman, then you're probably right — I am the most beautiful woman here." She sniffed her flowers, then looked up at Abe. "Thank you, Abe. Such a beautiful bouquet — and so thoughtful of you. How are you? It's truly good to see you again."

"It's good to see you, too, April. I'm fine, thank you."

April smiled, then glanced at Melissa and raised her eyebrows. "So, young lady, how about we gather these flowers together and find a vase or two to put them in — what do you say?" Her voice lowered a notch, taking on a conspiratorial tone. "Besides, if you and I go back into the kitchen, these two lovebirds will have a chance to say hello properly."

Melissa grinned. "Gotcha. Good plan." She reached for Toni's flowers, then followed April through the room, stopping in the doorway and turning back to give Toni and Abe an exaggerated wink before going into the kitchen. "Have fun," she called.

Toni shook her head, glad for the chance to be alone with Abe and happy to see her sister smiling and enjoying herself, in spite of the toll the past months had taken on her. Toni turned and looked up at Abe. His eyes shone with laughter and anticipation as he wrapped both arms around her and pulled her close. "I like the way they think," he said, kissing her fully this time, his lips lingering on hers and filling her with a warmth and sweetness that seemed to course through her entire body. Toni's eyes were closed as she pressed against the slight dampness of his parka and savored the moment. It was strange how Abe's presence and touch could generate such excitement within her yet at the same time fill her with such peace. It was a feeling she'd never experienced in her longtime relationship with her former high-school sweetheart and fiancé, Brad Anderson. True, she'd felt comfortable with Brad, having known him since they were children, but it had never been like this. Never. With Abe she felt as if she could stand in the middle of the living room floor with his strong arms holding her close and his warm lips on hers forever. A tremble coursed through her, and she sighed contentedly as he pulled back and looked down at her.

"You OK?" he asked.

Toni smiled. From the first day they'd met — not quite six months earlier — she'd thought Detective Abe Matthews had the most expressive eyes she'd ever seen. The concern she read in them now made her feel even more loved than when he'd been kissing her a moment earlier.

"I'm fine," she said, her voice husky. "Just glad to see you."

He held her gaze for a moment, then kissed her again. "Got a minute?" he asked.

"Or two, or three? I want to talk to you about something . . . important."

Toni raised her eyebrows. "Sure." She nodded toward the living room couch that faced the crackling fireplace. "In there OK?"

Abe glanced in the direction of the couch, then back at Toni. "I was thinking of somewhere a little more . . . private. How about going for a walk with me?"

The practical side of Toni kicked in then as she indicated the window with a nod of her head. "It's freezing out there," she said. "Are you sure you want to go for a walk?"

Abe smiled. "I'll keep you warm," he promised. "Come on. Get a jacket on, and let's go. Please?"

Toni's practicality melted, and she shook her head. "This could get to be a problem, Mr. Matthews. I can't seem to say no to you."

Abe raised his eyebrows, and his smile widened. "Now that's the best news I've heard in a while. I know I should tell you I won't take advantage of this new sense of power you've just handed me, but then again . . ."

His voice trailed off, and Toni forced herself to pull her eyes from his. "I'll be right back," she said, releasing herself from his embrace and turning toward the kitchen.

When she reached the doorway, she stopped, her back toward Abe, who still stood between the entryway and the living room. "Abe and I are going for a walk," she announced. "Will you two be OK till we get back?"

Almost in unison, the elderly lady and the teenaged girl turned their shining eyes on Toni. "What do you mean, will we be OK?" Melissa asked. "Don't you think we can handle things in the kitchen without you? Go on. Get out of here. Everything is under control."

"That's right, my dear," April agreed, her cheek smudged with flour and her lips spread in a broad smile. "You and your young man take all the time you need. Melissa and I are doing just fine. We've got the last pie baking in one oven, and the turkey's more than half done in the other. Now we're going to start on the salads, so you just go on and don't worry about us. We're fine."

"The last pie?" Toni asked. "How many pies are you making? And how many salads? There are only four of us — well, five if Abe's Aunt Sophie shows up, which I seriously doubt. How much food can we possibly eat?"

April lifted her apron and pretended to

shoo Toni out of the room. "Don't waste your time worrying about details," she admonished. "We'll take care of our end of things. You just go do what you need to do." She raised her eyebrows. "Something tells me this walk of yours may be a bit more important than how many pies or salads we have left over."

Toni shrugged in mock resignation. "OK, fine. You two have all the fun while I'm out walking in the freezing cold." She turned and headed back toward Abe, grinning widely. "Honestly, the sacrifices I make around this place."

Toni reached into the closet by the front door and grabbed her down parka along with a pair of boots. Abe helped her into the jacket, then watched approvingly as she changed from tennis shoes to boots and then pulled gloves from the jacket pocket and slipped them on.

"How do I look?" she asked, eyeing him questioningly.

"Warm," he answered, looking her up and down approvingly. "And very beautiful."

She smiled as Abe slipped back into his own gloves and then reached out and opened the front door. With his hand on her elbow, he guided her down the steps and out the walkway onto the sidewalk.

"Which way?" she asked as they stood together in front of the house.

Abe glanced both ways, then smiled. "How about the park? It's only a couple of blocks away."

"A couple? Try five or six, at least."

Abe smiled and shrugged. "Well, my math is off a little. So sue me, as my Uncle Sol used to say. . . ."

Abe's voice trailed off, and his smile faded. Toni, the recent loss of her father still fresh in her own mind, reached up and touched his cheek with her gloved hand. "You miss him, don't you?"

Abe nodded. "He was all the family I had left after Mom and Dad died . . . except for Aunt Sophie, of course."

"And now she's upset with you." Toni paused, then asked softly, "Do you think she'll show up?"

"I doubt it. The snow will be her excuse, I'm sure, but I don't think she would have come if the sun was shining and it was seventy-five degrees outside." His smile was forced. "I guess it's part of the price I have to pay, right?"

Toni nodded. "I suppose, but it's so sad."

Abe nodded. "Yes, it is. But sad is not what today is about, is it? So let's change the subject. Come on, let's get moving

24

before we freeze."

Her arm tucked inside his, they quickly covered the half-dozen blocks to the deserted park, keeping the conversation light and cheerful along the way, with Toni trying unsuccessfully to still the pounding of her heart as she anticipated what was coming. Suddenly Abe broke free and started to run. "I'll race you!" he called, heading for the empty swings swaying in the cold breeze.

Toni stared after him, her mouth open in amazement. Just when she thought they were headed for a romantic, serious discussion about the future, this unpredictable man threw her a curve and took off running like an exuberant child. It was one of the many things she loved about Abe Matthews.

Thankful she'd taken the time to change into her boots, Toni willed her semifrozen feet to move. Catching up to Abe, she plunked down into a swing next to his. They immediately linked hands, laughing as they gently began to swing back and forth a few inches by pushing with their toes through the soft white layer that was beginning to cover the hard ground beneath. Their breath taking shape in front of them as they talked, Toni found herself silently thanking God for bringing this strong but gentle man into her life, even though their relationship had been born out of such tragic loss for both of them.

"A penny for your thoughts," Abe said, interrupting her reverie.

"A penny?" Toni teased. "At today's prices it's going to take a lot more than a penny to get me to tell you anything."

Once again, Abe raised his eyebrows. "Oh, you think so, do you? Well, never let it be said that I came unprepared. In fact, I think I may have just the thing to loosen your lips and get you to confess your innermost thoughts. Now, if I could just remember where I put it. . . ." Standing up, Abe made a pretense of searching through all the pockets of his jacket and pants and coming up empty. Then, when it looked as if he were about to give up, his eyes began to glow mischievously as he unzipped his parka and reached down inside to his shirt pocket. "Ah," he said, "now I remember where I put it."

Toni's eyes grew wide as Abe pulled out a tiny white box, then gracefully knelt down in the snow beside her swing. With an almost imperceptible trembling of his hands and a light dusting of snow landing on his head as he looked up at her, Abe opened the box to reveal a shining diamond ring, a cluster of six delicate stones set in gold and nestled against a tiny swatch of blue velvet. Toni barely suppressed a gasp as he began to speak.

"This was my mother's," he said, his eyes as dark as coal and more serious than she'd ever seen them before, "and my grandmother's before that. But now I want you to have it. I love you, Toni Matthews, more than anything or anyone in this world. I think I've loved you since the first day we met, but I love you more with each day that passes. I can't imagine my life without you ever again. I know this is too soon, I know I should have waited . . . and I tried . . . but I just couldn't. Please, sweetheart, make me the happiest man in the world and tell me you'll marry me."

Toni swallowed. She wanted to laugh and cry and run and shout, "Yes, yes, of course I'll marry you!" But she felt frozen in place — not just because of the cold and the snow, but because her heart was pounding so hard she was afraid to move. Afraid she might wake up and find this had all been a dream, that she was still stuck in the nightmare of the previous months, trying to prove her father had been murdered, trying to enlist someone's help to track down the murderer, trying to resist her attraction to Abe and go through with her marriage to

Brad, trying to rescue Melissa from the kidnappers before . . .

She shook her head and swallowed again. She had to move, had to say something. Poor Abe was kneeling in the snow, holding out the ring, and waiting expectantly for her to respond, and there she sat, like a frightened child, on a motionless swing in the middle of an empty park on a cold and snowy Thanksgiving afternoon. Suddenly the ridiculousness of the entire situation struck her, and she began to giggle. Abe looked as if she'd slapped him. Obviously this was not the response he'd anticipated — or hoped for. She tried to talk but couldn't. Instead, she reached out and wrapped her arms around his neck, slid out of the swing onto his lap, and let him hold her as her laughter turned to tears of joy. When she nodded her answer, he joyfully removed the ring from its box and slipped it onto her finger. They sat together like that for several minutes before Abe said, "You're a strange one, Miss Matthews, but I love you anyway. I assume this is a yes?"

Toni had finally composed herself enough to speak. "Yes," she whispered. "Most definitely, yes, yes, yes." Then he kissed her, the cold and snow forgotten in the warmth of their embrace.

"Here they come!" Melissa had been sneaking out of the kitchen and peeking out the front window of the living room every few minutes since they left, watching for Abe and Toni's return. Now, at last, they were in sight.

"That's wonderful," said April, coming up behind her. "Now get away from that window before they see you. The turkey is almost ready to take out of the oven, and we can mash the potatoes soon. Let's get back in the kitchen and let them tell us their news — if there is any — in their own way and in their own time."

"What do you mean, 'if'?" Melissa was incredulous. "They're going to get married, I know it!"

"I imagine you're right, my dear," April agreed, gently pulling her away from the window. "Eventually. But we'll just have to wait and see what happens. For now, let's get back to work on that dinner."

By the time Abe and Toni had hung up their jackets, removed their boots, and made their way into the kitchen, April and Melissa were hard at work on the finishing touches of their holiday feast. "Oh, you're back,"

Melissa exclaimed, feigning surprise.

April smiled. "Did you have a nice walk?"

Abe and Toni looked at each other. "Wonderful," Toni murmured. Abe just gazed into her eyes and grinned. Melissa thought she would burst with excitement. *Wasn't anyone going to say anything?*

April cleared her throat. "Well," she said, "would someone like to set the table?"

Toni turned from Abe and looked straight at April and Melissa, but the dreamy look in her eyes made Melissa wonder if her sister even saw them standing there.

"Sure," Toni answered. "I'd be glad to."

"I'll help you," Abe offered, following Toni to the cupboard, where she handed him the good china, their hands lingering as they touched. April and Melissa exchanged looks, raising their eyebrows questioningly. Then Melissa saw it. She shrieked, and Toni jumped.

"What is it?" she demanded. "You scared me half to death. I almost dropped the dishes."

"A ring," Melissa cried. "I knew it! I knew it! You're getting married!"

Toni and Abe looked at each other and grinned, then Toni set the dishes on the counter and held out her hand to display the shining diamonds. "Yes," she said, "we are."

Abe, standing at Toni's side, put down his dishes and slipped his arm around her waist. "I proposed to your sister in the snow," he announced, "and she said yes. Can you believe it?"

Melissa ran to them and threw her arms around Toni and Abe simultaneously. "Of course, I can believe it," she said, laughing excitedly. "Why wouldn't she? You're perfect for each other!"

"I couldn't agree more," said April, coming up behind Melissa. "My congratulations to both of you."

Melissa stepped away to give April room to hug Toni and Abe. "So, when is the big event?" April asked, standing back to look at them. "I need to make my plans early, you know. This is one wedding I wouldn't miss for anything."

Abe and Toni looked at each other. "I don't know," Toni said. "We didn't really get that far."

"Tomorrow would be fine with me," said Abe, "but I have a feeling I may have to wait a little longer than that. What do you think, Toni? A week? Two? Three at the most, right?"

Toni grinned. "A little longer than that, I

think. We'll have to talk about it, look at the calendar, work out the details . . ."

Abe looked at Melissa and rolled his eyes. "Uh-oh. Here we go with details already. Something tells me I just gave up total control of my life."

Melissa laughed. "Count on it. Toni is a detail freak." She smiled happily at her older sister, then grabbed her left hand and studied the sparkling gems on her finger. "It's beautiful," she breathed. "Absolutely beautiful."

The tears came then, stinging Melissa's eyes as they threatened to overflow onto her cheeks. But she didn't mind. Life was good once again in spite of the losses of the past few months. She could hardly wait to get back to school the next week and tell her friends the wonderful news.

CHAPTER 2

Huddling facedown next to her fallen friend, her long auburn hair spilling over onto the floor, Melissa wondered if the gunfire would ever end. Then suddenly it stopped, almost as quickly as it had begun. The screams and the moans continued, however, along with the sounds of doors slamming and people running. Chaos and confusion enveloped Melissa, and the only rational thought that registered in her mind was, *Not Carrie too! Please, God, not Carrie. . . .*

It had been only six months since Melissa's father, Paul Matthews, had died. What everyone had assumed was a heart attack had instead turned out to be murder, and Toni and Melissa had been devastated by the gruesome revelation, particularly in light of the fact that the murder had been committed by one of Paul Matthews's most trusted friends, Dr. Bruce Jensen. It was Toni's investigative work — with the assistance of Detective Abe Matthews — that had uncovered the awful truth about Paul Matthews's death and exposed the baby-selling ring in which Dr. Jensen and Abe's late uncle, Sol Levitz, were involved. But the murder of Melissa's father and the betrayal by longtime family friend and physician, Dr. Jensen, weren't the only traumas the young girl had been forced to endure. In an effort to get Abe and Toni to back off the investigation into Paul Matthews's death, someone from the baby-selling ring had kidnapped Melissa and held her hostage for several days before a daring rescue by Abe and Toni, during which Abe's uncle was killed. Melissa had only recently begun to recover from the trauma and to come to a place where she felt safe and secure once again — and now this.

Melissa had no idea how long she'd been on the floor next to her friend — seconds, minutes . . . ? She knew only that Carrie was not moving. Melissa was sure she'd heard Carrie moan soon after the shooting had begun, but she'd heard nothing from her since. It amazed her that in the midst of all the noise and turmoil her own breathing seemed to echo in her ears. And although she was terrified for her friend, she hadn't yet experienced any fear for herself — not until she felt the hands grasp her arms from behind and gently but firmly lift her from her prone position. It was then that she began to scream, and she wondered if she'd ever be able to stop.

Abe and Toni sat across from each other at what used to be Paul Matthews's desk at Matthews and Matthews Detective Agency. Paul and Marilyn Matthews had opened the agency soon after their marriage, with Marilyn handling the administrative end of the business while Paul did all the fieldwork. Marilyn, however, had died of cancer when Toni was fourteen and Melissa was two. Paul Matthews had kept the agency going, hiring a secretary and retaining the Matthews and Matthews name in the hope that one or both of his daughters would someday join him in the business. Although Toni's original inclination upon learning of her father's death was to sell the agency, she was now rethinking the entire matter.

"So, what's the verdict?" Abe asked, grinning mischievously. "Are we going to try to keep this place running, or do we have to go out and look for real jobs?"

Toni smiled. It was obvious that this persistent detective who'd so captured her heart was not going to let her off easily. She knew exactly what he was talking about. They'd discussed it many times before — her dream of writing novels while working as a teacher and his return to the force once the baby-selling-ring trials and Abe's leave of absence were over, or working together and perpetuating the Matthews and Matthews Detective Agency started by her parents. Toni was putting off the inevitable — one way or the other — regarding the decision to liquidate or keep the agency. Why, she wasn't sure. She had, after all, completed her master's degree and was ready to forge ahead into full-time teaching, which had been her plan for years; but every time she thought she'd made up her mind, something else would come along to change it. At this particular moment, she was leaning toward selling the agency and getting on with life with as few complications as possible. So, what was the holdup?

"I need to make a decision, don't I?" she said, her voice soft with acceptance.

Abe nodded. "Yes. Either way, a decision will help us move on to the next step of our lives."

Toni grinned. "Meaning our wedding?"

"Absolutely. And all that goes with it. Where will we go on our honeymoon?

Where will we live? How many children will we have, and what will we name them?"

"Whoa! We haven't even picked a date yet, and already we're naming our children?"

"You want children, don't you?"

Toni's heart constricted. "Of course, I want to have children — our children. I can't imagine anything more wonderful."

Abe smiled and reached across the desk to take her hand. "So, how many? Ten? Fifteen? Twenty?"

"Very funny, detective. I'm afraid I was thinking more along the lines of two or three — four, tops."

Abe raised his dark eyebrows in an obvious expression of disappointment. "That's it? Four kids? No more?" He shook his head. "Well, all right, if you say so, but I have one condition."

"What's that?"

"They all have to look like you — beautiful little girls with sky-blue eyes and curly blonde hair."

Toni laughed. "No way, Mr. Matthews. We have to have at least one little boy with dark wavy hair and gorgeous brown eyes — Abe, Junior — so I can watch him grow up and become a handsome, strong man like his father."

Abe released her hand and stood up, walking around to her side of the desk and gently pulling her from the chair into his arms. Just as his lips touched hers and she felt herself melting into his embrace, the phone rang. She began to pull away and reach for the receiver, but Abe stopped her.

"Let it ring," he whispered. "Whoever it is will leave a message."

He was right, of course. Tuning out the phone, she returned fully to his embrace. However, when the ringing stopped and the answering machine clicked on, they both came to full attention as April Lippincott's anxious voice called their names.

"Toni? Abe? Are you there? Oh, please answer. Something awful has happened. A shooting at Melissa's school. Please, please pick up!"

Toni snatched up the receiver and pressed it to her ear. "April? What happened? What are you talking about? Is Melissa all right?"

"I have no idea," April answered, her voice quavering. "I was just watching television when the program was interrupted with a newsflash about a shooting at Melissa's school. It must have just happened — no details yet. But I can see dozens of police cars and ambulances behind the reporter. Do you want me to try calling the school or

the police? I thought I should call you first.
. . ."

"You did the right thing," Toni assured her. "Abe and I are on our way. You go ahead and call around and see what you can find out. I have my cell phone so you can call me, or I'll call you as soon as we know something."

She hung up the receiver and turned to Abe.

"What?" he said, grabbing Toni gently by the shoulders. "What happened to Melissa?"

Toni shook her head. "We don't know. April just saw on TV that there was a shooting at Melissa's school, but no one seems to know any details yet. It must have just happened."

"Let's go." Abe took her by the elbow and steered her out onto the sidewalk where his black, late-model Honda Accord was parked. "I'll drive," he announced, closing the door to Matthews and Matthews Detective Agency behind him. They were in the car and gone before either of them spoke another word.

April was frantic. She'd called everyone she could think of who might be able to shed some light on the tragic incident at Melissa's school but had learned nothing. Either she got a busy signal, or the person who answered had no more information than she did. Frustrated, she hung up the phone and went back to the TV, which she had left on while making her phone calls. Maybe the reporter had learned something new during that time.

Settling down on the sofa, the elderly lady grabbed the remote and turned up the volume. The on-scene reporter, a woman in her early to mid-thirties, wore a red wool blazer over a white blouse with navy blue pants. Her medium-length black hair tossed around her face and shoulders in the cool afternoon breeze. The dark, ominous clouds gathering behind her seemed almost prophetic.

". . . nothing definite from anyone inside the building at this point," the reporter was saying, her microphone gripped tightly in her right hand. "Police have cordoned off the area, keeping anxious parents waiting for news of their children. We understand that the few students and teachers who managed to escape when the shooting began are being kept together in a covered area near the cafeteria."

The camera cut to a shot of a closed building, presumably the cafeteria, but no students or teachers were visible. Police, however, were everywhere, and a growing throng of agitated parents and other relatives was pressing in as close as the police cordon would allow, some crying, some shouting, some praying, some just staring, straining for a glimpse of their loved ones. The reporter was angling for emotional input from distressed parents and had just isolated one distraught man for questioning when April spotted them.

Toni and Abe, their faces tense and anxious, pressed, along with the others, as close as they dared, questioning, interrogating, and pleading for information. April's heart went out to them. It had been such a short time since she'd lost her only grandchild, sixteen-year-old Julie, who'd been murdered by the same man who'd later kidnapped Melissa, only to be murdered himself by two of his cohorts. April was, in fact, staying with Toni and Melissa while the trials were underway, not only because she expected to be called as a witness for the prosecution, but also because she felt the need to be nearby — for Julie's sake — until the verdicts were reached. It was difficult being away from her daughter and son-in-law, particularly during the holidays, but being with Toni and Melissa had made the separation from her family a little easier.

And because Toni and Melissa, as well as Abe, had also experienced tragic personal losses at almost the same time she lost Julie, they'd all bonded immediately. Now, however, it looked as if another tragedy might be upon them.

April jumped when the phone rang. She knew it couldn't be Abe or Toni calling from a cell phone, as she could still see them on television jostling for position near the police cordon. She grabbed the receiver, a bit confused by the vaguely familiar voice on the other end.

"April? April Lippincott? This is Brad Anderson. I'm calling to see if Melissa is all right."

April frowned. *Brad Anderson?* She knew she should know the name, but somehow she just couldn't place it.

"I'm sorry," she stammered. "I . . ."

"That's all right, Mrs. Lippincott. This is Brad Anderson, Toni's former fiancé. We met a few months ago when Toni and I were still —"

"Of course," April interrupted. "Brad. I remember now. How are you?"

"I'm fine, but I just heard about the shooting at Melissa's school. Do you know if she's OK?"

April shook her head, then realized he

couldn't see her. "I . . . I don't know," she answered, her voice revealing her fear. "I'm afraid I don't know anything. I've tried and tried to call, but . . ."

"What about Toni? Is she there with you? Can I speak to her?"

"No. She and Abe are down at the school right now, trying to see what they can learn about Melissa. In fact, I saw them just a moment ago on television."

Brad paused, and April wondered if it was because she had mentioned Abe, who only recently had replaced Brad as Toni's fiancé. But it was too late to take back the words now and hardly the time to worry about Brad's feelings when Melissa's very life could be at stake.

"All right," Brad said. "I'll do some checking of my own and see what I can find out. I'll let you know if I come up with anything. Will you do the same?"

"Of course," April answered, "but where do I reach you?"

"I'm at the law office right now — I imagine the number is still in Toni's address book. Thank you, Mrs. Lippincott. I'll be praying."

April nodded. "As will I." She hung up the phone and slid to her knees, grateful that she, too, could turn to God, the only one who could bring something good out of such a terrifying situation.

Abe breathed deeply, knowing he had to stay calm for Toni's sake — and for Melissa's. They'd been at the school for almost fifteen minutes now but had only been able to glean minimal amounts of information. Because Abe was on a paid leave of absence from the River View Police Department, due to his indirect involvement with the baby-selling ring and the current trials of its masterminds, he didn't have his badge and couldn't use it to gain access to cordoned areas. However, he'd managed to find one of his friends from the force and gather a few details, including the fact that the reason for the almost immediate response by police was the presence of two officers within the school at the time of the shooting.

"It seems that some sort of assembly was scheduled to start just minutes after the shooting began," Abe had explained to Toni. "It was one of those anti-drug, anti-violence programs sponsored by our department, which is why two officers were in the building when all this went down. I'm assuming that's where most of what little information we have came from and why the authorities responded so quickly. When the shooting started, most of the kids were already in the auditorium or making their way toward it. It was the students still in the hallways, headed toward the assembly, who got hit by the shooter — or shooters. My buddy didn't say why, but the police seem to think, at least at this point, that only one gunman was involved. I don't know if he's been apprehended yet, and I couldn't find out anything about anyone who may have been shot. I'm sorry, sweetheart. That's the best I can do for right now."

Toni nodded, leaning her head against Abe's chest as he pulled her close. She felt so small and vulnerable in his arms. He wanted to protect her yet felt helpless to do so. The frustration was overwhelming. If only he could do something — anything — to resolve the situation, but all he could do at the moment was to stand there and hold her . . . and hope and pray for the best.

"Excuse me," someone was saying. "Are you the mother of one of the students here today? Can I speak with you for a moment?"

Abe and Toni turned to see a dark-haired woman with a microphone — obviously a reporter — directing her attention to a distraught woman standing next to them. The sobbing woman appeared dazed.

"Why?" she asked, her voice barely above a whisper. "Do you know something about my children? My sons? They're both in there — inside the school. Please, I just want to know —"

"I'm afraid I don't have any answers for you, at least not yet," the reporter said, a cameraman at her side. "Can you tell us your name and the names and ages of your children?"

"I —" The poor woman seemed at a loss to answer the simple questions, perplexed at why they were being asked. "Please," she repeated. "I just want to know if my boys are all right."

"I'm sure you do," the reporter agreed. "You must be beside yourself with worry over their safety. How exactly are you feeling, Mrs. . . . ?"

The unnamed woman stared, still appearing unable to grasp the situation or answer the questions coherently. Abe could stand it no longer.

"Leave her alone," he said to the reporter. "Can't you see she's upset, just like everyone else here today? Why don't you take that microphone of yours and go find some self-important city official to interview, someone who's looking for some public exposure before election day, and just leave these people alone."

The reporter's mouth dropped open, but only briefly. She quickly regained her composure and thrust the microphone in Abe's direction. "May I ask your name?" she said, glancing first at Abe and then at Toni. "Is this your wife? You seem a bit young to have a child here. Are you related in some way to one of the students at River View High?"

Toni opened her mouth as if to speak, but Abe interrupted her. "Look, lady, our age or relationship to any of these students is none of your business, OK? Just like what the rest of these people are feeling right now is none of your business either." His voice was rising and gaining momentum as the muscles in his jaws twitched furiously. "What is it with you people, anyway? You're like a school of piranha that smells fresh blood and goes in for the kill. Don't you have any compassion? Any decency? Is an exclusive so important that you'd sacrifice people's privacy and dignity to get it? Or are you just trying to kill time until you can find out the real gory stuff and air that?"

Toni laid her hand on Abe's arm. He was about to shake her off when he looked down and saw the expression on her face. She was hurting and scared, unable to deal with any added pressure or emotion. He realized then that he'd overreacted, but the reporter had just pushed the wrong buttons at the wrong time.

"Sorry, sweetheart," he said. "I didn't mean to make it worse." He looked back at the reporter, started to apologize, then changed his mind. Yes, he'd overreacted, but he hadn't said anything that wasn't true. Maybe this woman would take his words to heart and show a little sensitivity to these people. Putting an arm around Toni's shoulders, he said, "Come on. Let's get out of here and see if we can find somebody who knows something."

Leaving the red-faced reporter holding the microphone out in front of her, Abe and Toni inched their way through the crowd, back to where Abe had talked with his friend from the force. As they neared the spot where Abe had last seen him, he heard an almost inhuman wailing rising up from somewhere in the crowd, swelling to a crescendo of grief. "Please," a voice cried out between sobs, "please, won't someone tell us if our babies are dead or alive? Please!"

Abe shuddered, wondering if the voice had come from the mother of the sons — the one who'd been assaulted by the tactless reporter — or if it was another of the many mothers in the crowd, wailing over her inability to help her child and her frustration at not knowing where or how that child was. Either way, it tore at Abe's heart, and his hold on Toni's shoulders tightened as he pressed toward the spot where he hoped his friend would still be standing, possibly with something new to tell them.

How is it possible that such a thing could happen here? Abe wondered. In River View! It's not like this was some big metropolitan area with gangs and drive-by shootings. River View was a nice, quiet community, filled with families and churches and parks. . . .

And crime rings, he reminded himself. After all, hadn't he and Toni just uncovered one of the largest baby-selling rings in the world? And it had been based in River View, Washington. So why should he be shocked that something like a high school shooting should happen here as well?

He was shocked, though, just as were all these other people gathered around waiting for news of their children. That respected members of their community had been involved in something as despicable as black-market baby selling — not to mention kidnapping and murder — was one thing. But that one or more of their high schoolers would be involved in shooting other students was just too much to accept.

Then it hit him. Maybe it wasn't a student doing the shooting. He'd just assumed. . . . But what had he learned at the academy, as well as in his years of service on the force, about the folly of assuming? Suddenly he found himself hoping — as pointless as it seemed at the moment — that the shooter was not one of the students but rather some deranged adult who'd somehow gained access to the school and begun firing indiscriminately. He knew that if the shooter was an adult the pain and loss that both individual families and the community in general sustained this day wouldn't be lessened, but somehow just a shred of the innocence that most people associated with childhood would be protected.

"Is that your friend?" Toni asked, pointing to a uniformed policeman standing beside his open-doored police cruiser, a looming sentry stationed to help restrain the swelling crowd of nearly hysterical onlookers.

Abe followed the direction of Toni's pointing finger. He nodded. "Yes. Let's try to get to him and see if he can tell us anything new."

Before they could move, a frantic woman,

unknown to Abe, grabbed Toni's arm.

"Toni," she cried, her face tearstained and contorted with fear. "Toni Matthews! Thank God. Have you heard anything about Melissa or Carrie?"

"Mrs. Bosworth," Toni said, acknowledging the woman who still clung to her arm. "I'm sorry, I don't know anything about either of them. We're trying to find out all we can, but —"

"I know," Donna Bosworth moaned. "They won't tell us anything. It's driving me crazy! What are we going to do? We've got to do something. We can't just leave them in there. . . ."

Abe intervened as the woman's voice trailed off. "Mrs. Bosworth," he said, "I'm Abe Matthews, Toni's fiancé. I assume you're Carrie's mother?" When she nodded in the affirmative, Abe went on, his voice calm and reassuring. "I'm sure Carrie and Melissa are fine. Toni and I were just about to go talk to that police officer over there. He's a friend of mine, and if there's been any news in the last few minutes, he'll know about it. You just stay calm, and as soon as Toni and I talk with him, we'll come right back and tell you what he says. Would that be all right?"

The woman nodded again. "Oh, yes,

thank you," she said. "It would be wonderful if you could just find out something. . . ."

Abe and Toni broke away and finally managed to get through to Abe's friend, Officer Ted Malloy.

"Ted," Abe said. "Anything new since we last talked?"

The tall policeman's face was grim. "Actually, yes," he said. "But I'm afraid we've got both good news and bad news. The good news is, they got the shooter. The officers who were here to do the presentation at the assembly were able to pin him down. He's shot, but I don't know how seriously, and at least he's not shooting anyone else. The bad news is, several students and faculty members are down. The extent of their wounds — or if any of them are dead — we don't know yet."

Abe heard Toni gasp, and he pulled her close. "Do they know who it was? The shooter, I mean."

"We don't have a positive ID," Officer Malloy answered. "But unofficially — and this part stays between us — a couple of the students identified him as a former River View High student, some loser who couldn't cut it — a dropout who never made it to graduation. You know, got into the drug scene and all that. Said his name was

Blevins, I think. Tom Blevins. Ring a bell to you?"

Before Abe could answer, he felt Toni's body tense. Looking down at her, he saw the shock in her blue eyes. "It can't be," she whispered. "Not Tom Blevins. I know that boy. He . . . he's a problem child, yes, but . . . a killer? No way. It must be a mistake. It has to be!"

Abe looked back at his friend, who shrugged his shoulders. "Like I said, it's unofficial and not something we want any of those nosy reporters or a bunch of hysterical parents to get hold of, if you know what I mean. We've got enough problems with crowd control right now. We don't need a riot on our hands, and until we know something for sure, let's just pretend I never mentioned the name Tom Blevins."

Abe nodded. He'd never heard of the kid, but obviously Toni had. Regardless of what they learned about Melissa in the next few minutes or hours, he had a feeling that this situation was going to get very personal before it was over.

CHAPTER 3

April hadn't been praying for more than a couple of minutes when she became aware of Abe's voice. She opened her eyes and looked toward the TV in astonishment. There he was, jaws twitching and dark eyes blazing as he unleashed his fear and frustrations on the unsuspecting reporter, leaving her momentarily speechless as she clutched her microphone and blinked nervously. A quick shot of Toni, her anxious eyes fixed on Abe, completed the picture.

"Oh, Lord, help us!" April cried. "What are all those poor people going through? And those children inside . . . Oh Father, help them, please. . . ."

Her voice trailed off, and she could no longer speak. But even as she cried, she sensed that God was counting her tears and that he would somehow bring good out of the evil that had descended upon them.

■ ■ ■

Almost immediately after Abe and Toni had received their most recent update from Officer Malloy, a call came in on the policeman's car radio. By the time Abe's friend had finished his brief conversation, several ambulances had begun backing up to the school's main entrance. "Now that the suspect has been apprehended, they're going to start bringing out the wounded," the officer explained. "That's what my call was about. I still don't have any names for you, but you might want to get as close to the main entrance as you can. That's where they'll be bringing them out, so maybe you can see something from there."

Abe's jaw twitched once more, and he nodded, again taking a firm hold on Toni's shoulders and steering her through the crush of people in the direction of the waiting ambulances. Others in the crowd, having noticed the ambulances approaching the building, were also moving in that direction. Abe struggled to keep his hold on Toni and to press his way through without knocking anyone down. If they could just get close enough to see the faces of the wounded and to be sure that Melissa wasn't among them. . . .

Abe winced with guilt, then reminded himself that everyone else in the crowd was undoubtedly thinking the same thing: *Please, God, not my child!* If, however, several students and faculty members were down, as Ted Malloy had reported, then some of these people were not going to have their prayers answered — that is, not in the affirmative. It was as simple as that. Some mothers and fathers, grandmothers and grandfathers, aunts and uncles, brothers and sisters were going to recognize the face of a loved one being carried on a gurney to a waiting ambulance. Then the earnest bargaining and pleading with God for their lives would begin.

Through persistence, coupled with his sheer size and strength, Abe managed to maneuver himself and Toni to the front of the crowd and as near to the ambulances as they could get without crossing the police cordons. Members of the media, including the reporter they had encountered earlier, were there ahead of them. Abe and Toni watched in horror as the five most seriously wounded were brought out first. Of those five, they immediately recognized Carrie's deathly white face, her motionless body covered with a sheet. Melissa stumbled along beside her, sobbing hysterically and leaning against Valerie Myers, the assistant principal, as they made their way toward the open ambulance door.

The minute Toni spotted her younger sister, she broke free of Abe's restraining arm, ignored the police cordon, and rushed to Melissa's side. Abe was right behind her.

"Toni, wait . . ." But he knew it was no use trying to stop her. Others in the crowd were also breaking through, and Abe found himself wondering if Donna Bosworth had been close enough to catch a glimpse of her daughter. He glanced around but didn't see her. Should he look for her? He and Toni had promised to let her know if they learned anything new. But he couldn't leave Toni and Melissa. Still, he made a mental note to have Officer Malloy find Mrs. Bosworth and let her know about Carrie — not that they really knew anything definite at this point. It seemed the girl was still alive, but for how long? Melissa was up and walking, and thank God for that. But what about the others? How many wounded were there? And how serious were their injuries? Abe prayed fervently that none of those injuries were fatal.

Melissa had fallen into her older sister's arms the minute Toni spoke her name and placed her hands on her shoulders. As the two of them cried, Abe hovered beside them, watching the ambulance attendants load Carrie into the emergency vehicle. The doors closed, and the ambulance began to crawl through the crowd, sounding its siren in an almost pointless attempt to clear the way. The bloody scene was now beginning to make its way from the school to the emergency room of the local hospital. Abe wondered what awful news awaited them all once they finally got there.

April was horrified. When the camera had cut to the ambulances backed up to the school's main entrance with their doors open and waiting, the elderly woman held her breath, her eyes wide as the first gurneys were wheeled outside. And then she saw Melissa — sobbing and seemingly held up on her feet by a middle-aged woman with coffee-colored skin and dark hair pulled back into a bun at the nape of her neck, her lips pressed together in an obviously futile attempt to restrain the tears that trickled down her cheeks. The woman's charcoal gray suit seemed ominously appropriate in the gathering darkness of the sky just visible above the school's rooftop.

Suddenly Toni burst into the picture, taking Melissa into her arms. Abe stood beside them, his handsome face appearing pained but relieved at the sight of the two sisters clinging to one another and sobbing. A few others in the crowd were also being reunited with loved ones, some crying with joy at the sight of an unharmed child, others screaming and crying out to God for help as they accompanied a gurney to one of the waiting ambulances. In the midst of it all, the woman reporter's voice chattered excitedly at the recent developments, undoubtedly relieved to have something new to relate, yet careful to maintain a proper sense of horror over the almost unimaginable tragedy. April wondered how anyone, regardless of professionalism or training, could ever come to the point of being able to report such a gruesome scene without collapsing in tears.

Relieved that Melissa was all right, April's thoughts turned immediately to the injured students and faculty being loaded into the ambulances. Too many people were crowded around to see the faces of the wounded, but she knew from personal experience the pain and terror of wondering if a loved one would live or die. Her tears started afresh then as she pictured the beautiful face of her recently deceased granddaughter, and

59

she prayed that none of the wounded children from River View High would end up like Julie. April was grateful to know that her beloved grandchild was safe with God, but oh, how she missed her, and how she wished she could hold her just once more.

How long? she wondered. How long until she could see a young girl with blonde hair and blue eyes, or hear a laugh or a song, or smell a particular fragrance and not be crushed with grief? How long until she could admit to anyone that at times she was angry with God for allowing such a young and promising life to come to an end while she, long since widowed and retired, continued on with no verifiable purpose? And yet April knew that she couldn't change her feelings. She would simply have to trust that God already knew how she felt and that he loved her anyway, as he always had. She also had to believe that, even if she never received the answers to her questions in this life, she would someday stand in God's presence, and then it would all make sense. In the meantime the pain was excruciating — and scenes like the one unfolding on the screen in front of her made the reality of her granddaughter's brutal murder almost unbearable.

■ ■ ■ ■

Sophie Jacobson wept silently as she sat
before the television in her living room,
watching the grisly scene that was even now
being lived out less than an hour's drive
south of her modest home in Olympia,
Washington. A school shooting right in their
own quiet corner of the Pacific Northwest!
It had been bad enough to think that anyone, however deranged and for whatever
self-justified reasons, had actually begun firing on school-aged children. However, when
she saw her own nephew on the screen and
realized his personal involvement due to his
relationship with Toni Matthews and her
younger sister, Melissa, Sophie's shock had
turned to anguish.

Oh, Avraham, she cried silently. *First your
parents, then Sol, and now . . . Why? Why did
it have to happen like this? Is it because your
mother deserted* HaShem *and adopted the
ways of the* goyim? *Is that how all this began?
Or was there something else, something
much further back . . . ?*

Her sigh was jagged, like lightning slicing
through her chest. *Why, Avraham? Why did
you have to follow in your mother's footsteps?
Why couldn't you have walked in the ways of*

Avraham avinu, *after whom you were named? If only you would return to the Holy One, blessed be he, then he would return to you as he has promised. But you have turned away, not only from* Adonai, *but from your own people, from me. . . . Oh, Avraham, you are all the family I have left, and now I must count you as dead to me as well. Why, Avraham? Why?*

Despite the hospital staff's almost constant attempts to keep the noise at a manageable level, chaos reigned in the emergency room. Ambulances continued to arrive at the back door, unloading students and faculty members with varying degrees of injuries. Three, including Carrie Bosworth, were critical; others had injuries that were considered serious, while some were minor or superficial. But even those without life-threatening injuries seemed terrified, shell-shocked, or dazed. Few spoke coherently. The family members arriving in the waiting room were worse.

"I demand to see my child!"

"Is my baby all right?"

"Where is my daughter? I want to see her!"

"I'm here to take my son home. Where is he? When can he leave? Why can't I see him?

Is there something you're not telling me?"

Although the parents were taken to their injured children as soon as proper identification was made, the process took longer than most hysterical family members thought it should. Emergency medical personnel had been called in from all over southwest Washington. Some had been flown in; others were still en route. Those who had already arrived were scrubbing for surgery, hoping and praying there would be enough operating rooms to accommodate the seemingly endless number of broken and battered victims.

Toni sat between Abe and Melissa, knowing it would be quite a while before anyone would have time to take a look at her sister, who was shaken up but otherwise unharmed. Their primary concern at that point was Carrie. Donna Bosworth had only recently arrived and was immediately ushered into a tiny, curtain-drawn cubicle to sign consent forms and to see her daughter one last time before she was wheeled away into surgery. Mr. Bosworth, who had been out of town on business, had been notified of the tragedy and would be catching the first available flight home. Meanwhile, Toni was determined to wait at the hospital with Melissa until Carrie's operation was over.

She was also keeping an eye out for April, who would be arriving any moment.

As soon as Toni had called Mrs. Lippincott to fill her in on what was happening, including Carrie's condition, April had insisted on coming right down, even though Toni had tried to convince her otherwise. She couldn't imagine what possible good could come from one more person being added to the ranks of the frantic, grieving, and injured who already swelled the emergency room facilities to the breaking point, but she knew she could not dissuade April from coming. So they waited — for April to show up, for some sort of update from Mrs. Bosworth regarding Carrie's condition, for Mr. Bosworth to arrive from the airport, and for news of the others who had been injured in the brutal attack.

It was still hard to believe that anything like this could have happened. Each time a fresh wave of reality swept over Toni, she squeezed Melissa's hand a little tighter, thankful beyond words that her sister had made it out alive, but terrified to learn of those who had not.

By now it was widely rumored that at least one of the critically injured victims had died since arriving at the hospital. Abe, who had spoken to two of the uniformed police officers standing guard near the emergency room entrance, was unable to obtain confirmation of the rumor or any information on who the fatality — if indeed there was one — might be. Still, he had asked them to fill him in on any further information as they received it, and they had assured him they would do so. They had also given him one piece of news that had rocked Toni to her core.

"It's still unofficial," Abe had told her after speaking with them, "but they do believe Tom Blevins was the shooter and that he acted alone. He's been shot himself and is in surgery right now, but they think he'll make it. That's all they seemed to know about his situation, at least for now."

Tom Blevins. Toni thought of the times she had seen the young man over the years. He was a year or so older than Melissa and, Toni thought, immature for his age. She remembered that he often got into trouble at school, but never for anything malicious. His pranks were usually just that — attention-getting devices from a lonely boy with no friends and, as far as Toni knew, very little family life. Tom Blevins had struck her as a chronically low achiever, pathetic in his need for attention, a loner who desperately but futilely, sought acceptance and friendship. Never would she have thought of him as a menace, though, and certainly not someone capable of wreaking the kind of destruction that had engulfed River View High that day. Surely there was a mistake. Surely someone else was involved. Surely she hadn't so misread the boy. Yet the police seemed to believe otherwise.

"Toni." She felt Abe's hand on her arm, breaking into her thoughts even as he spoke her name. Looking up, she followed his nod and saw April Lippincott standing in the doorway, searching for them among the sea of faces. Toni waved until she caught April's attention. The elderly lady picked her way gingerly through the crowd, gratefully accepting Abe's vacated seat beside Toni.

"I'll be right back," Abe assured them after he'd stood up. "I'm going to go see if I can dig up anything new."

Toni nodded, hugging April, who then reached across her and squeezed Melissa's hand. "Oh, my dear," she exclaimed, "I'm so thankful you're all right. When I saw you on television, walking toward the ambulance . . ." Her voice trailed off, and she shook her head, turning her attention back to Toni. "What a terrible tragedy this is. How could this happen? Do you know anything more about the injured? How is Carrie? Is her mother here?"

Toni gave her a brief rundown on what they knew, explaining that they were waiting for news from Mrs. Bosworth, who had gone to see Carrie and to sign the necessary papers. "I would think she'll wait out Carrie's operation in the waiting area near the operating rooms, but she did promise to come and fill us in as soon as she could," Toni said. "If they'll let us, we'll go and wait with her, at least until her husband arrives."

Melissa agreed, her voice shaky but resolute. "I'm not going anywhere until I know Carrie is all right."

Toni turned and looked at her younger sister. Melissa's green eyes and long, dark lashes seemed perpetually wet as an unending stream of tears trickled down her blotched and puffy face.

"She will be all right, won't she, Toni?" Melissa's question was more of a plea. "I mean, they're going to do the operation and then she'll be fine, right?"

Toni's heart constricted. She wanted to reassure Melissa, but she couldn't lie to her. From what little information Abe had been able to glean about Carrie's condition, it sounded very serious, possibly even life-threatening. If there was one truth Toni had come to know through the years, it was that there are no guarantees when it comes to life and death. The loss of both of their parents when Toni and Melissa were so young attested to that fact. Still, she had to say something to encourage the traumatized teenager.

Toni pulled Melissa to her, gently stroking her long auburn hair. "Don't worry, Melissa. We'll just keep on praying, and God will take care of Carrie. You'll see."

"That's right, dear," April agreed. "We must keep praying — for Carrie and for all the victims."

"I know," Melissa answered, her voice shaking as she pulled back and looked from Toni to April and then back again. "I'm trying. Really, I am. Sometimes it's just hard to know what to say."

April smiled. "I know exactly what you mean. But you know something? I don't think God is that concerned about what we say, only that it comes from our hearts. Sometimes even our tears are a prayer."

Melissa's smile was tentative. "Thanks. I think I needed to hear that. And I also need to remember how God took care of me and brought me back home safely when . . . when I was . . . kidnapped."

Toni closed her eyes. Melissa was right.

That was exactly what they needed to focus on right now. God had only recently brought them through some of the worst trials they'd ever faced. He certainly wasn't going to abandon them now.

"Toni?"

She looked up and saw Abe standing over them. Her heart skipped a beat, and she felt almost guilty for having such a positive response to his presence in the midst of such tragedy. She released Melissa and stood to face Abe. "What did you find out? Anything new?"

Abe's eyes were clouded, the tone of his voice guarded. "Yes. A little, anyway." He glanced briefly at April and Melissa, then looked back at Toni. "Can we walk a minute?"

"What is it?" Toni asked as soon as they had reached the front doors.

Abe didn't answer right away. As they stepped outside into the brisk, late-afternoon air, he pulled her close. "A teacher is dead," he said, his voice still low. "That's the only fatality at this point. The principal is injured too — how seriously, I don't know. Besides Carrie — and Tom Blevins, of course — two others are seriously injured, both students. But Carrie seems to be the worst."

Toni caught her breath. *Dead? A teacher was dead? Oh, dear God . . .*

A cold wind blew against them as they huddled together on the hospital steps — Toni trying to hold back the tears, trying to be strong for Melissa, trying not to fall apart completely. She clung more tightly to Abe, grateful for his arms holding her up, stunned by his words. *Carrie, the most seriously injured. . . .* Carrie — the sweet, quiet, dark-haired little girl who had been Melissa's best friend since kindergarten. Carrie Bosworth, her parents' only child . . .

Abe was speaking to her again. What was he saying? Something about going back inside, that he had seen Donna Bosworth through the glass doors . . . Toni released herself from Abe's embrace and allowed him to walk her back inside to the waiting room, over to where Carrie's mother had just approached April and Melissa. The elderly lady and the teenager stood to greet her, but no one seemed able to speak. Toni and Abe walked up to them, and Toni reached out and laid her hand on Donna's arm. The woman was trembling.

Mrs. Bosworth turned to Toni, her face chalky white, her gray eyes wide with fear. "Oh, Toni," she whispered, wringing her hands, "what are we going to do? What's going to happen to my daughter?"

Toni, instinctively trying to calm the poor woman, took her hands and held them tightly in her own. "What is it, Mrs. Bosworth? What did the doctors say about Carrie? How is she?"

The middle-aged mother, who seemed to have aged ten years in a matter of hours, opened her mouth to speak. Her voice cracked. "She . . . might not make it." The tears were coursing down her cheeks now, and dark streaks of mascara were beginning to run as well. "And even if she does . . ." She stopped, and her body shook violently. "Even if she does," she continued, her voice barely above a whisper, "she might never walk again. A bullet has lodged in her spinal cord. Right now she has no feeling from her waist down, but they won't know how serious it is until they do the surgery. If the cord is severed . . ."

The sobbing woman fell into Toni's arms. Toni glanced at Melissa. The young girl had heard every word, and her green eyes stared in disbelief as she slowly rose from her chair. Abe and April stationed themselves on either side of the grief-stricken teenager, who seemed too dazed to utter a sound.

As darkness began to fall outside River View Memorial Hospital, eerily snaking its way inside and wrapping its tendrils around the waiting room's already terrified and beleaguered inhabitants, Toni realized it would be a very long night.

CHAPTER 4

In spite of the cloudless, windless day, Melissa shivered in the mid-December air. Bundled in her dark green, down-filled parka, she'd removed her gloves so she could write in her journal, as she often did, particularly when she visited the cemetery. She sat cross-legged, leaning against the stately pine tree that overshadowed her parents' graves, wondering if she would ever stop aching inside.

It was noon on Saturday, just over three weeks since they'd celebrated Thanksgiving, as well as Abe and Toni's engagement. Melissa had come to believe that the worst was finally behind them, that God was indeed watching over and blessing them, and that he would, in time, mend their broken hearts. Now, exactly nineteen days since her sense of peace and security had been shattered by an assassin's bullets, her newfound faith was beginning to waver, and she found herself wondering if God really cared for her at all.

I don't want to think that way, God, she prayed silently, closing her eyes and laying down her pen. *Truly I don't! I know it seems so ungrateful, especially after you protected and rescued me when I was . . . kidnapped.* She shuddered at the still fresh memory. *But . . . but how could you let something like this happen to Carrie? I've already lost my dad, I hardly remember my mom, and now my best friend might spend the rest of her life in a wheelchair. Why, God? I thought you were supposed to have a plan for our lives, a good plan — especially for people who love you. And I know Carrie loves you. I know she does! Her faith is so much stronger than mine, and she's helped me with my own doubts so many times. I just don't understand. Why her, God? Why Carrie?*

The lonesome wail of a freighters' foghorn making its way down the nearby Columbia River was her only answer. She sighed, opened her eyes, and began to write.

I miss you, Dad. More today than ever, I think. If only I had you to talk to! Maybe you could help me make some sense of all this. I just feel so alone right now. I know I have Toni, but . . . she's engaged to Abe, and they have so much going on in their own lives. And poor

April, trying to get through these awful trials of the people who killed her granddaughter. . . . I don't even want to think of my part in the trials. I know I'll be called to testify, but . . . She swallowed, then continued to write. *I'm just not ready to think about that yet, Dad. Not yet . . . and I also know that Toni and Abe and April all mean well, trying to cheer me up and include me in the things they do, but . . . it's just not the same. It's like I've lost two best friends — first you, and now Carrie, even though she's not dead, but still . . .*

The tears burned behind her eyelids, blurring her vision until she had to lay down her pen once more. She sighed and leaned her head back against the rough tree trunk, letting the tears flow freely down her cheeks. The picture of Carrie in her wheelchair, pale and thin and trying to smile as her father wheeled her down the hospital walkway to the waiting car, was too vivid to dismiss.

Two days earlier Carrie had been released to go home. Melissa and Toni had been at the hospital to help escort her out the door, and they'd done their best to maintain a positive and upbeat attitude. However, the moment Carrie was loaded into the family car and driven away, Melissa had broken into sobs, collapsing into Toni's arms as she voiced the questions that now seemed to echo through her mind day and night: *Why? Why Carrie? Why the wheelchair? Why the shooting? Why River View High? Why that day, in that particular spot in the hallway? And why Tom Blevins?* There seemed to be no end to the whys; nor were there any satisfactory answers. She recalled reviewing those same questions the day of the memorial service for the slain teacher, only a couple of weeks earlier. It seemed that the entire community had turned out for the event; yet what Melissa had hoped would be a time of healing simply intensified her confusion.

Melissa jumped at the unexpected sound of her name. She hadn't heard anyone approaching, but she looked up and there stood Brad Anderson, Toni's former fiancé and a family friend for as long as Melissa could remember. A shock of sandy blond hair fell across Brad's forehead, and his hazel eyes were warm with concern. "Are you all right?" His voice was gentle, familiar in a way that comforted and calmed her. She nodded.

"Yes. I'm fine. I . . ." She stopped. Why was she lying to Brad? She'd known him all her life and trusted him implicitly. "No. I'm not fine. I'm sad and scared and confused. Most of all I just feel so . . . alone."

Brad didn't answer. He simply sat down beside her and took her hand in his, supplying the wordless companionship she so desperately needed. Suddenly the silence didn't seem so overwhelming, or God so far away. Maybe somehow, someday, she would find her way out of the darkness and back into the light, but she knew she could never do it alone.

"Barukh atah Adonai Elohenu melekh ha-olam. . . ." As Sophie Jacobson recited the familiar prayer and lit the *shamash* candle on this sixth day of Hanukkah, a flicker of something vaguely familiar yet totally unknown to her stopped her hand. She frowned, puzzled at the tug of memory toward something she could not identify. Was it something as simple as déjà vu? Or could it be that *HaShem* himself, blessed be he, was speaking to her?

She shook her head. Impossible. Her imagination was just running away with her. After all, why should she be surprised that the traditional lighting of the Hanukkah candles whispered of familiarity? She'd been lighting them every year at this time throughout her entire life. Yet, there was something different this time, a blending of something both new and ancient in the message of the tall center candle — the *sha-mash,* or servant candle — bending down to give its light to the shorter candles on each side of the menorah. Surely Hanuk-kah's message — that of God's intervention to save and bring eternal light to his people — could not change, for God himself did not change.

Sophie sighed abruptly and shook her head again, purposely blocking out the questions as she continued with the age-old ceremony and its recited prayers of praise to *Adonai,* the God of her fathers from the time of the great patriarch *Avraham.* If the Almighty wanted to tell her something different from what she had already learned through her seventy-three years of diligently practicing her faith, he was going to have to be a lot more specific.

With only ten days left until Christmas, Toni had finally agreed to go to the mall with April and do some shopping. Unlike most females she knew, Toni was not a shopper. Melissa had insisted it was a serious character fault, so serious, in fact, that she should consider getting counseling to help her overcome it. Toni always smiled and ignored her younger sister's teasing on the subject, but sometimes she wondered if there was at least a little truth in it. Even under the best of circumstances, shopping seemed to her a pointless pastime. Now, in the aftermath of her father's death and the school shootings, it was more difficult than ever to convince herself to spend time at what she considered a frivolous pursuit.

Yet, it was Christmas. Toni knew Melissa needed as much normalcy as possible in her life right now, and that wasn't easy to come by with the media constantly keeping the drama of the last few weeks in front of everyone's eyes. Media notwithstanding, Toni was determined to make the best of the holidays, especially for Melissa's sake. Their father had always made a big deal of shopping for just the right gift for each of his daughters — not to mention the hours he spent picking out the perfect tree and getting it set up in the living room so they could all spend an evening in front of a crackling fireplace hanging decorations and enjoying each other's company. Remembering those special times together, Toni had finally decided that she'd do her best to replicate the event for her sister. In addition, she knew April needed to be able to do some shopping so she would have gifts for her daughter and son-in-law when she flew home to Colorado for the holidays. She would be leaving in two days, so it was now or never.

"OK, we're off," Toni announced, backing out of the driveway. "I just wish we had a better day for our outing."

The rain was coming down in sheets, blown about by an angry north wind that seemed to vent its fury on anyone foolish enough to think an umbrella would keep them from getting wet. Toni was sure the umbrella April had brought along would be blown inside out between the car and the mall, but they would just have to manage.

April laughed. "Don't worry about it, my dear. I've been wet before. And who knows? We just might have a good time — weather, crowds, and all."

Toni groaned silently. Even though it was a weekday, she knew April was right. The weather wasn't the only negative element they would be facing. The closer it got to Christmas, the more frantic last-minute shoppers invaded the mall. And because of her procrastination, she and April were now doomed to be a part of it.

"I don't know about having a good time," she said. "Right now I'd settle for surviving and getting home in one piece."

April chuckled again, but Toni recognized the pain, even in her laughter. It was no wonder she and Melissa had bonded so quickly with the bereaved grandmother. They had all been through so much in the last year. Dare she hope that the year to come would be different?

Toni immediately thought of Abe and the joy she'd experienced when he'd asked her to be his wife. Had it truly been less than a month since that snowy afternoon at the park when life had finally seemed full of promise once again? How grateful she was for the strong, handsome detective who had only recently but totally captured her heart. She prayed that nothing would happen to interfere with their plans. Marrying Abe was the bright spot in her future, and she couldn't bear to think of life without him.

Her thoughts shifted to what things had been like only one year earlier. Finishing her last year of school, she'd looked forward to graduation and then teaching, as well as marriage to her high school sweetheart, Brad Anderson. Life seemed certain; everything was falling into place exactly as she'd planned. Then her father had been murdered, and nothing had been the same since.

"A penny for your thoughts," April said, interrupting Toni's reverie. She started, almost having forgotten for a moment where she was.

"Oh, I was just thinking about how much has changed since this time last year," she answered, glancing at April with a sad smile. "For all of us."

April nodded. "Julie hadn't yet run away, I was still in Colorado, your father was here with you and Melissa, and you were still in school and engaged to marry Brad. Not to mention the shootings, Carrie's paralysis, the death of a teacher. . . . Life does have a way of throwing us some curves at times, doesn't it?"

"Curves I could handle," Toni answered. "It's the crushing blows that are a bit much, especially when they seem to come one right after the other."

April reached over and patted Toni's shoulder. "Just remember, my dear, God is still in control. I remind myself of that daily. No matter how things may appear, none of this has caught him by surprise. That doesn't mean that violence and death don't grieve him. They do, of course. But he will still bring good out of it all somehow."

Toni nodded again. "I know you're right, truly I do. But sometimes it all just seems so overwhelming."

"Try to concentrate on the positive, my dear. In the midst of all this pain and loss, you have found the love of your life. Some people never do, you know."

Toni thought again of her broken engagement to Brad, of what a sweet and gentle man he was, and yet how grateful she was that she hadn't gone through with her plans to marry him. If she had, she might have led a pleasant and quiet life, but she'd never have known the joy of loving someone so completely as she did with Abe. If she was sure of nothing else in these turbulent times, she knew without a doubt that Abe was the one man created by God to be her husband. With that in mind, the shopping trip took on a slightly brighter hue as she wondered what very special gift she might buy for this man she loved so dearly.

The rain had let up only slightly as they pulled into the mall and began to cruise around searching for a vacant parking place. "How about if I let you out by the entrance?" Toni offered. "I'll go find a spot and meet you inside. It looks like I might have to park pretty far away."

"Don't bother, my dear," April answered. "As I said, I've been wet before. A little rain doesn't bother me, and I love to walk, so just keep driving and looking. I'm sure we'll find something."

Just then Toni slammed on her brakes and laid on her horn as a careless driver backed into their path without looking. The woman jerked her head around in apparent amazement to find someone blocking her way. Toni's immediate irritation melted as she realized the near accident hadn't been intentional. Besides, they now had a parking space.

Once the woman backed out and Toni's red Ford Taurus was safely parked in the recently vacated space, they gathered up their purses and April's umbrella, ready to make a run for it. Despite Toni's misgivings, April's umbrella survived the dash from the car to the mall, and they were soon warm and dry inside, dodging harried shoppers and whining children as they made their way from one store to another.

It didn't take April long to pick out the perfect gift for her daughter and son-in-law. She spotted it in a window at The Treasure Trove, an antique store that she claimed made her nostalgic. "Especially this time of year," she'd confessed, "when I'm missing Lawrence more than ever. He's been gone fifteen years now, but something about the holidays makes me want to look for a gift for him, as if he's going to be there when I get home. . . ."

Toni's heart squeezed with longing for Abe. She had no idea what she'd buy him for Christmas, but she knew it would be something very, very special and that she would recognize it the moment she saw it, just as April did when she spotted the gift for her daughter and son-in-law.

"That's it," she'd announced. "That's what I'm going to buy for Carolyn and Ted. It will be perfect for their sitting room."

The double-orbed milk glass table lamp was soon paid for, and arrangements were made for it to be shipped home. "I don't want to take any chances trying to carry it on the plane with me," April had declared. "I'll just have to call Carolyn and Ted and tell them not to open it if it arrives before I do. My daughter has always been that way — searching for hidden gifts and trying to peek at them before Christmas. Julie was like that too. . . ."

April's voice had trailed off then, and Toni had given the elderly lady's shoulder a squeeze. It would be a difficult holiday for all of them. The important thing, Toni knew, was not the gifts or the tree or the food, but their remembrance and celebration of all that Christmas represented — the best gift of all, God's Son, given freely to all who would receive him. So long as she kept her thoughts focused on God, who gave everything to those who deserved nothing, all the rest seemed to stay in proper perspective. She resolved to do just that and to help April, Melissa, and Abe to do the same.

By early afternoon they'd finished all their shopping, except Toni's gift for Abe. Toni had even managed to pick up a little something for April while she was distracted with something else. But now Toni's feet ached and her stomach growled, and though she wasn't about to give up on her quest for Abe's gift, she had to think of April, who wasn't one to complain but who was obviously in need of a rest.

"How about some lunch?" Toni asked. "There's a nice little cafeteria at the far end of the mall."

April readily agreed, and they were soon seated in a booth near the window, watching the rain come down outside while they enjoyed hot chicken noodle soup and fresh sourdough bread. Toni was relieved to draw away from the frenzy of rushed shoppers and unwind a little before pressing on with her mission.

"This is nice, isn't it?" April observed.

Toni nodded in agreement. "Yes, I must admit, this is probably the highlight of my day so far."

"Melissa will love the watch you bought her. I heard her mention just the other day how she wished she had one like that."

"Yes, I heard her too. It certainly simplified things when I saw it in the jeweler's window. I think I have everyone else covered, except Abe, of course. I just hope I can find something he'll like."

April smiled. "If you bought him the ugliest tie in the mall, he'd love it. I really don't think you need to worry about that."

Toni laughed. "You're probably right. Still, I want to get something special, something that will remind him of me — of us — all year long. For the rest of our lives, actually. After all, this is our first Christmas together — his first Christmas as a believer, for that matter. It has to be just right."

"I'm sure it will be, my dear. You'll see."

Toni nodded absently and picked at her bread. "You know, April, I'm trying very hard to keep focused on the positive as you suggested. And I think I'm doing a pretty good job — most of the time. But every now and then . . ."

"I know. It's the same for me. Don't be so hard on yourself, my dear. It's natural. We loved them . . . and we miss them."

Spreading a dab of butter on her bread, Toni went on. "It isn't just Dad . . . or Julie, or Abe's uncle. It's hard to lose someone to death, especially when it happens so violently, and I suppose that's the worst part of all this. I still can't help thinking about Carrie though. She's always been such a sweet, quiet girl but so vibrant in her faith and her zest for life. She had so many plans for the future. Did you know she talked about being a missionary? Ever since she was a little girl that's what she's wanted to do. But now . . . I don't see how her dreams can ever be realized from a wheelchair. It just seems such a waste."

"No life is wasted unless the one living it chooses to waste it," April said, her voice gentle but firm. "God can use anyone, anywhere, in any condition, so long as that person is willing. From what little I know of Carrie, she's quite willing to do whatever God calls her to. Don't you agree?"

Toni nodded. April was right. In her own quiet way, Carrie was a fighter. Toni was sure the wheelchair-bound teenager would not grow bitter or give up on her dreams, but it all seemed so unfair. A young, vibrant life derailed so abruptly and pointlessly, all because another teen, however emotionally disturbed, had selfishly chosen to vent his frustrations in a deadly way. Whatever had happened to Tom Blevins in his nearly eighteen years of life that could possibly have pushed him over the edge in such a destructive manner?

"It's so hard to understand," she said, thinking out loud. "Not just Tom Blevins, but all these school shootings. Kids shooting kids. It makes no sense."

"That's because human life is sacred, my dear. Each one of us, deep inside, knows that. That's why murder is so abhorrent to us, as it should be. I pray we never get so accustomed to hearing about it that we fail to be devastated by it. But to think that someone so young could have become so hardened . . . I suppose that's the most difficult of all to accept."

"You're right. How else could it have happened? Tom must have become hardened, as you said. But . . . how? What could have led him to such deadly behavior? I'll admit, I don't know Tom or the Blevins family well. But this is a small town, and Tom attended the same schools as Melissa all these years. Even if I didn't see him often enough to realize how troubled he was, surely someone else did. A teacher, his parents . . . I don't know. It just seems there must be something more to this than an angry teenager with a grudge."

April reached across the table and patted Toni's hand, the buttered bread long forgotten. "I think it's natural for you to feel this way, my dear, but I imagine others have thought the same thing in every one of these horrible school-shooting incidents. No one wants to believe that a child — and Tom is scarcely more than that — would simply, on his own, turn a gun on his former class-mates. Yet, that seems to have been the case in the previous shootings, and I suppose we'll find that to be the case with Tom as well."

"Maybe, but I'm not so sure. Something is nagging at me, telling me there's more to this ugly situation than the obvious. I can't explain it, but it reminds me of the feeling I had about Dad — that his death was some-thing other than a heart attack." She fixed her eyes on the silver-haired lady sitting across from her. "You know, April, even as I say the words, I'm sensing that not only is there more to this situation than meets the eye, but I'm going to somehow be involved in finding out what it is. Please tell me I'm wrong. I know I'm a detective's daughter and I even have my private investigator's license, but the last thing I need right now is another mystery to solve. All I want to do is go find that perfect gift for the man I love and get on with my life. Is that too much to ask?"

April raised her eyebrows and shrugged.

"I must confess, my dear, I don't have an answer for you. All I can say is that if there truly is more to this shooting than what the police seem to believe, and if God is calling you to be a part of uncovering the truth, then you really have no choice, do you?"

Their eyes locked, and Toni wished she'd never voiced her suspicions about Tom Blevins to April. For some inexplicable reason, she now felt as if she'd painted herself into a corner and didn't have a way out, except to dive into an investigation of Tom Blevins's life and all that had led up to the deadly attack at River View High. She also knew that the very next person she would have to talk to about her decision was Abe. It was hardly the Christmas present she'd hoped to give him.

CHAPTER 5

Even as Melissa laughed, she caught herself. How could she be so selfish? What kind of person was she that she could have a good time singing Christmas carols and decorating a tree while her best friend was confined to a wheelchair, possibly for the rest of her life?

It was Christmas Eve, and Melissa knew Toni was doing her best to keep up the Matthews's tradition of spending the afternoon locating the biggest tree that would fit in the living room, then decorating it together in the evening before going to church to attend a candlelight service. Throughout their childhood years, no matter how much Toni and Melissa had begged their father to put up the tree at least by mid-December, he had refused, saying trees should be fresh on Christmas morning. Somehow he'd always managed to turn the tree-trimming occasion into a fun-filled event despite the haunting absence of Marilyn Matthews, whose picture still called to them from the mantelpiece.

Until now, Christmas Eve had been Melissa's favorite day of the year, but things had changed drastically in the past months. Now, each time she felt a tug of joy or excitement or laughter begin to take hold in her heart, the cloud of guilt and sorrow descended upon her, threatening to envelop her completely. She couldn't seem to escape it.

Still, she had to admit, it had been a nice day. The snow they'd hoped for hadn't arrived, but the freezing rain that had pelted the windows most of the day made the crackle of the logs in the fireplace that much more welcome. Melissa had wrapped the last of her gifts that morning and planned to place them under the tree as soon as she and Abe and Toni finished decorating it. Then the three of them would leave for church.

Melissa knew that Carrie and her parents were hoping to attend the service, so long as Carrie felt up to it. She still tired easily but enjoyed getting out, even in her wheelchair. Melissa wondered if she could be as cheerful and positive as her friend if she were the one who had been shot rather than Carrie.

That, of course, was the source of her guilt. Not only had Carrie been shot instead of Melissa as they walked side by side toward the auditorium, but it had been Melissa's insistence that they go to their lockers to put away their books before going to the assembly that had placed the girls directly in the line of fire when the shooting began. If Melissa had just agreed to take the books to the auditorium with them, as Carrie had wanted, Melissa's once active best friend would not now be confined to a wheelchair, quite possibly a paraplegic for the rest of her life. Indirectly, Carrie's accident was Melissa's fault, and it was the worst thing she'd ever had to deal with — worse even than her father's murder or her own kidnapping ordeal earlier in the year, simply because those tragedies were caused by someone else. The responsibility for this one had landed right in her lap — hers and Tom Blevins's, of course.

Melissa tried to shake off her negative thoughts and rejoin the festivities, as Abe and Toni urged her on to another round of "Deck the Halls," but though she forced the words from her lips, her heart wouldn't respond. Listlessly, she draped a few more strands of tinsel on the tree and wondered again why Tom had done something so awful. She'd known him for years — ever since she started kindergarten — although they'd never been close, particularly since Tom was a year ahead of her in school. But River View was a small town, and Melissa thought she'd known Tom well enough to be sure he would never do anything as mean and hateful as purposely hurting or shooting someone. Melissa's friends, including Carrie, had expressed the same confusion and concern over Tom's behavior. How could it have happened? And if it happened with Tom Blevins, what was to stop it from happening again with someone else? The corridors of River View High — indeed, the entire city of River View — had suddenly become haunted by dark and ominous shadows.

Melissa shivered. The guilt, the fear, the grief — it was all so overwhelming at times. She wished she had someone to talk to about it, but she didn't feel right dumping her feelings on Toni. After all, her sister had enough emotions and plans of her own to deal with at the moment. Nor could she talk with Mrs. Lippincott, who was now back in Colorado with her daughter and son-in-law for the holidays. Melissa was happy that April would be with her family for a couple of weeks. She wasn't happy, however, that almost immediately following the elderly lady's return, the trials would begin once again, which meant Melissa's turn to testify was drawing near.

She closed her eyes, refusing to let herself dwell on the dreaded upcoming event or the horrifying experiences that had led up to it, refocusing instead on April Lippincott. Even though she missed her, Melissa knew April was right where she needed to be, especially since this would be her family's first Christmas without Julie . . . just as it would be Melissa's first Christmas without her father.

The reminder of Paul Matthews's death was so painful that Melissa had to excuse herself before she ruined Abe and Toni's evening with a fresh onslaught of tears. Hurrying to the bathroom, she closed and locked the door behind her, sat down on the edge of the bathtub, buried her face in her hands, and let the tears come, being careful not to sob out loud. *Oh, God,* she prayed silently. *Here I go again! Won't this ever stop? Will I ever feel normal again? Or is it going to be like this forever?*

The candles flickering in the semi-darkness of the church seemed to whisper of hope and promise, of better things to come. Toni prayed that Melissa would hear that whisper, as faint as it might be.

As the final strains of "Silent Night" faded to a close, Toni glanced over at her sister, who sat on her right. The girl's face was expressionless, her eyes dry but still a bit puffy from what Toni was sure had been another crying episode. She'd been watching her all day and knew she was struggling with a myriad of emotions. Yet each time Toni had tried to reach out to her, Melissa had assured her she was fine and admonished her not to worry. So far, Toni had not been able to take her advice.

She laid her hand gently on Melissa's arm, who then turned and gave her a shaky smile. Toni knew her sister was disappointed and concerned that Carrie and her parents hadn't shown up for the service. It was just one more weight for Melissa to carry on her already overburdened young shoulders. "Merry Christmas," Toni mouthed, wishing she could say or do something more to take some of the burden from her sister, but frustrated over her inability to do so.

Melissa nodded in response, then turned back to the front of the church. Abe, sitting on Toni's left, squeezed her hand. She looked at him and smiled, grateful for his understanding, knowing he shared her concern for Melissa.

The lights were slowly turned on, allowing time for people's eyes to adjust. The Christmas Eve service was over, and it was time to head home for hot chocolate. As they stood and began to merge with others making their way toward the exit, the familiar face of Brad Anderson loomed in front of them. Before Toni could speak, Brad had embraced Melissa, then stepped back and smiled down at her.

"Merry Christmas," he said softly. "How are you doing?"

A sad smile flickered across Melissa's face as she answered. "About the same as when I saw you at the cemetery the other day."

Brad nodded, then glanced at Abe and Toni in acknowledgment. "Toni, Abe. Merry Christmas."

"Merry Christmas," they answered in unison as Abe's arm slipped around Toni's waist to draw her near. She knew this was an awkward moment for all of them. Still, someone had to try to ease the tension.

"How are you, Brad?" she asked. "And your parents? I imagine you're planning your usual family get-together tomorrow."

Brad nodded. "We're all fine, thank you, and you're right. The family is already gathering for the big feast. Mom's been cooking for days."

Toni tried to laugh. "I can imagine. Your mother thrives on company, and she loves to cook."

"The more the merrier," Brad agreed, his smile tight as the tension between them grew. "The perfect hostess. Well, I'd better get going. I told Mom I'd drop by this evening and help her with a few last-minute things. So . . ."

As his voice trailed off, Melissa seemed to brighten. Looking intently at Brad as she laid her hand on his arm, she asked, "Can I come with you? I mean, just to say hello to your parents? I haven't seen much of them lately, and besides, like you said, the more the merrier, right?"

Brad grinned. "Absolutely. I don't see why not. We could pop some popcorn, make some hot chocolate. Sound good?"

Before Melissa could answer, Toni felt Abe's arm tighten around her waist. She cleared her throat. "Uh, Melissa, I thought that's what we were going to do, remember? We've got the tree decorated, and we were just about to go home and make some hot chocolate ourselves, then sit around and admire our handiwork. Besides, you don't want to intrude on the Andersons."

Melissa's green eyes opened in surprise. "Intrude? Toni, we're practically family. We've known the Andersons forever. We've been there on Christmas Eve lots of times."

"That's true," Brad agreed. "Melissa could never intrude. In fact, my dad was saying just the other day how much he missed having her around." When Toni hesitated, he added, "I'll bring her home in a couple of hours. OK?"

With the two of them eyeing her expectantly, Toni felt the tension thicken once again. Why was she having such a difficult time with this simple request? Was it because she didn't want Melissa spending Christmas Eve with someone else? No, there was more to it than that. After all, she'd half expected the Bosworths to invite Melissa over, and she would've been OK with that. Was it because Brad was her former fiancé and she was uncomfortable with the reminder of their broken relationship and her sister's continued association with Brad's family? She supposed that was some of it, but there was more, something she couldn't quite put her finger on. An apprehension of some sort, or . . .

She took a deep breath. She was being ridiculous. This was Brad, after all. Someone she'd known her entire life, someone she trusted implicitly. How could she deny Melissa, who'd already been through so much, a chance for a few hours of fun? "Sure," she answered. "That would be fine. Have a nice time, both of you."

Yet even as Toni watched them walk away, Brad's arm draped across Melissa's shoulders protectively and the suddenly animated teenager looking up at him and chatting eagerly, she wondered if she'd made a serious mistake by letting Melissa go.

It wasn't fair. It wasn't right! None of this was working out the way they'd planned. They were supposed to be relaxing on some distant tropical beach by now, sipping cold drinks and laughing at the price they'd extracted from those who'd hurt them. Instead, here he sat, three days after Christmas, on the edge of a hard bunk, locked up in a tiny, windowless cell, isolated from the rest of the inmates because of his age and the seriousness of the charges against him.

For that he was glad. If he had to be in this awful place, he sure didn't want any of the other prisoners to be able to get near him. He'd heard what happens to young guys in jail, and he was terrified. He'd even expressed those very concerns before agreeing to open fire on the students and faculty

101

at his former high school, but he'd been assured the plan was foolproof, that no one would ever catch him or lock him up anywhere. And he'd believed it, just as he'd believed everything he'd been told before the shooting. Now he had to work hard to convince himself that although he sat in jail awaiting a trial that could cost him his life, the rest of what he'd been told was not a lie. It was, after all, the only thing he had to hold on to. That, and the memories . . .

He sighed and shuddered, the pain of those memories and the longing they evoked overshadowing his fear of what lay ahead. He'd spent the first week after the shootings lying in a hospital bed, recovering from the surgery that had successfully removed a bullet from his side and wondering why it hadn't landed a few inches higher, ending his life once and for all and saving the state the cost of a trial and an execution. He was sure that even the death penalty would be preferable to spending whatever was left of his life behind bars, thrust into a prison population that would abuse him and take advantage of his young age and small stature. Or, was it possible that maybe — just maybe, in spite of their failed plans — the promises could still come true and he might one day be free to pursue the dreams that had kept him going over the past year?

He was about to stretch out on his bunk and try to take a nap when he heard a guard speaking to the man in the next cell. He frowned when he realized that prisoner was being escorted down the hallway for a personal visit. Tom couldn't help but wonder who the visitor might be. He also wondered if he would ever have any visitors of his own. So far, with the exception of his court-appointed lawyer, no one had come to see him — not even at Christmas.

Tom, of course, knew that his stepfather would never allow his mother to visit, even if he happened to be sober enough to drive her. After all, they hadn't even bothered to come for Christmas. And both of his older sisters had left home years ago, running at the first possible opportunity of escape. Even if they knew about what had happened, he couldn't imagine either of them coming all this way just to visit him in jail. There was no one else — except, of course . . .

No. He wouldn't let himself think about that. Besides, he could not put that name on his list of visitors. He would just have to wait and see if he was contacted some other way — by mail perhaps. That, too, could be risky, but it was at least a possibility, which a personal visit was not. And so, with every ounce of strength he possessed, he hung onto the hope of a letter.

Though trying to appear natural, Abe sat stiffly as he waited for his longtime friend Harold Barnett to return from the outer office. Harold was a crusader, a court-appointed defense attorney who believed in protecting the rights of his clients — regardless of their crimes. This time Harold had been appointed to defend Tom Blevins. It was not a popular assignment, given the current public sentiment of River View citizens, but one Abe was sure that Harold would carry out with energy and enthusiasm. Harold was the best and would fight valiantly for Tom within the legal boundaries he was obliged to honor.

Abe and Harold had been friends for years. Thus Abe knew he would be granted an appointment with the popular defense lawyer. However, because of the nature of his visit — and because he hadn't told Toni of his plans to talk with Harold — Abe was tense, knowing he had to couch his words carefully so as not to cross any lines, legally or personally. On top of that, Harold knew Abe too well not to recognize his obvious discomfort when he first showed up for their meeting. Immediately after escorting Abe into his office, Harold had excused himself to go after two cups of coffee.

So Abe sat, waiting for his friend's return. He wished he'd planned better what he would say to Harold, how he would broach this very sensitive subject. He had attorney-client privilege to consider, not to mention his current status with the police force. All in all, Abe knew he was on very thin ice even being in Harold's office. But ever since Toni had told him how strongly she felt about the situation with Tom — that there was more to the case than a solitary, emotionally disturbed teenager going over the edge and taking potshots at faculty and students in a high school corridor, as well as the fact that she was determined to launch an investigation of her own to find out the whole story — Abe had wanted to find a way of going ahead of her, of paving the way as much as possible. How to do that had been his greatest dilemma.

His first choice would have been a visit to Tom himself, but he knew that was out of the question. As a police officer — active or on paid leave, it made no difference — he would never be allowed to talk with Tom. Then there were Abe's contacts on the force, but even they had given him minimal information. Abe hadn't felt free to push for more without raising suspicions or being accused of interfering with an investigation — a serious charge that could even result in his permanent dismissal from the force. So he'd settled for the scraps they'd fed him, which had included information regarding the source of Tom's gun, which was licensed to Tom's stepfather and ostensibly taken without his knowledge; the fact that there were no computer files or other telltale clues in Tom's room; and that they'd been unable to gain any insight from Tom's parents or sisters or even former teachers or classmates that would shed any new light on the troubled teen's life. The only thing the extensive police investigation into Tom Blevins's life had produced was confirmation of the existing profile of an antisocial loner, a misfit with no friends or outside interests, who confided in absolutely no one and seemed to live in his own fantasy world.

None of that would be enough to dissuade Toni from her own investigation. Abe needed more — something solid to present to Toni to convince her that Tom had acted alone and that she was just wasting her time pursuing her suspicions. That brought him to Harold. Abe only hoped he could get through this visit without alienating Harold of stirring up a whole new pack of trouble.

He sighed. He didn't like doing anything behind Toni's back. He had, in fact, thought seriously about telling her of his plans, but he knew she would have insisted on joining him. This meeting with Harold was going to be difficult enough without Toni's presence to further complicate matters. If he could just get something from Harold, something concrete about Tom's personality or demeanor that would help him explain to Toni what the young man was really like, what made him tick, why he would — entirely on his own — go off and commit such a despicable crime, then maybe she'd back off and let the police do their job.

A smile played on his lips as he honestly considered his chances of that happening. How many people had tried to convince this stubborn fiancée of his to stop investigating her father's death, to simply accept the coroner's verdict that Paul Matthews had died of a heart attack, and to go on with her life? Yet she'd forged ahead, convinced there was something more.

Something more. The very words Toni now used to describe her suspicions about Tom Blevins and the high school shooting were the same words she'd used about her father's death, and she'd been right ab that. Was it possible that she was right about Tom as well?

Abe, lost in thought, flinched when Harold reentered the room.

"Hey, buddy," Harold announced in his booming voice. "Here's that java I promised you. Had to go clear down the hall to get it. You'd think the county could spring for more than one coffeepot per floor, wouldn't you? Especially when the building has only two floors."

The big man with the balding head and the laughing eyes plunked down behind his desk, across from Abe, then leaned back in his squeaky chair and studied his friend. "OK, this isn't just your everyday, let's-do-lunch-on-Friday social call, is it? You've got something on your mind, Matthews. What's up?"

Abe swallowed a smile and feigned surprise. "Now, Harold, what makes you think I'm here for any reason other than just to say hello? Are you trying to imply I have an ulterior motive?"

Harold laughed. "I'm not trying to imply anything. I'm saying it. You have an ulterior motive. So what is it?"

Abe's eyes narrowed as he smiled. "You'd ave made a good detective."

I am a detective. That's half of being a

good lawyer. Ideally our clients tell us the truth, the whole truth, and nothing but the truth, and we just take it from there. But in case you haven't noticed, we don't live in an ideal world — and my cases don't involve ideal clients. Sometimes — maybe even most of the time — they don't tell me the truth, at least not all of it. That's when I put on my detective hat and start digging. Sometimes I come up with something, sometimes I don't." He paused. "And sometimes I come up with something that makes things worse for my client, but I still have to do it."

Abe nodded. "I know. If you don't have all the facts . . ." His voice trailed off, and he took a deep breath. Harold was probably going to send him packing when he found out why he was here, but it wasn't going to get any better by putting it off.

"OK," Abe began, watching his friend closely for any reaction. "Here are the facts — all of them. My fiancée's younger sister was in the hallway when the Blevins kid opened fire. She was with her best friend, Carrie Bosworth . . ." Harold's face immediately registered recognition, and Abe knew he'd hit a nerve. "Obviously you know the name and the extent of Carrie's injuries." Harold nodded curtly, and Abe continued. "But that's not why I'm here — not about Carrie, anyway. It's my fiancée, Toni Matthews . . ."

Another flicker of recognition crossed Harold's face, this time followed by a grin. "So that's what this is all about. The temporarily-on-paid-leave detective and his wannabe-detective girlfriend are on a case — the Blevins case, to be exact — and you're here to see what you can find out from me." He leaned forward, his grin widening. "I've heard about this fiancée of yours. Who hasn't? She practically cracked her father's murder investigation single-handedly. Made the River View PD look like a bunch of buffoons. Of course, they didn't know they were being stymied by some of their own . . . including your uncle."

Abe pressed his lips together and nodded in acceptance. It was still a painful subject for him, even if his rogue-cop uncle turned bad guy had died trying to save Abe's life. Before he could respond, Harold went on.

"Sorry. I shouldn't have mentioned it, but you have to know that Matthews girl you're hooked up with has quite a reputation around here — as a real pain sometimes, but as a dynamite detective too. Guess she gets that from her father. I never knew the guy, but he had a good reputation — honest, fair, a real bulldog when he got his teeth into something. Sounds as if his daughter has followed in his footsteps."

"You can say that again," Abe admitted. "She's a wonderful lady. She really is, but she can be a bit . . . stubborn, if you know what I mean."

Harold laughed. "I've known a few of those in my life. But what's all that got to do with me? Or should I say, with Tom Blevins? How are the two of you involved in his case?"

"We're not, at least not officially. But Toni has this fixation, this obsession, that . . ." He paused, then took a deep breath and plunged in. "Toni doesn't think Tom acted alone. She's sure that others were involved in the planning. I can't give you any concrete reasons why she feels that way; she just does. She keeps insisting there's 'something more' than the accepted lone-gunman theory, and she's bound and determined to find out what it is."

Harold's face had turned serious, and he was leaning back in his chair once more, his fingers tented together in front of him. Abe waited. Finally Harold spoke. "And what do you think?"

"I don't know," Abe answered honestly. "I've talked to some people on the force, but I really haven't learned anything to support Toni's suspicions. Yet —"

"Yet you wonder," Harold interrupted. His eyes narrowed slightly. "I don't know why I'm telling you this," he said, "but I've wondered the same thing myself. Even though I've done my digging, just like the police, and I've come up with nothing. Absolutely nothing. I've talked to his family — as much as anyone can, I suppose. You'd think they'd be more cooperative with the lawyer who's supposed to be fighting to save their kid's life, but they didn't tell me much. In fact, Tom's mother hardly spoke a word the entire time I was at their house. She never opened her mouth without first looking at her husband to make sure it was OK. He was half-crocked, so I didn't find out much from him either — other than he didn't like Tom much, and he was *real* mad about his gun being used to commit the crime. I don't think he's too broken up over the idea of Tom's being locked up for life — or even being given the death penalty, for that matter. What a family . . ."

"That's pretty much the same impression I got from the guys I talked to on the force," Abe said. "Look . . . Harold, I know all about attorney-client privilege, OK? I'm not trying to get you to tell me anything that would violate that, but can't you give me something? Anything at all you can tell me that would help me convince Toni to back off this thing?"

"You could reassure her that the police are looking into the very things she suspects. Certainly she's not naïve enough to believe she's the only one checking out these possibilities, is she?"

"I've already tried that. She knows they're checking into it, but she's convinced they're overlooking something. Sounds crazy, I know, but —"

"But she was right about her dad."

"Exactly."

Harold sighed, rose from his desk, crossed to a small window overlooking the parking lot, and stared. Abe waited. Finally Harold turned. "OK, Matthews. Here's what I've got — and it's not much, believe me. Nothing, really, when it comes to evidence. Just a gut feeling that there's . . . something more, as your girlfriend says. To be more specific, I think someone else is involved. It makes no sense to think that way, since absolutely nothing has turned up to substantiate it, but Tom has said a couple of things that make me wonder." Harold sat back down, his chair squeaking again. "Either someone else was involved, or Tom wishes there were."

Abe frowned. "What do you mean?"

"Look, the kid's lonely. That's obvious, right? He's been described as having a vivid imagination, of living in a dream world. So maybe he's just fantasizing about someone else, but a couple of times when I mentioned that I'd try to get his mother to come and visit him so he wouldn't be so lonely, he got real defensive. Told me not to bother his mother, but then he also said that he wasn't as lonely as everybody thought he was, that there was somebody who really cared about him and who he was sure he'd hear from any day. When I asked his parents and sisters about it, they couldn't imagine who it could be. And he won't say anything else about it. Clams up the minute I try to get any more out of him."

"What do you make of it? Do you think he has some sort of partner somewhere? A girlfriend, maybe?"

"If he does, she's invisible. No one around here has ever seen or heard of her."

"But you think she might exist."

"He, she. Who knows? Maybe just in his imagination."

Abe raised his eyebrows and sighed. "If I tell Toni any of this, it'll just add fuel to the flames; you know that."

Harold nodded. "I can imagine. Maybe it's best if you don't mention it."

"You're probably right. No sense getting her any more fired up than she already is." Abe smiled. "But I appreciate your telling me. Maybe Toni isn't so far off in her suspicions after all."

"Maybe not," Harold agreed. "And maybe she inherited more of her father's detective genes than you realize." He winked at Abe and grinned again. "Better watch it, Matthews. Doesn't sound like you'll be able to get much past that one. Seriously, though, if she does manage to find out something, will you let me in on it?"

"You got it. And thanks . . . for everything."

CHAPTER 6

The restaurant was elegant, the background music romantic and muted. The food, though known for its excellence, was almost inconsequential, at least as far as Toni was concerned. Sitting beside Abe at the intimate window table overlooking the Columbia, Toni watched the lights from other New Year's Eve celebrations along the waterfront dance on the dark waters of the majestic river, while she lovingly fingered the cluster of diamonds on her left ring finger. Life was good in spite of all they'd been through and all they still had to face in the weeks and months ahead. She missed her father desperately, but God had brought her together with the man she was sure he intended for her to marry, and she was more grateful than she could ever express.

Abe's voice in her ear was soft as it coursed through her body. "Beautiful," was all he said, but it seemed so much more.

"Mmm," she agreed. "It is, isn't it?"

"Not the river — you."

Smiling, she turned from the window and looked at Abe, his dark eyes only inches from hers. She was glad for the high-backed booth that gave them privacy from the other patrons. As his lips touched hers, her eyes closed and she wondered why they hadn't already set a wedding date — and the sooner the better. She'd tentatively thought of late spring, but Abe was leaning toward something much sooner. Valentine's Day had been his most recent suggestion. "A day for lovers," he'd whispered as he held her in his arms, much as he did at this moment. "A day . . . and a night too. It would be romantic, Toni, and it's a lot sooner than spring, especially late spring. Come on, sweetheart, why wait that long — unless you're having second thoughts?"

Toni had insisted that second thoughts were the furthest thing from her mind and that spring would arrive before they knew it. But as she melted in his arms on this eve of a new year together, their mutual longing an almost tangible heat between them, February was beginning to sound better all the time. Maybe she should just give in and tell him that Valentine's Day would be perfect. . . .

The waiter cleared his throat, and Abe and Toni parted lips. "Sorry," Abe said, looking up at the middle-aged man with the close-cropped dark hair and self-conscious smile who'd earlier identified himself as David. "We didn't realize you were there."

"That's quite all right," David answered, carefully setting their salads in front of them. "This is a romantic restaurant, and this, of course, is a romantic night. We're used to seeing couples in love, who care more for one another than for food — which is how it should be, don't you agree? Still, our food is excellent. Would you care for some freshly ground pepper?"

Abe and Toni declined, and the waiter moved on. Abe looked at Toni and smiled sheepishly. "Sorry. I didn't mean to embarrass you."

Toni returned his smile. "You didn't, and I don't think we embarrassed good old David much either."

Abe chuckled, then took Toni's hand and offered a prayer of thanks. Picking up his fork and stabbing a cherry tomato, he said, "Our waiter just might be right about my caring more for you than eating, but that doesn't mean I'm not hungry. How about you?"

"Starved," she admitted.

As they worked their way through their salads, interspersing bites with conversation, Toni found herself reliving their last kiss and wondering if and when she should tell Abe that his Valentine wedding date sounded great to her. After all, where was it written that a wedding had to be a big, expensive affair with months of planning and preparation? Maybe they could arrange something small and quiet with Pastor Michael from their church officiating and just a few close friends and family members in attendance. . . .

Abe's question interrupted her thoughts. "So, how's Melissa dealing with her upcoming testimony? She'll probably be called in the next couple of weeks. I know I'm expecting to be put on the stand any day now — April too, I'm sure. It's not going to be a cakewalk for any of us, but it'll be hardest for Melissa."

Toni nodded in agreement. Second only to Melissa's concern for Carrie was her dread over the testimony she would soon be called to give. It would mean reliving every moment of the horrible kidnapping ordeal, including the cold-blooded killing in Melissa's presence of one member of the baby-selling ring by two other members. Toni knew the inevitable event of giving her testimony was always playing on Melissa's mind, but the girl never seemed to want to discuss it in any detail.

"I've already talked about it to the district attorney," she'd told Toni. "He says we'll go over it more carefully just before I have to go on the stand. So let's just drop it for now, please."

That was that. Toni had left it alone from then on, but she couldn't help but wonder if she didn't worry about it almost as much as Melissa. How glad she would be to have these issues behind them once and for all.

"You're right," Toni said, pulling herself back to the present and refocusing on Abe. "But I just can't get her to talk about it. I'm hoping she might open up a little with April when she returns from Colorado this week. Since they'll each be testifying and it will be difficult for both of them, maybe that will create a bond between them that will help Melissa voice her concerns. So much is going on in her life right now, especially Carrie's situation. It's absolutely devastated Melissa."

Abe nodded. "I've noticed. But we can all hold on to that shred of hope the doctor gave us about the possibility that Carrie could one day regain use of her legs since the nerves in her spinal cord weren't severed."

"Thank God for that. We have to keep praying for that miracle to happen, but we also have to help Melissa get through this if it doesn't. From what I understand, Carrie seems to be coping with the situation better than Melissa, although it's probably too early to be sure of that. We'll just have to give it time and see what happens, I suppose."

Abe tore off a piece of sourdough bread and spread it with butter. Before popping it into his mouth he said, "This thing is going to have a lot more repercussions than any of us realize. Something like this has a monumental impact on so many lives. And then there's the gun control thing."

"That issue sure seems to be raising its ugly, controversial head again, doesn't it?" Toni observed. "I heard on the news today that some sort of anti-gun rally will take place in front of the courthouse next week."

"I heard that too. As a law enforcement officer, I'm not sure exactly where I stand on that issue. There's nothing I'd like better than to see some good, strong legislation put into place that could actually keep lethal weapons out of the hands of criminals. The problem is, so many laws already on the books are designed to do just that and none of them really work, which makes me wonder how more laws would make any difference. The only ones who pay any attention to the existing laws are people who aren't going to use guns for anything illegal anyway. Still, every time something like a school shooting takes place, it's pretty hard to argue against gun control when more and more people see readily available guns used to destroy innocent lives."

Toni sighed and set her fork down on her almost empty salad plate. "It's all so sad, isn't it? One young person goes off the deep end and ruins the lives of so many others. I still have a hard time accepting that Tom Blevins acted alone though. Regardless of what the police think, there's got to be more to it. That's why I've decided to try to get in to see Tom this week. I'm not sure how far I'll get, since I'm obviously not on his approved visitors list, but I've got to try. I just can't put it off any longer."

Abe set his fork down as well, then hesitated before answering. "Toni, I . . . I don't see how visiting Tom is going to make any difference in any of this. Besides, even if you can find a way to get in, what makes you think he'll talk to you anyway?"

"I told you, sweetheart, it's just something

I have to do. Maybe I won't get anywhere, but I have to try. I can't ignore this hunch that there's more to what Tom did than what the police and media seem to believe." She laid her hand on his. "Will you go with me? I'd really like for us to do this together."

Abe's jaws twitched, and he hesitated. "Actually, I . . . don't think that would be a very good idea. In fact, it would be impossible. I may be on paid leave right now, but I'm still a member of the force. The authorities would never let me in to see him."

"Then I'll go alone."

"You'll never get in, Toni. You said yourself, you're not on his visitors list."

"I know the jail chaplain. He and Dad were friends for years, and I know he got him in to see people a few times. It's a long shot, but I'm going to call him and see what he says."

Abe sighed. "Toni, I . . . Look, I might as well just tell you. I talked to a friend of mine a couple of days ago, Harold Barnett. He —"

Toni was stunned. "Harold Barnett?" she interrupted. "Isn't he Tom's lawyer?"

"Yes. I've known him for years, and —"

"Abe, why didn't you tell me?"

"I . . . was going to, but . . . Toni, I didn't really find out anything, so I didn't see the point. Because of attorney-client privilege he couldn't say much —"

"I know all about attorney-client privilege, and you knew about it before you went to see him. So why did you go if you didn't think you were going to learn anything? Abe, what are you keeping from me?"

"Nothing, sweetheart. Honest. Harold just said —"

Toni could feel her frustration mounting. "He just said what? What did Harold Barnett say about Tom? If he could tell you, then you can tell me. He wouldn't have broken attorney-client privilege, so you have no reason to keep it from me."

Abe looked at her for a moment, the brief indecision on his face finally dissolving into resignation. "OK, I'll tell you. But it's nothing, really. Harold just said that . . . that he feels the same about Tom as you do — that there's something more to the case — but Toni, he's talked to everyone, done his research, and he can't find a thing. Neither can the police. What in the world makes you think you can uncover what all these trained professionals seem unable to do?"

Toni bristled, her frustration quickly turning to resentment. "They may be trained professionals," she said, her voice cool but resolute, "but those same professionals failed to find out the truth about my father's death, didn't they?" When Abe didn't answer, she went on. "I don't understand you, Abe. I thought we were partners, a team. Partners don't keep secrets from each other."

Abe once again found his voice. "I know," he answered, "and I should have said something sooner, but Harold and I agreed it wouldn't serve any purpose, so I . . . didn't."

"You and Harold decided that telling me wouldn't serve any purpose?" Toni was incredulous. "I'm sorry, Abe, but I don't think that's the reason. I think you decided not to tell me about your visit with Harold because you don't want me pursuing this case, and you knew Harold's suspicions would only fuel my own. Well, you were right. That's absolutely what's happened. Now I'm more determined than ever to see Tom, and anyone else I have to, so I can get to the bottom of this. You can help me or not, that's up to you. But, please . . ." Her voice softened slightly, but her throat felt tight, and her heart hurt. "No more secrets. Please."

Yet even as Abe nodded his agreement, Toni was surprised to find herself thinking that she was glad she hadn't said anything to him about moving up the wedding date.

As much as she loved Abe and longed to be his wife, maybe they needed more time after all.

Melissa marveled at how she could suddenly feel so out of place in the Bosworths' home, where she had spent almost as much time over the years as she had in her own. She recalled all the special times with Carrie — the many dinners and sleepovers, late nights doing homework and talking about boys, styling each other's hair, experimenting with makeup, talking about their future plans and dreams. . . .

Now, after being let in by Mrs. Bosworth, Melissa stood stiffly in the doorway of Carrie's bedroom, trying to keep her smile in place and her voice cheerful as she greeted her friend. If only Carrie didn't look so pale and thin, propped up against the pillows on her bed. She was absorbed in a book and seemed not to notice she had company.

"Hi," Melissa said, her voice far too enthusiastic. "I thought I'd come by and see what you were doing."

Carrie's face brightened the moment she looked up. "Melissa, come on in. How are you?"

"Fine," Melissa answered, crossing the

room and taking a seat in the chair next to the bed, ignoring the empty wheelchair that sat waiting less than a foot away from her. "How are you?"

Carrie's smile was accepting. She shrugged her thin shoulders and laid her book in her lap. "OK, I guess. Not running any races yet, but the doctors say that could change. I'm just glad this hasn't affected my arms. It would be awful if I couldn't hold books to read."

Melissa did her best to smile. "That's for sure. I can't imagine you without one in your hand. So . . . what are you reading anyway?"

"A history book," Carrie said, laying it down on the bed beside her. "Just trying to keep up with homework. I don't want to get too far behind. I sure hope I can go back to school when the new semester starts."

Melissa nodded. How could her friend be so cheerful and optimistic about doing homework and running races and going back to school when she couldn't even get out of bed without help? Why would she even *want* to go back to school after what had happened to her there? Didn't Carrie wrestle with the same fears and confusion that haunted so many other River View students, including Melissa herself? Maybe it was because, regardless of whatever else Carrie had to deal with, at least she didn't have the guilt.

Melissa looked for a safe subject, anything that might keep her from breaking into tears. "I . . . so . . . your mom says your physical therapy is going good."

"Yep, but it's really hard and exhausting. And I've just started. The therapist says it's going to get a lot tougher before we're through. But if it helps me to walk again, it's worth it, right?"

"I . . ." The tears were threatening once more, and Melissa took a deep breath. "What if . . . what if it doesn't work? I mean, what if you never . . . ?" She couldn't bring herself to say the words, but she knew Carrie understood. Still, when she didn't answer right away, Melissa began to berate herself for asking such an insensitive question.

Finally Carrie spoke, her delicate hand brushing away a tear from the corner of her eye. Her short dark hair shone in the bedroom light as she smiled once again. "Then I guess I'll become a world champion wheelchair racer, what do you think? After all, I can't spend the rest of my life sitting here in this bed, waiting for the world to come to me, can I?"

"But . . . all your plans for the future . . . wanting to become a missionary . . . to get married someday and have lots of kids . . ."

Carrie shrugged again. "Who says I can't still do all that? I've read lots of stories of people in wheelchairs doing just about anything and everything that other people do . . . sometimes better. I'll just have to work a little harder at it, that's all." She smiled her familiar smile, her dimples deepening as she spoke. "Besides, just think how much fun I'd have racing after all those kids I'm going to have. They wouldn't stand a chance of outrunning my wheels." Her dark eyes danced. "Neither will my future husband, once I finally meet him."

Melissa knew she should laugh, but the effort only released the tears she'd been trying so hard to hold back. As they slid down her cheeks she whispered, "Oh, Carrie, I'm so sorry. It's all my fault."

Carrie's smile dissolved into a puzzled frown. "Your fault? Melissa, what are you talking about? How could any of this be your fault? It was Tom Blevins who shot me, remember? Not you."

"Yes, but . . . if I hadn't made you go back to our lockers before we went to the assembly —"

"OK, stop right there." Carrie's voice rang

with a note of authority Melissa had never before heard from her friend. "First of all, that is absolutely ridiculous. How could you have known what was going to happen? Besides, going to our lockers first made a lot of sense. Most of the other kids were doing the same thing. So just forget that part, OK? And second . . ." She paused and reached over to Melissa, taking her by the hand. Melissa was amazed at the strength she sensed in Carrie's grip.

"Second," she went on, "if anybody has a reason to feel sorry for herself around here, it's me. And if I'm not having a pity party, I'm sure not going to let you have one."

Melissa, wiping the tears from her cheeks with her free hand, studied Carrie's face. She knew her friend was trying to make light of the situation, but she also knew Carrie's words were true. The girl had not once fallen into the "poor me" trap of self-pity; in fact, here she was, paralyzed — at least temporarily — from the waist down, trying to cheer up Melissa, who had walked into the room on her own two feet. Melissa felt more ashamed than ever.

"You're right. I know you are. It's just —"

"Hard?"

Melissa nodded, determined not to break down again.

Carrie smiled. "So who lied and told you life was easy? You, if anybody, should know better. We might only be fifteen, but we've lived long enough to know that bad things happen, right? To everyone. You lost your mom when you were so young you can't even remember her. Then you lost your dad, and then that horrible kidnapping thing. . . . But Melissa, you're still sitting here in my room safe and sound. What does that tell you?"

It was Melissa's turn to frown. "I . . . don't know."

Carrie shook her head exasperatedly. "Don't you get it? Can't you see? Melissa, you were kidnapped by the very people who killed your dad . . . and Mrs. Lippincott's granddaughter, but you're still alive, and so am I. I don't know if I'll ever get to be a missionary or get married and have a bunch of kids — even if I'll walk again, there's no guarantee of that. But I do know one thing; God has a plan for our lives, and it's a good plan. Jeremiah 29:11 promises us that. " 'For I know the plans I have for you," declares the LORD, "plans to prosper you and not to harm you, plans to give you hope and a future.' " That's been my favorite verse for a long time, and it's even more special to me now. It's true for both of us, if

131

we'll just trust him to work those plans out in our lives." She squeezed Melissa's hand. "Besides, what choice do we have? Do you think we're smart enough to figure out all these things on our own?"

Melissa forced a smile. *How did Carrie stay so positive?* "You're right," she admitted, meaning it. "I just wish I had your faith."

"You do. The Bible says that God has given a measure of faith to each of us. We just have to make sure we place it in him and nothing else. Then it'll begin to grow."

Donna Bosworth knocked on the door then, bringing two steaming mugs of hot chocolate and a plate of freshly baked oatmeal cookies. After she'd gone, Carrie smiled. "Didn't I tell you God has good plans for us?"

Melissa laughed in spite of herself. "I have to admit," she said, taking a big bite, "it doesn't get much better than homemade oatmeal cookies."

Carrie nodded in agreement, then nibbled absently at a cookie. "Melissa," she said, looking intently at her friend, "what's going on with Tom Blevins? My parents don't tell me much, and they try to keep me from seeing or hearing the news. Has he been arraigned?"

"Yes. He's been held over for trial — as

an adult."

"I figured that would happen. He's almost eighteen. I wonder what they'll do to him."

"He'll probably go to prison for the rest of his life, don't you think? It's what he deserves. He killed a teacher and wounded you and a lot of others."

"You don't think it's possible they'll give him the death penalty, do you?"

Melissa raised her eyebrows. "I hadn't even thought of that. I hope not. I mean . . . he's just a kid like us. Well, sort of."

Carrie nodded. "Yeah. Sort of."

Melissa was shocked. The possibility of Tom's getting the death penalty had never really crossed her mind. How did she feel about it? What did she think? More importantly . . .

"What . . . what do *you* think?" she asked, watching Carrie's face closely. "About what happens to Tom, I mean."

"I'm not sure. If he's convicted — and we all know he did it — he should probably get life in prison, right? But death? Melissa, he's only seventeen."

"I know. One year older than us. I still can't believe it."

"He must be so scared. I feel sorry for him."

Melissa's eyes opened wide. "You feel

sorry for Tom Blevins? Carrie, he shot you. He pulled the trigger, and now you can't walk. How can you feel sorry for him? Anybody else would hate him."

"I won't deny that I'm angry with him at times. But hate him? No. I can't hate him. I have to forgive him. In fact, I've been thinking of writing him a letter."

"A letter? Carrie, what are you talking about?"

"I'm talking about writing to Tom and telling him that I forgive him. Maybe that might help him somehow. I know for sure it'll help me. I can't very well ask God to heal me if I'm all angry and full of hate inside. Besides, Tom doesn't know the Lord, I'm sure of it. And that's the most important thing. I've been praying for him every day, but now I think it's time to put some feet to my prayers." She smiled. "Since my legs aren't working right now, I thought I'd let my fingers do the walking by way of a letter. What do you think?"

Melissa stared in amazement. She'd known Carrie all her life. They were the same age; they'd grown up together. Suddenly, though, Melissa felt so much younger and more immature than her friend. What did Melissa *think?* She thought Carrie was a saint, and she thought she could never be like her.

"I don't know what to say," she answered. "I know you're right — about forgiving him and everything — but I don't know if I could do it."

"Sure you could. God would help you just like he's helping me. Otherwise, I couldn't do it either. But if Jesus forgave the ones who killed him, and if God forgave us for all our sins, shouldn't we follow his example?"

An unbidden image of Bruce Jensen, the Matthews's family's longtime friend and physician, popped into Melissa's mind, and she flinched. Surely God wasn't telling her she had to forgive him, was he? After all, Dr. Jensen had pretended to be their friend, but he'd killed her father and was part of the baby-selling ring that had kidnapped her. How could she ever forgive him for something like that?

Yet, even as she silently asked the question, she already knew the answer.

It had taken a lot of string pulling — on both her part and Abe's — for Toni to wangle a visit with Tom Blevins. She'd put in a call to the jail chaplain, who'd agreed to put her on Tom's visitors list if Harold Barnett would allow it. Abe had convinced

Harold to agree to Toni's visit on three conditions — if Tom was open to it, if Toni promised not to get into any legal aspects of the case during the visit, and if she promised to pass along to Harold any information she might obtain from Tom.

So here she sat, waiting for Tom to be brought into the visiting cell on the other side of the Plexiglas partition, still amazed that he had agreed to see her. Toni imagined that he had consented to the visit more out of curiosity and loneliness than anything else, but she was grateful, whatever the reasons.

What in the world am I going to say to Tom? she wondered. Tom, of course, knew her as Melissa's older sister, but where would that leave her? It wasn't as if she'd been a friend of the Blevinses' family over the years, although she'd met them on occasion. And, of course, depending on how her visit with Tom went today, she might very well have to be in touch with them soon. But what would happen when Tom walked through that metal door, she had no idea.

Help me, Father, she prayed silently. *I believe you've sent me here for a purpose, that you're calling me to look into Tom's situation and uncover the truth. If that's so, Lord, you're going to have to lead me in what to say and do. . . .*

That was as far as she got before the door opened and Tom was led into the tiny room by a burly, grim-faced guard. The young prisoner was dressed in jailhouse orange, his dull eyes displaying a hostile indifference. Behind the hard mask, however, Toni detected fear and confusion.

As she watched him sit down in the chair opposite her, Toni was surprised by Tom's frail frame and the extreme boyishness of his features. It had been a while since she'd seen him, so she wasn't prepared for his extremely young and immature appearance. Despite his defiant stare, Toni was sure that somewhere inside Tom Blevins was a scared boy, desperately seeking an ally, and if she was right in her assessment of Tom's family, he wasn't getting the support he needed from them. Maybe — with God's help — she could somehow support him, even as she sought to uncover the coconspirators in this young man's crime.

Wait a minute, Toni warned herself. *Don't let his innocent looks get to you. He might have the face of a little boy, but he has the heart of a killer. He's already proven that. So stay focused on the reason you're here.*

Taking a deep breath, Toni picked up the phone, wondering if Tom would do the same. He stared, stone-faced and unmoving for a moment, as if to let her know who was in charge, then slowly reached out and picked up the receiver and put it to his ear.

"Yeah?" he said. "What do you want?"

Toni swallowed. "Hello, Tom. How are you?"

His forehead drew together in a frown. "Why do you want to know? And what are you doing here anyway? My lawyer said you wanted to talk to me, but he didn't say why. I know you're Melissa Matthews's sister, but so what? She's nothin' to me, and neither are you. So what's your story?"

Toni measured her words carefully, continuing to watch Tom's face for any revealing expressions. She took another deep breath. This was no time for games. She knew that if she wasn't straightforward with him he'd walk out that metal door and never talk to her again. He might do that anyway, no matter what she said to him, but she had to take a chance — and truth was the only chance she had.

"I . . . I think there's more to your story than what the police or media believe. I don't know you well, Tom, but I've seen you through the years and . . . well, I can't put my finger on it, but something doesn't add up. I just can't accept the fact that you walked into that school — completely on your own, with no prodding from anyone else — and shot all those people. Oh, I know you were alone when you pulled the trigger, but . . . the bottom line is, I think other people were involved, and for some reason, you're covering for them." She paused, waiting for some sign of a reaction to her words, and praying that she wasn't crossing the legal lines Abe and Harold had warned her about. A flicker of what appeared to be alarm was all she saw on Tom's face before everything went hard.

"Tom, listen to me," she went on, desperately trying to make contact before he shut her out completely. "If other people are involved, it can only help your case to tell someone about it. If not me, then tell someone else — your lawyer or your mother or —"

"You leave my mother out of this." His response was quick, his eyes cold. "Look, lady, I don't need your help, OK? If that's what you came here for, forget it. And don't bother comin' back here again. We've got nothin' to say to each other." He rose from his seat, then turned to bang on the door. "Guard!" he shouted, "I'm ready to go back to my cell." The conversation was obviously over, and Toni had gotten absolutely nowhere.

The day had dawned clear but cold, the raw winds of January taking their toll on anyone who ventured outside. Toni and Abe had taken a walk earlier but had cut it short and opted for a quiet afternoon in front of the fireplace with April and Melissa.

It was Saturday, two weeks into the new year, and Toni had made no effort to try to see Tom Blevins again. She felt it was pointless and that she would probably find out more by talking to people who knew Tom better than she did. So far she'd been unable to reach Tom's mother, having run into a brick wall when she'd tried to get past Tom's stepfather. From what Toni could gather from talking to Melissa and a couple of the town gossips, Tom's mother and stepfather were married when Tom was still a baby. Tom's real father had disappeared soon after Tom was born, and Tom had carried his stepfather's name almost his entire life. The one time Toni had ventured over to the Blevinses' home, Sam Blevins had met her at the door, drunk and angry, and promptly sent her on her way, threatening to call the police if she didn't stay off their property. His wife had cowered silently at his side throughout the brief confrontation.

When she told Abe of the incident, he'd encouraged her to follow Mr. Blevins's warning, reminding her that she could easily get herself into legal trouble if she appeared to be interfering with an ongoing police investigation. She would have to be very careful in the future about whom she talked to concerning Tom Blevins.

Meanwhile, the topic of the day seemed to be the ongoing trials. April, who'd returned the first week of January from her visit with her family in Colorado, had completed her testimony earlier that week, and Abe had begun his on Friday. He would pick up where he'd left off on Monday.

Toni couldn't help but notice that Melissa was paying close attention to all that was said regarding the trial. She knew her little sister was trying to prepare herself for her own testimony, which would begin as soon as Abe's was finished. Toni prayed it would go smoothly for Melissa and be over as soon as possible, even though she recognized that this was only the first of several trials involving the baby-selling ring, so repeats of the testimonies would be required in the months to come. Toni just wished Melissa would enter into their conversation rather than sitting silently, listening and keeping her thoughts and concerns to herself.

The phone rang, and Toni reached for the receiver. The moment Brad identified himself, Toni felt uncomfortable, even though she knew she needn't be.

"Hello, Brad," she said, wondering why she felt the urge to avert her eyes from Abe as she spoke. She opted to fix her gaze on Melissa, noticing immediately how her sister had perked up at the sound of Brad's name. "How are you?"

"I'm fine. And you?"

"Fine, thank you. What can I do for you?"

"Actually, I called to speak to Melissa. Is she there?"

Toni hesitated, raising her eyebrows questioningly at Melissa. "Yes," she answered, "she's right here."

Melissa's smile lit up her entire face. "For me?"

Toni nodded, holding out the phone. Melissa jumped up. "I'll take it in my room," she said, hurrying toward the hallway. "Just hang it up when I get in there, will you?"

Toni's eyebrows were still raised as she waited to hear Melissa pick up the phone. Then she hung up. Before she could say anything, April Lippincott excused herself to go into the kitchen and fix some tea.

Toni turned to Abe. "Why does that

bother me?" she asked, hoping he would have some sort of answer for her but not really expecting one. "Why am I uncomfortable about Brad calling here for Melissa? They've known each other for years, but . . ."

She studied Abe's face. His jaws twitched, but she couldn't read his dark eyes. Should she have kept her concerns to herself? No, not if she was going to be true to her own convictions of keeping everything honest and aboveboard between them as she wished Abe had done in the matter of visiting Tom Blevins's lawyer. She waited for his response.

"Maybe," he said finally, "it just sounds strange to you to hear his voice asking for Melissa instead of you. After all, you two were an item for years, and it hasn't been that long since you were planning to marry him."

His words hung in the air, and their eyes locked. What was wrong? What was happening to them? Couldn't Abe see the reason for Toni's concern? It was so obvious to Toni. Didn't he care about Melissa's vulnerability, her growing dependence on Brad? Was Toni reading something into Abe's words that wasn't there, or was he implying that she still had feelings for Brad Anderson?

Whatever it was, Toni decided, she didn't like it one bit.

CHAPTER 7

Just the day before, as Toni had sat in the courtroom and prayed while she watched Melissa struggle through the final portion of her testimony, she'd noticed Valerie Myers, River View High's assistant principal, whom Toni knew only casually, sitting to her left a few rows back. Toni had hoped to get a chance to say hello and to thank the woman for her kindness in escorting Melissa from the school after the shootings, but Valerie had left before she could get over to her. She'd made a mental note then to seek her out at her first opportunity but didn't realize that opportunity would present itself so quickly and that she would have to do absolutely nothing to make it happen.

It was early afternoon on Thursday, an unseasonably warm day for January, with clear skies and temperatures approaching sixty. With Melissa in school and April at the hairdresser, Toni had decided to take advantage of the good weather and get outside for some exercise. After a two-mile walk around the park, she'd settled down on a bench, the winter sun at her back and a mystery novel in her lap.

She sighed as she opened it. Would life ever settle down enough so that she could pursue her dream of writing? With scarcely enough time to read books written by others, she knew that writing her own wasn't even an option at the moment. Maybe that would change someday. Maybe when she'd finally worked through all the unknowns in her future. . . .

Before she could get sidetracked thinking of those unknowns, she heard a familiar voice. "Toni? Toni Matthews?"

Toni looked up. There stood Valerie Myers, wearing a pale blue sweat suit and slightly scuffed walking shoes. Her long salt and pepper hair, normally pulled back into a bun at the nape of her neck, hung loose past her shoulders. Large ebony eyes set in a fiftyish yet youthful face smiled down at Tony expectantly.

"Valerie Myers. What a nice surprise." Toni closed her book and set it beside her. "I see you're out taking advantage of this great weather too."

Valerie smiled. "Absolutely. While Principal Duffield was healing from his gunshot wound, I pulled double duty — worked almost nonstop for a month." She paused, glancing at the empty spot on the bench next to Toni. "Mind if I join you? I've walked my three miles for the day, and I'm ready for a break." Before Toni could answer, Valerie had plunked down beside her, continuing with her story. "Once Jeff — Mr. Duffield — returned, he gave me some extra time off to take at my discretion. When I woke up this morning and realized what kind of day it would be . . . well, needless to say, my discretion told me to use some of that time." She laughed, the sound of it warm and musical.

"I don't blame you." Toni's smile was wistful. "These days are few and far between around here, and we've all been through some really hard times lately."

Valerie's eyes softened. "I saw you in the courtroom yesterday. How is Melissa doing with all this? I've been so concerned for her. That's why I made a point of dropping in on the proceedings during her testimony."

"She's as well as can be expected, I suppose. Thank you for asking — and for caring enough to show your support by showing up at court yesterday. That means a lot."

Valerie nodded slightly, paused as if

unsure about what more to say, then unhooked the sports bottle attached to her waistband and took a drink of water. "Whew. It sure feels good to sit down. I have to confess, I'm not used to walking much. I enjoy it, but I just don't get the chance very often. When I do, I realize how out of shape I am."

It was Toni's turn to laugh. "You look great to me. I just hope I look half that good when I'm your age."

Valerie raised her eyebrows. "Spoken like a true twenty-something. Believe it or not, I remember being twenty-something, when middle age was as far away as the heavens themselves. Take it from me — it sneaks up on you when you aren't looking, so be careful!"

"I will," Toni promised, wondering for a brief instant what her life would be like when she reached Valerie's age. Before the unknowns of the future could begin to plague her once again, she said, "You know, I've been wanting to thank you for what you did for Melissa after the shootings. She was devastated over Carrie's injury and in no condition to walk out of that school building on her own."

Valerie nodded. "I could see that. In fact, when I found her she was huddled facedown over Carrie, hanging onto her as if she could somehow keep her friend's life from slipping away. I had a hard time getting Melissa up so the paramedics could get to Carrie." She shook her head. "What a nightmare that day was. It's funny how some things are almost a blur to me, while others — like finding Melissa huddled over Carrie — are as clear as if I were standing there right now."

"Were you there . . . in the hallway . . . when the shooting began?"

"No. I would have been, but . . ." She sighed. "Actually, I was on my way to the auditorium, walking beside Mr. Duffield, when I realized I'd forgotten the notes I needed to introduce the police officers who were doing the presentation at the assembly. So I turned to Jeff and excused myself, and by the time I was able to get back into that hallway, the shooting was over and Jeff was lying on the floor along with several others. I couldn't believe what I was seeing. If I hadn't left him there and gone back to my office when I did, well . . . who knows where I might be today?"

Toni took a moment to absorb what Valerie had told her. *How quickly our lives can change with one choice, one turn, one changed circumstance,* she thought. Jeff

Duffield, River View's high school principal, had been wounded in the attack but had recovered, along with several others. Carrie, however, was in a wheelchair, and one teacher was dead. What would Valerie's fate have been had she not walked away when she did?

As if she could read her thoughts, Valerie said, "It's an amazing thing, isn't it? Our futures can change in a split second. The morning of the assembly it was business as usual, and by afternoon . . ." Her voice trailed off and she seemed lost in the memory of that tragic day.

Suddenly conscious of Abe's warning about not interfering with an ongoing police investigation, Toni wondered whether or not she should ask Valerie about Tom. Maybe if she was careful about what she said, how far she went with her questions . . . maintaining a casual attitude she asked, "So, what do you think of Tom Blevins? Did you know him well?"

Valerie shook her head. "No one knew Tom well, I'm afraid. He was a real loner. From what I've been able to gather, he's been that way from the beginning, although on occasion he tried to make friends. Unfortunately, he failed — especially with the girls. He was always trying to strike up relationships and continually being rejected. It was as if he desperately wanted to fit in but simply didn't know how to go about it. And you know how cruel kids can be sometimes, especially when his failed attempts at socialization were common knowledge."

Toni nodded. She knew that everything Valerie was saying about Tom was typical of the lone gunman profile, and logic told her to let go of her suspicions and accept what the police and seemingly everyone else had already accepted — that Tom Blevins had acted without any accomplices or coconspirators — but something just didn't add up. She had to know more.

"What about his family? Have you talked with them since the shooting?"

Valerie sighed. "I wish I could. I wish *somebody* besides the police could talk with them, but they are completely unreceptive and uncooperative. Even before this happened, way back when Tom was faltering in school and on the verge of dropping out, I went to see his parents, hoping we could work together to keep Tom in school, but I never made it past the front door. That Mr. Blevins is a real piece of work, let me tell you. I don't think he's ever held a job for any length of time, and I understand that drinking problem of his is pretty chronic. I couldn't get past him to talk to Mrs. Blevins." She frowned. "I do know that Mr. Blevins is Tom's stepfather and that Tom has gone by his name ever since he's been in school. What happened to his real father, I have no idea."

"Sounds like a duplicate of the experience I had when I went over there," Toni said. "Tom's mother seems completely dominated by her husband, even fearful of him."

"I'm sure that's true. I've seen that scenario so many times." She shook her head. "Must be a very unhealthy way for a child to grow up. Both of his older sisters left home as soon as they were able. Can't say I blame them. From what I understand, they don't come home to visit much, if at all."

Toni raised her eyebrows. She'd forgotten about Tom's older sisters. If she couldn't get to Tom's mother, she might be able to find the sisters and learn something from them. She was sure the police had already talked with them, but that didn't mean she couldn't try it herself, although she doubted Abe would be very excited about the idea. Still, regardless of Abe's reaction and with or without his help, Toni knew she would follow through on whatever leads came along as she pursued this puzzling situation with Tom Blevins.

"Well," Valerie said, rising to her feet as she glanced at her watch and then re-clipped her sports bottle to her waistband, "I'm off. Got an appointment in an hour." She gave Toni a parting smile. "I'm glad we ran into each other. Please give my best to Melissa. And if there's anything I can do . . ."

Toni nodded and smiled. "Thank you, Valerie. You've been a big help already."

It had been a long day — a long week, actually — and Brad Anderson was glad it was over. Being the junior partner in his father's law firm, he'd been buried in research on a pending case. His mind, however, had been elsewhere, which was not unusual these days. Ever since the breakup of his engagement with Toni earlier in the year and her subsequent engagement to Abe Matthews, Brad had a hard time thinking of anything other than what might have been. *If only . . .* How those words plagued him. He some-how sensed, however — and reluctantly admitted to himself if to no one else — that Toni and Abe were right for each other, but that didn't stop the aching in his heart, particularly when he saw them together. The previous week had been especially difficult, as Brad thought of Melissa giving her testimony at the trial and what the effect of reliving her experiences must have been on both her and Toni.

He stretched his long legs and rested his shoeless feet on the coffee table, relaxing on the couch and wondering if he had anything in the kitchen worth fixing for dinner or if he should just call and have a pizza delivered. Before he could decide, the doorbell rang.

It was Melissa, her eyebrows arched and her green eyes wide as she awaited Brad's reaction. Brad was as close to Melissa as if she were his own sister, and she'd been to Brad's apartment many times — although never without Toni — but Brad couldn't imagine why she had come to his apartment alone on a Friday evening.

"Can . . . I come in?" she asked, her voice younger even than her sixteen years.

"I . . . sure. But . . ."

Melissa stepped inside, wrapped snugly in her parka and mittens. Her cheeks were pink, as if she'd been walking in the cold.

"What are you doing out?" Brad asked. "It's dark, you know. And cold."

Melissa smiled. "You sound just like my dad. He always makes . . . *made* . . . obvious remarks like that. You know, like he was the only one who knew it was dark or cold, or whatever."

Brad nodded. Where did he go from here? Melissa wouldn't have come unless it was something important. But why hadn't Toni — or April Lippincott, for that matter — driven her, rather than allowing her to walk? And why hadn't someone phoned and let him know she was coming? He could have met her somewhere, or picked her up. . . .

"So, can I sit down?" She headed for the couch, unbuttoning her parka along the way. Whatever this was about — and he assumed it had something to do with her testimony at the trial — it was apparently going to be discussed right here.

Melissa plopped down on one end of the couch, while Brad purposely situated himself at the opposite end. After all the years he and Melissa had known each other, he knew he was being ridiculous, but his legal training made him wary of potentially awkward or compromising situations — especially with a minor.

As he watched her place her parka and mittens on the seat between them, he couldn't help noticing the underlying sadness in Melissa's actions. She'd been that way ever since her father had died in the spring, but Brad thought he'd seen some improvement after her miraculous escape

155

from the kidnappers. Since the school shooting, however, she'd begun to sink back into depression and fear, and despite his efforts to cheer her up, Melissa's upbeat moods never seemed to last. Brad wished he felt free to talk with Toni about it, but he doubted that either Toni or Abe would welcome his interference. For now he would simply listen, try to encourage, and continue to pray for this young girl who'd experienced so much tragedy in her short life.

"What is it, Melissa?" He kept his voice soft, steady, and reassuring. "I know you weren't just passing by. You came for a reason, didn't you?"

Melissa dropped her head and nodded.

"Does it have to do with the trial, the testimony you had to give?"

Melissa looked up, her eyes brimming with tears. "It was awful," she whispered. "I had to tell them . . . everything. In front of all those people. The way that terrible Carlo put his hands on me . . . what he was threatening to do just before they killed him, and . . ." She swallowed, and Brad could tell she was struggling to maintain her composure. "I know I had to do it — give my testimony, I mean — but it was so . . . humiliating. And . . . I'm going to have to do it again, you know. At the other tri-als."

Brad pressed his lips together and nod-ded. He had no easy answers, no magic words to say to make her feel better, and he sensed she knew that. She simply needed someone to talk to, and she'd chosen him. This wasn't the first time, of course. Ever since he'd come upon her at the cemetery sitting beside her parents' graves and writ-ing in her journal soon after the shootings, Brad had tried to do what he could to help Melissa. He'd invited her to his parents' home on Christmas Eve and called to check on her occasionally. However, discussing her kidnapping ordeal and the trial, espe-cially here at his apartment, with the two of them alone together, somehow seemed too intimate. He wondered if Melissa had already had this conversation with Toni, or if she had kept her feelings inside until she could share them with him.

"Have you talked with Toni about any of this?"

She shook her head. "I can't. She tries to get me to talk about it, but I just can't. I don't know why. But with you . . ." Her long lashes were still wet as she fixed her eyes on his. "I feel safe here. Like you understand me. Almost like it was when I was with my

father. Like . . ." She shrugged. "Like we're
. . . family, I guess."

Brad smiled. "I'm glad you feel that way. I
always want you to feel safe with me. And
you are like family, Melissa — like my own
little sister, you know that. But . . ." He
paused, wondering if he was making a big
thing out of nothing. What harm could it do
to let her vent, to listen while she poured
out her feelings? Listening was really about
all he could do for her, so why not? If it
made her feel better, what problem could
come of it? But he knew his apartment was
not the right place for this conversation.

He reached over and took her hand. "I'm
always here for you, Melissa. Always. You
can trust me, no matter what. How about if
we go out and get something to eat? I'm
starved. How about you? Have you had any
dinner?"

"No. Abe and Toni went out for the
afternoon and haven't come home yet. April
and I were going to eat at home, but she
called and had to stay late at her church.
They're getting ready for a rummage sale
tomorrow, and they needed her help, so I
told her I'd warm up some leftovers. But
. . . I wasn't really hungry, and I got lonely,
so I decided to go for a walk, and . . . I
ended up here."

Brad smiled as he released Melissa's hand and rose from the couch. "I'm glad you did. OK, let's go eat. But before we do, I want you to call your house and leave a message on the machine for April or Toni, whoever gets home first, OK? I don't want anyone to be worried about you."

Melissa stood to her feet, a hint of a smile tugging at the corners of her mouth. The sadness in her eyes faded momentarily as she took a step toward Brad, then stood on her tiptoes and planted a kiss on his cheek. "Thanks, Bro. You're the best."

Brad nodded in acknowledgment, swallowing the lump in his throat as Melissa's pet name for him echoed in his memory. How many times had she called him "Bro" during the years when he and Toni were dating? It was no wonder that he and Melissa thought of one another as being "almost family" — they had nearly been so at one time. In fact, had it not been for Abe Matthews, they might truly be a family right now.

It was Sunday morning, and the brief respite from the cold, damp Washington weather had ended. Winter had returned with a vengeance. As Abe maneuvered his Honda Accord through the icy streets, he wondered how many of the faithful would even attempt the slippery trek to church. Not many, he supposed, but he'd promised Toni and Melissa he would pick them up and get them there, so he'd left early to allow some extra time.

As he drove, he wondered how and when to tell Toni what he'd just heard about Tom Blevins. He had no doubt the news would only cause her to dig in her heels that much deeper in her attempt to find out what she called "something more" about the case. But tell her he must. He was pretty sure she'd finally forgiven him for not telling her about his plans to visit Tom's lawyer, but he didn't want to push his luck. Keeping another secret about Tom — especially since it was inevitable that she would learn about it on Monday anyway — might be fatal to their relationship. Still, he hoped to put it off until later in the day, after church and a nice lunch out somewhere. For once Toni got hold of it, there would be no letting go. It would become the sole topic of conversation.

That, of course, would be his excuse for putting it off. Melissa would be with them on the ride to and from church, as well as during lunch. He couldn't very well introduce news about Tom Blevins with Melissa there. He'd wait until they were back at Toni's place after they ate. Maybe they could slip away somewhere, just the two of them, and he could tell her what he'd learned from his contact on the police force.

The call had come as Abe was getting out of the shower. His first thought was that it was Toni, calling to say they should cancel out on going to church because of the weather. Instead, he was surprised to hear a male voice — a former partner of his who knew of Abe's interest in Tom Blevins — calling to give him the latest information about the case.

Guilty, he thought. *Why would Tom change his plea from not guilty to guilty? It doesn't make any sense. Everyone knows he did it, but if he was going with a not guilty plea before, why would Harold suddenly advise him to change it? Or was all this Tom's idea?* Abe shook his head. For the first time since Toni had told him of her suspicions that there was something more to Tom's case, he had to admit she might be right. And if he had to guess about Tom's reason for the change of plea, he'd go with a cover-up. Tom just might be protecting someone, but whom? That's when he'd put in a call to Harold, who'd confirmed Tom's change of plea, adding that he thought the possibility of a lesser sentence was only part of the reason Tom had made the change. He, too, wondered if it was really about protecting someone else.

Abe sighed, slowing to a stop a couple of blocks from Toni's house. Who could Tom be protecting? And why? These were the very questions Toni would jump on the minute she heard the news, which Abe was going to make sure she heard from him before it was released to the media on Monday morning. Just when the sensationalism of the high school shooting was beginning to die down and the lives of River View's citizens were starting to return to normal, fresh meat was about to be thrown to the wolves. What a field day the press would have with this one. Abe wondered if things would ever settle down enough for him to get Toni to refocus on their wedding plans, which ever since his revelation to Toni of his visit to Harold Barnett, seemed to have been put on hold.

"Mail call."

Tom didn't even move from his prone position on his bunk when he heard the guard give the announcement. He'd never had any mail before. Why should today be any different? Even if someone were re-

sponding to this morning's media announcement of his plea change, there
wouldn't have been time for anyone to write
him a letter about it.

"Blevins. A letter for you."

Tom jumped. A letter? For him?

He bolted from the bunk and across the
tiny space to the slot in his door where an
envelope poked through. His hands shook
as he grabbed it and returned to his bunk.
He quickly turned it over to look at the
return address, aware that it had already
been opened and read. Standard screening
procedure, he imagined.

Tom's heart sank as he saw the name in
the top left corner. Carrie Bosworth. Who
in the world was she, and why was she writing to him? More important, why couldn't
it have been from . . . ?

He shook his head. He couldn't let himself
think of that now. He would hear in time.
He just had to be patient.

Still trembling, he tore the single sheet of
paper from the envelope. The letter was
handwritten, the words neat and in straight
lines across the page. He looked at the
signature at the bottom. "Carrie." Carrie
Bosworth . . . oh yeah, now he remembered.
One of Melissa Matthews's friends. Another
one of those stuck-up girls who thought she

163

was too good for him. Why in the world was she writing to him now?

He lay back on his thin mattress, put one arm under his head, and began to read.

Dear Tom:

This is a very difficult letter for me to write, but I feel I must, for my sake as well as yours. I pray you will read it thoughtfully and consider what I am going to say.

I know we haven't been close friends over the years, but I imagine you know me well enough to recognize my name. I also know you weren't aiming at me specifically when you pulled the trigger in the hallway that Monday after Thanksgiving, but one of your bullets hit me in the lower back, and I'm now partially paralyzed.

Tom clutched the paper in his hand, fighting the emotion that welled up inside him. He'd heard from his lawyer that, in addition to the death of a teacher and several injured students, one student had been hurt seriously. She might, in fact, never walk again. He had not wanted to know who it was. He didn't want a face or a name to go with that vague "somebody," but now he knew. And it made him sick.

Why had she written to him? To punish him? To twist the knife that was already permanently lodged in his gut? Well, he wasn't going to let her. He wasn't about to read any more about her injury or her self-pity or her anger at him. If this was the only letter he was going to receive while he sat rotting in jail, he would never accept another piece of mail again. He crumpled the letter and threw it into the far corner of his cell.

CHAPTER 8

April was stunned. What did it mean, Tom's changing his plea from not guilty to guilty? Did he suddenly remember that he'd committed the crime, whereas before he thought he hadn't? Ludicrous. It didn't make any sense at all. She shook her head as she stirred the tuna salad. She'd been listening to the radio in the kitchen as she prepared lunch when she first heard the shocking news. If she'd had the television on that morning she would probably already have known about it, but she'd spent the early hours of the day in prayer and meditation, enjoying her time alone with God. Now she was putting the finishing touches on the soup and salad lunch she'd planned for Toni, Abe, Melissa, and herself.

Abe had dropped by about thirty minutes earlier, offering to take Toni to pick up Melissa at Carrie's, where she'd spent the night. April expected them all back soon, and she'd been looking forward to their lunch together. She now hoped she'd have a chance to talk with Abe and Toni alone about this latest development in the case, not knowing if Melissa knew about it or how she might react to the situation.

The salad was ready. April placed it on the table and then went to check the vegetable soup simmering on the stove. It was good to have someone to cook for again. How she missed Lawrence! It had been years since she'd had anyone to share her meals with. Her daughter and son-in-law had always included her when possible, but they were busy with their own lives and often forgot how lonely an elderly widow can be, especially at mealtime. There was nothing sadder, April believed, than sitting down at the kitchen table, day after day, meal after meal, with no one to talk to. In her loneliness she'd become accustomed to turning on the radio or television while she prepared and ate her meals. It was the only company she'd had for several years — except for Julie, of course.

She sighed, carefully folding the napkins and placing them beside each plate, recalling the many times over the years when her granddaughter had dropped by for a meal and a chat. Poor, sweet Julie. How April's heart grieved for her only grandchild, her short life having ended in such a tragic way. The misguided teen had run off with a member of the baby-selling ring, believing they were in love and were going to start a new life together on the West Coast. Instead, she became pregnant and then miscarried, ultimately dying a violent death at the hands of the man who had impregnated her and claimed to love her. Still, April had the solace of knowing, through the testimony of a female member of the ring who'd spent quite a bit of time with Julie and whose trial was currently in progress, that in the last weeks of her life the wayward girl had returned to her childhood teachings and had started to pray and talk about God. She'd even begun repeating Bible verses she'd learned as a little girl. The woman said Julie seemed to be at peace before she died, and that gave April some measure of peace now.

It didn't take away the aching or the loneliness, though. How grateful she was that Toni and Melissa had taken her in — and how deeply concerned she was about anything that affected their lives. Right now that meant the entire situation with Tom Blevins.

Guilty. She shook her head as she heard

the car pull into the driveway, then flipped off the switch on the radio. No sense taking a chance that Melissa might hear the news for the first time as they all sat having lunch together. April would keep silent on the subject and see if anyone else brought it up first. If not, she'd find a way to take Toni and Abe aside and ask them what they thought of Tom's actions. Why would an obviously guilty young man enter a plea of not guilty, only to change it as the trial date approached? What did Tom Blevins have to gain — or lose — by this sudden about-face of his plea? April was hopeful that Abe would be able to shed some light on her questions.

This Monday, like all days spent in the dingy, confining cell, seemed to drag. Tom felt as if he'd been awake for at least an entire day, but it was only lunchtime. The only thing he had to look forward to at this point was a visit from his lawyer the next day. Tom didn't like his court-appointed attorney much, and he certainly didn't have much confidence in him, but right now the man was all he had.

For that reason, Tom had thought long and hard about Harold Barnett's advice concerning his plea. They'd originally entered a plea of not guilty, but Mr. Barnett had told Tom that he had almost no chance of winning in court. More than likely, the best they could hope for was LWOP — life without parole. Realistically, with public sentiment concerning the rash of school shootings running at an all-time high, Tom could very well end up with the death penalty. Consequently, Mr. Barnett thought Tom should at least consider changing his plea to guilty *if* — and the attorney made no promises on this one — he could get the D.A. to deal. In other words, if they could be assured the state wouldn't go for the death penalty if Tom pleaded guilty and avoided a trial, the boy might want to grab the compromise of LWOP, if indeed the offer was made. Mr. Barnett had even said there was a slight chance — *if* they all agreed to deal — of getting Tom off with twenty-five to life, which at least allowed for the possibility of parole at some point in the future.

However, the possibility of a lesser sentence wasn't the only reason Tom had changed his plea. Although he was somewhat relieved when Mr. Barnett told him it looked as if the D.A. would drop his option of seeking the death penalty if Tom pled guilty, the lonely prisoner was also hoping that his choice to avoid a trial would bring his partner out of hiding, convinced once and for all that Tom wasn't going to implicate anyone else in the shooting. Surely then Tom would finally hear something from the one with whom he'd planned the entire incident. . . .

Why had it turned out like this? Why had he botched it so badly? Instead of the two of them lying on some remote beach somewhere, enjoying themselves as they'd talked and dreamed of so often, he was stuck in this hole alone, hoping to get off with as little as twenty-five years behind bars. This wasn't at all what he'd expected.

He knew, of course, that it was no one's fault but his own. Still, it would help if he could at least have some contact, some hope that something was being done to help him. But then again, what could be done? What could anyone possibly do to get him out of this mess? Yet, after all they'd been through together, Tom thought at least some effort would be made. . . .

Was it because Tom hadn't fulfilled his mission? He'd tried — he truly had. He thought he'd had it all planned out, and by the time he stopped shooting, he thought he'd accomplished exactly what he'd set out to do. He also thought, in the midst of all the chaos and confusion, that he would be able to escape and be long gone before the police showed up. What he hadn't counted on was that two cops would already be in the building when he began firing. He would never forgive himself for being so stupid.

Bored, he sat up, wishing he at least had something to read. That's when he noticed the crumpled letter in the corner. His lip curled into a sneer. *So, Carrie Bosworth, Miss High-and-Mighty who thought you were too good for someone like me, now you're stuck in a wheelchair. Too bad. Guess you were just in the wrong place at the wrong time, weren't you? Like I've been all my life. Not much fun to be the one with all the bad luck, is it? So now you want to unload on me, tell me what a creep I am and how much you hate me for ruining your life.* Tom snorted. *Well, why not? If it makes you feel better . . .*

Telling himself he was doing it only to mock her, he got up from his bunk and retrieved the crumpled paper, smoothing it out as he returned to his bed. Perching on the edge, he began reading from the top, determined to make it through the entire letter this time to find out just what this paralyzed girl had to say to the one she undoubtedly blamed for ruining her life.

Dear Tom:

This is a very difficult letter for me to write, but I feel I must, for my sake as well as yours. I pray you will read it thoughtfully and consider what I am going to say.

I know we haven't been close friends over the years . . .

Tom snorted again. "That's an understatement," he said aloud, then read on.

. . . but I imagine you know me well enough to recognize my name. I also know you weren't aiming at me specifically when you pulled the trigger in the hallway that Monday after Thanksgiving, but one of your bullets hit me in the lower back, and I am now partially paralyzed.

Tom suppressed a shudder. That was as far as he'd read so far. From here on out, it was virgin territory. He steeled his emotions.

I am in therapy right now, and the doctors say I have a chance of regaining at least partial use of my legs someday. I'm praying that will happen. But I'm also praying about something else — about you, Tom — about what all this has done to you, and about the things that must have happened in your life before the shooting to make you do such a desperate thing.

In some ways I wish I could sit down with you and look you in the eyes and ask you why. But even if I would be allowed to come and see you — which I'm not too sure I would be — I'm not ready for something like that yet. You probably aren't either. Maybe someday . . .

Meanwhile, I want you to know that I'm praying for you, that somehow God will get hold of your life before it's too late, and that you'll realize just how much he really loves you. Because he does, you know, just as he loves me. I don't know why you did what you did, and I don't know why God allowed me to be in your line of fire and end up here in this wheelchair. But I do know that his plans for my life are good plans, and they haven't changed. His plans for you are good, too, Tom, if you'll just let him into your heart and allow him to love you and guide you from here on out. God's Son, Jesus, has already died to pay the price for your sin, just as he has for mine. Now all you have to do is ask

God to forgive you and to help you. That's all he's waiting for. If you'll do that, Tom, he will change your life. I promise.

One more thing. If you're thinking that what you've done is too awful for God to forgive, you're wrong. Nothing is too bad for God to forgive. And I forgive you.

Carrie

Long after he'd finished the letter, Tom sat staring at the wrinkled paper. What kind of a nut was this girl? He'd heard of religious fanatics before, but this one was beyond weird. Here she was, stuck in a wheelchair, writing to the guy who put her there and telling him that God loved him and wanted to forgive him — and that she forgave him. He muttered an oath, crumpled the letter once again, and this time tossed it into the toilet. He had enough to deal with already. He didn't need any reminders that he'd shot someone who talked about God as if she really knew him.

The smell of homemade vegetable soup teased their nostrils as they opened the front door and stepped inside. Cold wind from outside hurried them along as they closed the door behind them and hung up their coats in the entryway closet. At least they hadn't needed their umbrellas; the expected rain hadn't yet materialized. From the looks of the sky, though, it wouldn't be long.

Toni was the first one into the kitchen. Her grin was mischievous. "Well, I see I've stayed away long enough for you to do everything, including setting the table."

April smiled. "It was my pleasure. Everything's just about ready. I assume you're all hungry?"

"You assumed correctly," Abe said, entering the kitchen as he rubbed his cold hands together. "I slept in this morning and didn't even bother with breakfast."

Toni looked from Abe to April and smiled. The two of them got along famously. In fact, everyone seemed to get along with April. She was a very special lady, and they were blessed to have her in their lives. It was hard to imagine that someday the trials would be over and she would leave them to go back to Colorado permanently. "It's awfully nice of you to do all this, April," Toni said. "I hope you know how much we appreciate you."

"Actually, no, I don't," April answered with a chuckle. "Why don't you all sit down and tell me while I get the soup?" As she carried the steaming tureen to the table, she frowned. "Wait a minute. Where's Melissa? Didn't she come home with you?"

"She's in her room," Toni said, trying not to let her concern show through in her voice. "She had to make a quick phone call." Melissa hadn't specified whom she was calling. Toni hoped it was Carrie, possibly to discuss something Melissa had forgotten to tell her friend while they were together, but somehow Toni doubted it.

April hesitated, then sat down. "In that case, I want to ask you something before she comes in. Have you heard the news today? About Tom Blevins changing his plea?"

Toni nodded as Abe's jaws twitched. "Abe told me yesterday," Toni explained. "He heard it from a friend on the force and wanted me to know before it hit the media today."

"I see," said April. She looked at Abe. "What do you make of it? What's this change of plea business all about?"

Abe looked at Toni, hesitated, then looked back at April. "I'm not sure, of course. Only Tom knows the real reason. The media's playing up the plea bargain theory — you know, plead guilty, spare the taxpayers and families of the victims a huge trial, and come away with a reduced sentence. That may very well be it."

April raised her eyebrows. "But you don't buy it?"

"Not necessarily, although that may be part of the reason."

"And the other part?"

Toni sensed Abe's hesitancy even before she heard it in his voice. He, like Toni, trusted April completely. But how wise or responsible was it to toss around unsubstantiated theories concerning a murder trial?

"I'm . . . not sure," Abe answered. "Toni and I think that maybe — just maybe, mind you — there could be something else to this plea change. What that something else might be, we really don't know. All we know for sure is what everyone else in River View — and probably the entire nation — knows by now. Tom Blevins, for whatever reason, has decided to plead guilty. About all that leaves now is for a judge to hand down a sentence. Of course, with Tom pleading guilty, the court will order a psychiatric evaluation first, but I don't see that making much difference with the verdict."

"What do you suppose the verdict will be?"

Abe shrugged and shook his head. "I really don't know that either, but a plea bargain almost assures that it won't be the death penalty."

April seemed shocked. "You mean that was an actual possibility without the plea bargain? He's not even eighteen years old. Surely they wouldn't give the death penalty to a child."

"He may not be quite eighteen yet, April, but he will be by the time he's ready to be moved to a state institution. And he's certainly not a child; he's a killer. I'm sure you know that teenagers younger than Tom have been tried as adults. And with the pressure of public sentiment to do whatever is necessary to stop these shootings, I'd have to say the death penalty would have been a strong possibility without the plea bargain, yes."

Melissa's voice caught them all by surprise when she asked, "But it won't be now, will it?"

Toni winced, wondering how long her younger sister had been standing there listening. Toni had talked to Donna Bosworth about the plea change when she and Abe had stopped by to pick up Melissa earlier, and Donna had assured her that Carrie knew nothing about it — which meant Melissa probably didn't either. The Bosworths planned to tell Carrie after

Melissa went home. Toni had planned to do the same with Melissa, but not like this.

Melissa rephrased her question. "Are you saying that Tom isn't going to get the death penalty?"

Abe motioned Melissa into the room. "Why don't you come on in and sit down? We'll talk about it over lunch."

Melissa didn't move. "I hate what Tom did to Carrie and to the others, but I'd feel a lot better knowing he wasn't going to be put to death."

Toni resisted the impulse to gather Melissa into her arms and try to change the subject. She sensed it would be better to let Abe handle the explanation, so she sat still and waited for him to continue.

"I imagine a lot of people feel the same way you do," Abe said. "Of course, no one knows for sure yet what Tom's sentence will be, but Tom has changed his plea, from not guilty to guilty. That means he'll probably get off with a life sentence or —"

"I know all that. Brad and I were just talking about it on the phone. He said the same thing you said — that the change of plea will probably save Tom's life."

Toni was shocked. "Brad told you that? You were discussing this with Brad Anderson? I didn't know you even knew about

Tom's change of plea. Is that why you went to your room to make a call, so you could talk about this with Brad?"

Melissa frowned. "No. I just wanted to say hello to him, that's all. I didn't know anything about Tom changing his plea until Brad told me."

Toni was angry. Where did Brad get off telling Melissa something like this? Didn't he realize this sort of news should be shared among family members first? Her blue eyes narrowed. She was going to have to talk with him about overstepping his bounds.

Toni felt Abe lay his hand on her arm. *Leave it alone,* his gesture warned, but she had no intention of leaving it alone. Brad was out of line, and she certainly intended to tell him so.

"What time is Abe picking you up for dinner?"

Toni checked her watch, then smiled at April. "He should be here any minute. What are you and Melissa planning?"

"I'm sure if I left it up to her, we'd have pizza . . . again. But I convinced her to help me make a casserole instead." April chuckled. "I think that girl would eat pizza every day if we let her." Her smile faded as quickly as it had appeared, and her pale blue eyes dulled. "Julie was the same way — about pizza — from the time she was a little girl. . . ."

Toni nodded. As she and April sat together on the couch in the living room watching the warm flames flickering in the fireplace, Toni knew all too well how something as simple as pizza could evoke a fresh wave of grief. It had happened to her just this morning as she'd stepped outside and remembered how her father had loved the fresh smell of a rain-washed morning. The storm they'd expected the day before had indeed arrived, and it had rained through the night, clearing just before dawn. Since then the scattered clouds had danced across the sky, blown by a cold wind, not staying still long enough to dump any more precipitation. Toni had spent the day "sleuthing," as she called it, making only slight progress. She was ready for a break, and dinner out with Abe sounded perfect. Things had been a bit strained between them lately, and she was determined to do whatever was necessary to resolve any issues that threatened their relationship.

"By the way," April said, interrupting Toni's thoughts, "have you heard anything at all from Abe's aunt? Sophie, isn't it? You haven't mentioned her in a while, and I was just wondering . . ."

"I'm afraid not, although Abe's been saying we should try again to talk with her. We thought maybe we'd drive up there together one day soon — unannounced, of course, so she can't take off before we arrive — and see if we can get her to at least listen to us."

"Do you think it will work? After all, Abe is virtually all the family she has left, and you said she's always doted on him."

"True, but Abe doesn't hold out much hope that we'll change her mind. He says his aunt can be very stubborn when she sets her mind to something. And right now, she considers Abe dead. When he accepted Jesus — Yeshua, as Abe says — as the Messiah, Aunt Sophie believes he turned his back on God and on the Jewish people. Of course, we know that's not true, but that's just how she sees it. I suppose all we can do is continue to pray for her and try our best to show her God's unconditional love whenever we get the chance."

April nodded. "I suppose that's true, my dear. It just seems so sad to purposely cut yourself off from your own flesh and blood, never knowing what might happen . . ."

Her voice trailed off, and Toni knew her thoughts had returned to Julie. Before Toni could say anything, the doorbell rang.

"There's Abe," she said, rising from the couch. She'd no sooner opened the front door than he stepped inside and took her in his arms.

"I've missed you," he whispered, then kissed her deeply.

"Wow," she gasped. "I guess you did. But we just saw each other yesterday." She knew he was really referring to the distance they'd both sensed between them since the Harold Barnett incident and Abe's veiled remarks about Brad Anderson, but she now realized that they were both ready to put all that behind them and move on.

"Too long," he said, kissing her again. "Let's get out of here and go discuss the details for our wedding over dinner."

"But —"

"No buts. Let's just do it. We've been putting it off long enough. I love you, Toni Matthews, and I want you to be my wife — soon."

He was about to kiss her again when Melissa interrupted them. "Hey, you two. Can anyone else say hello around here?"

Abe released Toni and blushed slightly. "Sorry," he said, grinning. "Guess I got carried away."

"No kidding," Melissa exclaimed. "So where are you two lovebirds heading?"

Abe looked at Toni and raised his eyebrows questioningly. "Have we decided?"

"I don't think we got that far, Romeo," Toni answered, smiling coyly. "You had your mind on other things."

Abe appealed to April, who'd also come in to join them. "Did you hear that? She calls our wedding plans 'other things.' Wouldn't you think that would count as the most important thing? Isn't that how it's supposed to work?"

April laughed. "So I've heard. But this young lady always seems to have so many things on her mind . . ."

"Tell me about it," Abe moaned. "I'm just one of the items on her to-do list."

"Oh, poor baby," Melissa teased, then jumped at the sound of the phone. "I'll get it," she announced quickly, racing to her room.

Abe looked at Toni questioningly. "She must be expecting an important call."

Toni sighed. "Who knows? Melissa seems to be spending a lot more time than usual on the phone lately. I really need to talk with her about that. At least she's not depressed tonight, and for that I'm truly grateful. I was expecting a call myself. . . ."

As April returned to the kitchen, Abe took Toni's jacket from the closet and helped her into it. "Anyone I know?" he asked.

Toni looked at him and raised her eyebrows questioningly. She had no idea what he was talking about.

"The phone call you were expecting," he explained.

"Oh. Oh, no, it isn't. No one I know either. It's Tom Blevins's sister — the older one, although I'm not sure she'll call. I spent the day tracking down their numbers and reached the younger sister on my first try. She wouldn't even listen to what I had to say. Apparently she thought I was another reporter looking for an exclusive. She told me not to call back and hung up in my ear."

Abe looked impressed. "You actually got through to the other sister? You got her to talk to you about Tom?"

Toni pursed her lips. "No. All I got was her answering machine. I left a message and asked her to call, but . . . well, she may not. I'll give it a day or two and then try her again." She finished buttoning her jacket, then looked up at Abe and smiled. "OK, enough of that. We'll leave the phone calls to Melissa. Let's get out of here and go eat — and talk about our wedding."

Abe smiled, but before he could open the front door, Melissa reappeared in the entryway. "It's for you," she said, her voice flat, the animation of a few moments earlier vanished without a trace.

Toni frowned, wondering if Tom's sister had indeed returned her call. "For me? Who is it? Did she say?"

Melissa's disappointment was evident in her green eyes. "It's not a she. It's Brad. Says he's returning your call."

Toni caught her breath. She'd forgotten about her call to Brad. Ever since lunch the previous day, when Melissa had told them how Brad had discussed Tom's change of plea with her on the phone, Toni had been building steam. She'd called Brad first thing that morning, determined to let him know that she thought he'd been out of line and that she'd appreciate his not interfering with Melissa anymore. Friendship was one thing, she would tell him, but if the two of them were going to continue their relationship, some clear boundaries would have to be drawn — and followed. However, Brad had apparently left for the office early, and Toni hadn't wanted to call him at work to discuss such a personal matter, so she'd simply left a message on his answering machine at home. He must have just picked up his messages and decided to return her call. Toni glanced at Abe. He didn't look happy.

"Excuse me," she said. "I'd better take

that." As she walked to the end table next to the couch in the living room, she felt two sets of eyes following her every step. She sighed, her hand shaking slightly as she reached for the receiver. However her conversation with Brad turned out, she sensed her dinner conversation with Abe had just taken a turn for the worse.

CHAPTER 9

As Abe unlocked the door and entered his sparsely decorated but comfortable bachelor apartment, his step felt almost as heavy as his heart. It had been a long day, but his weariness, he knew, was not from physical exertion or extended hours. In fact, he was home quite a bit earlier than he'd expected.

Leaving the lights off, he crossed the room and plunked down in his favorite recliner, kicking off his shoes as he leaned back. He rubbed his eyes, trying to relieve the slight headache that had plagued him for the last several hours. It was an understatement to say the evening hadn't turned out as he'd hoped. Was it his fault? Was he making a big thing out of nothing? Was he allowing his own insecurities to cloud his judgment?

A probable yes to all of the above, he conceded. Toni hadn't really done or said anything to indicate that she was still carry-ing a flame for her former fiancé, but she hadn't really said anything to dispel the possibility either. He imagined that was because she was annoyed with Abe for even considering wrong motives in her concern for Melissa's growing attachment to Brad. And, Abe had to admit, she had a point. Brad was much too old to be a romantic interest for a fifteen-year-old girl, and although Brad and Melissa had known each other and maintained a big brother–little sister relationship for years, the teenager was very vulnerable and impressionable, particularly at this juncture in her life. It wouldn't take much for her to sustain yet another major heartache, of which she'd already experienced far too many.

Abe sighed and considered going to the refrigerator for something cold to drink but decided against it. He wasn't really thirsty enough to bother getting up. He also considered checking the answering machine by the phone next to his chair; he wouldn't have to get up for that. He decided against that option as well. It was just more effort than he cared to expend. And he was sure that he didn't have a message from Toni, as it had been less than an hour since he'd left her at her house.

Abe would have been home sooner, but he'd driven around for a while after dropping Toni off, trying to convince himself that everything between them was OK. For a time he'd believe it; then the nagging suspicions and insecurities would begin to erode his confidence. As he sat staring into the semi-darkness at the familiar outlines of his apartment, he wondered how someone of his physical stature, a trained law enforcement officer, could feel so weak and unsure of himself. He reminded himself again that Toni had returned Brad's engagement ring months ago and had joyfully accepted Abe's that snowy Thanksgiving at the park. Yet here they were, almost two months later, no closer to pinpointing a wedding date and finalizing their plans than they'd been when he'd first proposed.

He knew there were reasons — good reasons, at least as far as Toni was concerned — for postponing their wedding for a few months. However, Abe also knew that throughout her lengthy engagement to Brad, Toni had dragged her feet on these very same issues. That knowledge — and the fact that Brad very obviously still had feelings for Toni — concerned Abe deeply.

Abe closed his eyes and wondered if he would be able to drift off to sleep right where he was. If he got up and went to bed, he'd just lie there and think of how he'd stayed awake the night before, dreaming of what it would be like once he and Toni were finally married and he could fall asleep with her in his arms. It was then that he'd decided once again to broach the subject of speeding up their wedding date. He would talk to Toni over dinner and convince her that he simply couldn't live without her any longer. He would make her see that a big wedding was unimportant, that they could have a small ceremony anywhere, anytime, and get on with their lives together. Surely she would agree . . .

Yet after his initial introduction of the subject when he'd first arrived at her home to pick her up, he hadn't mentioned it again, nor had she. They spent much of the evening on small talk, picking at their food, and making occasional references to Toni's concerns for Melissa or her progress in pursuing her hunch about the Tom Blevins case. Overall, it had been a dismal disappointment when compared to the evening Abe had expected.

Abe took Toni home early, and neither of them mentioned when they would get together again. He only wondered if Toni missed him half as much at this moment as he missed her. He wondered, too, if he might be in for the biggest heartbreak of his life.

Toni awoke two mornings later to the dim gray light of dawn that was struggling to penetrate the winter darkness. Sunrise — although often hidden by heavy cloud cover — was especially late in arriving this time of year. Toni peered at her clock on the nightstand. Seven-thirty. She seldom slept this late, but she'd lain awake long after midnight, tossing and turning and resisting the urge to call Abe, while praying he'd call her. He hadn't.

Nearly two days had passed since they'd talked. Yet scarcely a moment had gone by without Toni's reliving the events of Monday evening. As she lay there curled up under the covers, remembering, she could almost feel Abe's warmth when he'd first arrived and scooped her into his arms, kissing her passionately and urging her to finalize their wedding plans over dinner. Her heart had leapt that evening, as it had on New Year's Eve, another occasion when she'd seriously considered agreeing to Abe's request of an early wedding date. Just as on New Year's Eve, however, something had happened on Monday evening to prevent her from voicing her desire to marry Abe quickly. Was

God trying to tell her something? Was he cautioning her to be patient? Or were circumstances simply conspiring against them to keep them from the altar? Toni chose to believe that the latter was most likely the case.

Whatever the reasons, she knew only that she missed Abe terribly. Why didn't she just pick up the phone and call him, tell him how she felt, and ask him to come and get her so they could run off and get married right away — today, if possible?

She also knew why she couldn't do that. In spite of her almost overwhelming love for Abe Matthews, she was concerned about the signs of a lack of mutual trust in their relationship. Ever since Abe had visited Harold Barnett without telling her, she'd found herself wondering if there might be anything else he hadn't told her. He'd certainly had his share of secrets when they first met.

She smiled in spite of herself at the memory of that day less than a year ago. It had been only a matter of weeks since her father had died, and Toni was in his office at the detective agency going through the files and trying to decide what to do with the mound of paperwork Paul Matthews had left behind. It was the very day Toni had first heard from April Lippincott and had subsequently discovered the clue in Julie Greene's file that started her on her quest for the truth regarding her father's death. Toni had been so lost in thought that she hadn't even heard Abe come into the office. When she'd finally heard his voice and looked up, she'd almost gasped aloud at the sight of the tall, handsome man standing in front of her desk. Thinking back, she decided it was Abe's dark, emotion-laden eyes that had impressed her the most.

Despite Toni's efforts from that day forward to keep her thoughts about Abe purely impersonal and professional, she hadn't succeeded. It was only a matter of months before her growing attraction to Abe had been the catalyst that ended her engagement to her high school sweetheart, with whom she'd long assumed she'd share her life.

Brad Anderson. Such a kind and honest man — and completely trustworthy. Why had she been so concerned about his interest in Melissa? They were, for all intents and purposes, a brother-and-sister team. Why did Toni think that relationship should end simply because she and Brad were no longer engaged? And why had she unleashed her worries and frustrations on Brad? He certainly hadn't deserved it, but that's exactly what she'd done when he'd called on Monday evening. Yet, despite the obvious hurt in his voice, he'd been so understanding, even as she railed at him for spilling the news of Tom's plea change to Melissa.

"You're right," he'd readily admitted, his voice soft with contrition. "I was way out of line. I never should have assumed she already knew. It wasn't my place, and I'm sorry, Toni. Please forgive me."

His lack of defensiveness had almost completely diffused her anger — almost. "I . . . yes, well . . . of course, I forgive you. I suppose I can understand how you'd think she already knew about it. It was all over the news, and . . ." She caught herself. He was missing the point here.

"It's not just your telling Melissa about Tom," she'd explained, trying to keep her voice firm but low enough that Melissa and Abe, still waiting by the front door, wouldn't hear every word. "It's . . . the intensity of your relationship. I think you and Melissa are spending too much time together, and she's becoming entirely too dependent on you. I'm concerned that —"

Brad had interrupted her then, the tone of his voice wounded, as if she'd punched him and knocked the air from his diaphragm. "Do you . . . want me to stop spending time with Melissa? Because if you do, I'll certainly honor your wishes, but . . ." His words trailed off, and the silence that followed seemed to echo in Toni's ears.

"I . . . I didn't say that. I just . . ." She took a deep breath. "Your friendship is very important to Melissa, as I'm sure it is to you. I would never ask you to sever that. I just think that maybe —"

"You'd like me to cool it a bit." It was the second time Brad had interrupted her. This time she was grateful.

"Yes. That's it exactly. She loves you, Brad. You know that."

"I love her too." Another pause. "I —"

Before he could go any farther, Toni jumped back in. "I just think it would be good for her to spend more time with . . . us . . . her family. To confide in us a little more. It seems lately as if you've become her sole confidante. I don't think that's healthy."

"Understood. I'll make the necessary adjustments." Brad's words were clipped, but not harshly so. Toni got the impression he was holding back his emotions, trying not to say any more than he knew she wanted to hear. Once again, she was grateful. Brad had always been that way — so considerate of others' feelings, particularly hers. He had, in fact, been the one to break their engagement when he realized how strongly she felt about Abe. Toni knew, even at the time, how very difficult it had been for Brad, but she simply hadn't had the courage to make the break herself. As she remembered that evening when she'd returned his engagement ring and he'd kissed her one last time, the respect and admiration she felt for Brad Anderson reassured her that she had nothing to worry about concerning the time he spent with Melissa. The man was completely above reproach.

"Thank you, Brad." This time it was her turn to exercise restraint over her emotions. "I knew you'd understand. You always do."

Even now, lying in bed in the growing morning light, the memory of that phone conversation tugged at her heart. She'd never meant to hurt Brad, and yet she had. Deeply. That was a fact she'd just have to live with.

But what about Abe? Had she hurt him too? Was there justification — at least from his viewpoint — for his obvious insecurities regarding Brad? Grudgingly, she admitted the possibility, although she rationalized that Abe should have had enough maturity —

and enough confidence in her — to know better. Again, that was the problem. The lack of trust between them. Would they ever be able to overcome it?

She thought once again of the secrets Abe had carried into their relationship — although, in all fairness to him, he'd made a point to tell her everything before pursuing a future with her.

Everything. Oh Abe, I pray you really have told me everything — that there's nothing left in the past that might someday come back to haunt us. You told me about Amanda, your college sweetheart, the pregnancy, being paid to give the baby up for adoption. And after that, about getting involved with the baby-selling ring to make some extra money . . . Oh, Abe, I forgave you for all that. And I forgave you for going to see Tom behind my back. But . . . is there anything else?

Toni closed her eyes. *This is ridiculous. And so unfair. I've got to stop mistrusting and judging him based on something I've already forgiven. I know that thing with his going to see Tom's lawyer was because he loves me, because he was trying to help me. I wish he hadn't gone about it the way he did, but . . . his motives were good. I need to put this mistrust behind me and focus on the future. I've got to show him that he truly is the love of my life, the man I want to marry and grow old with . . .*

Resolving to make the first move, she reached for the phone to call him. Before she could pick it up, it rang. Her heart sang as she pressed the receiver to her ear.

"Abe?"

Momentary silence echoed in the wake of her greeting. Then a woman's voice said, "Hello? Is this Toni Matthews?"

Toni frowned, puzzled. Who, besides Abe, would be calling her so early in the morning? "Yes, it is. And you are . . . ?"

"This is Megan Browning — formerly Megan Blevins. I . . . got your message the other day. I would have called sooner, but . . . I wanted to think about it first. About talking to you, I mean."

Toni was shocked. She'd prayed for this but really hadn't expected it — at least not so soon. Now that she actually had Tom's oldest sister on the line, what should she say to her?

"I . . . wasn't sure if you'd remember me — or Melissa — or even make the connection," Toni stammered. "I honestly didn't remember you at first. I'm not even sure if we ever really met. But my younger sister —"

"I don't remember you," Megan interrupted, "but I certainly remember Melissa. That's why I decided to return your call."

Toni was puzzled. "I'm not sure I understand."

"It was a long time ago. Tom and Melissa were in the early years of grammar school — I can't remember exactly what grades, but Tom was already having problems with the other kids. They were always teasing and bullying him. He never seemed to know how to fight back. He'd just hold it inside and then let it all out when he got home — mostly with me, never with Mom. I'm only a few years older than he is, so I wasn't much help, I'm afraid. No one was — except Melissa."

She paused, and Toni wondered if she should say something. Before she could decide, Megan went on with her story.

"A couple of the boys were picking on Tom during recess. Before any of the teachers or playground monitors noticed or could break it up, Melissa came in swinging. She actually knocked one of the boys down, and the other one took off running when she came after him." Megan laughed, yet her voice was sad. "I always wished I could have been there to see it."

Toni wished she had, too, although it wasn't a difficult scene to envision. It was just like Melissa to fight for the underdog. She was so like their father in that way. Toni still couldn't remember the incident, and she was surprised no one had told her about it at the time.

"I never heard anything about that," Toni admitted. "The school never called, and if Melissa said anything, I'm afraid I don't remember."

"You probably didn't get a call because it all happened so quickly and no one was hurt. I doubt they even knew about it. It did happen, I assure you. Tom told me all about it — more than once. He talked about Melissa for a long time after that."

A distant alarm bell sounded in Toni's mind, and she knew she had to see Megan in person — as soon as possible. "Can we . . . get together sometime? I'd really like to talk to you. I can come there. . . ."

Megan hesitated. "I . . . don't know. I hadn't really planned . . ."

"Please. I won't take much of your time, I promise. I just want to talk with you about Tom. Please."

"Why? What's in it for you? I'm sorry. I don't mean to be cynical, but no one has ever cared much for Tom before. Why should you care about him now? You're not part of his legal defense, are you? Because if you are, I've already talked to his lawyer. And the police. And reporters by the millions."

"No," Toni admitted. "I'm not part of his legal defense. I just want to help him if I can. I'm not sure how, and I'm not sure why, but I think there's more to his story than what he's telling, and finding out what it is might help him somehow."

Megan hesitated again. "I've thought the same thing, but . . . I haven't admitted that to anyone else. And I haven't told anyone what I just told you about Melissa. Actually, I'd forgotten about it until you called." Toni heard her sigh before she went on. "I guess it couldn't hurt to talk to you, but . . . you won't bring any reporters, will you?"

"No. Just me, and . . ." It was Toni's turn to pause. Should she go alone, or should she try to get Megan to agree to Abe's coming along? To go without him would only widen the gap of mistrust between them, and Toni wasn't willing to risk that. "I'd . . . like to bring my fiancé if that's OK."

A final pause. "OK. Just the two of you. And not for long. I'm pretty busy. I have a two-year-old who keeps me hopping. It would have to be during the day when my husband's at work. I . . . don't think he'd much like the idea of my talking to you about Tom."

"During the day is fine. Tomorrow?"

"Friday would be better. About ten or so?"

"Perfect. You live near the beach, right? That's about a ninety-minute drive from here. We'll leave early. Can you give me directions?" She grabbed a pen and paper from the nightstand as Megan recited the stops and turns that led to her home. Toni was so excited she could hardly write. She only hoped Abe would be equally excited about their trip to the coast, or if not excited, then at least willing.

Friday dawned crisp and clear with a steady breeze blowing from the west. Toni imagined the breeze would increase in intensity as they neared the coast. In their jeans and parkas, Toni and Abe were ready for the cool beach temperatures they were bound to encounter.

Leaning back in the passenger seat of Abe's Honda, Toni searched for something to say to ease the tension between them. As soon as Toni had hung up from talking with Megan on Wednesday, she'd called Abe. He'd answered on the first ring as if he'd been sitting by the phone. Although he was reserved, he sounded pleased to hear her voice and readily accepted her invitation to join her on her trek to visit Tom Blevins's sister on Friday. After that, however, they didn't speak until he arrived to pick her up that morning.

As they climbed into the car to leave, Abe had asked Toni if she'd like to stop for breakfast along the way, but she'd said she preferred not to risk being late. They decided to stop somewhere in the area and eat if they arrived at their destination early enough. Otherwise, they'd just wait until their meeting with Megan was over and then eat on the way home.

It was amazing, Toni thought, how much mileage you could get out of a topic like when and where to eat — or not eat, as the case might be. From the beginning of their relationship, Abe and Toni had never had trouble talking. Suddenly they were reaching for safe topics, searching for ways to fill the silence. She didn't like it.

Determined to do something about it, she sat forward and laid her hand on Abe's, which rested on the console between them. His jaw twitched, and he turned to her, his eyes soft.

"I've missed you," was all she said.

Taking her hand in his, he raised it to his lips. "I've missed you too." His voice was husky. "Let's not do this anymore."

She shook her head. "No more."

He smiled and looked back at the road. "I feel better now."

"Me too." Toni sighed and closed her eyes, leaning back in her seat and enjoying the feel of his hand holding hers. He had big hands — strong and gentle. She smiled. That was Abe — big, strong, gentle. Why had she taken so long to reach out to him? She resolved not to let it happen again.

The remainder of their trip was uneventful, yet blissfully peaceful, as the silence that only moments earlier had been a wall between them now seemed a soothing balm to Toni's very relieved heart. This was right, the two of them, side by side, communing with one another whether they spoke or not. No suspicions, no innuendos, no second thoughts or misgivings. Only the joy of being together.

As it turned out, Toni had been right in anticipating that the wind would be blowing much stronger by the time they reached the coast. Large drifts of sand were piled up against the older homes that lined the beach community where Megan lived. And, although the temperature was five degrees warmer than it had been when they left River View, it felt colder. Toni was glad for the warmth of her parka — and of Abe's hand enveloping hers.

Locating Megan's home almost half an hour ahead of schedule, they decided to grab a quick bite at a drive-through restaurant, then proceeded back to the Browning home. By the time they arrived and rang the doorbell, Megan was waiting for them, her two-year-old in tow.

"Come on in," she said as soon as they'd introduced themselves. "This is my little boy, Tommy. I . . . named him after my brother. My dad, too, I guess, although I don't remember him much." She cleared away some unfolded laundry from the couch in the small, cluttered living area. "Have a seat," she offered, chattering, Toni surmised, to hide her nervousness. "How about some coffee?"

They declined, and Toni studied Megan as she attempted to get Tommy situated in his playpen with some toys. He would have none of it. Megan finally conceded and perched him on her ample hip as she swept a section of newspaper from the only other chair in the room, then transferred Tommy to her lap and smiled as she took a seat opposite Toni and Abe.

"He keeps me busy," she explained, her voice apologetic. "Terrible twos, you know."

Abe and Toni nodded. Toni could still

remember Melissa at that age, but she'd been anything but the typical "terrible" two-year-old. That was the year Marilyn Matthews had died of cancer, and Melissa had gone through a long withdrawn period, scarcely speaking to anyone and whimpering for her mother almost incessantly. It was not a year Toni liked to think about.

Toni switched gears back to the present, marveling at how little the young mother resembled her only brother. Megan was rather pretty, with dark hair, large eyes, dimples, and a ready smile. She carried her extra twenty pounds well; weight Toni imagined she'd gained and never lost after her pregnancy. It was obvious she doted on her son, who was already fidgeting and wanting down. Megan finally yielded to his wishes and allowed him to jump to freedom, keeping a wary eye on him as he played with his blocks on the floor only a few feet from her. Toni wondered if Megan was a bit overprotective. If so, Toni decided, she probably had good reason to be.

Toni cleared her throat. She hated to jump right in, but she also wanted to honor her promise to Megan that their meeting would be as brief as possible. "I . . . I really appreciate your allowing us to come and talk with you. I wasn't even sure you'd return my call."

Megan cut a glance toward her son, then looked back at Toni. "I wasn't sure at first either. But, like I said, the more I thought about what Melissa had done for Tom that day . . . well, I felt I owed it to you somehow. Even though . . ." She paused as if wondering whether or not to complete her thought. Apparently she decided to go ahead. "Even though Tom said she turned on him later."

Toni frowned. "What do you mean by that?"

Megan picked at a spot on her worn jeans, obviously uncomfortable with the news she was about to divulge. "She . . . turned him down. . . . For a date, I mean. It was just a year or so ago, not long before Tom dropped out of school. He asked her to go to a movie or something, and she said no. He was pretty devastated — humiliated, really. He never had anything good to say about her after that. In fact, I can't remember that he ever mentioned her again. But since I wasn't living at home at the time and only talked to him on the phone now and then, I really don't know all the details. Still, Melissa was the only person who ever stuck up for Tommy — Tom — in all those years, and that's why I decided to return your call." She shook her head sadly. "Some of those kids picked on him real bad."

The distant alarm that Toni had heard on Wednesday when she first spoke with Megan over the phone was increasing in volume. She tried to ignore it and keep her mind on what she needed to learn from Megan about Tom, but she knew she would seriously have to consider talking to Melissa about both incidents. Even if Melissa hadn't mentioned them to Toni when they occurred, Toni thought it strange that she hadn't told her about them at the time of the shooting — at least the most recent situation of Tom asking her on a date. Something just didn't add up.

Refocusing on the conversation at hand, Toni said, "It must have been terrible for your brother."

Megan nodded. "It was. At school . . . *and* at home. Our old man . . ." She shuddered and took a deep breath before going on. "Our stepdad, that is. Like I said, I don't really remember our real father. He left when Tom was a baby. According to Mom, it was good riddance. Maybe so. But I never could figure out why she went and got hooked up with someone like . . . Sam." She spat out the name as if it were a curse word. "I can't believe our real father was any worse than that. Couldn't have been."

Toni felt Abe's hand cover hers. She glanced up at him. His face was expressionless, but she could sense the tension in his body as his leg pressed against hers. Toni knew that if there was one thing that Abe, as a police officer, could not tolerate, it was child abuse of any sort. He'd run across so many cases of it since he'd been on the force, and now it appeared that child abuse might have been an everyday occurrence in the lives of the Blevins children.

Megan continued with her story. Toni was glad. It was so much easier than trying to drag information from a reluctant witness.

"It was awful," Megan said, averting her eyes from Abe and Toni and focusing them on her son. "Not so much for me and Jenny — my sister — but for Tom. He always got the worst of it. Sam said he was a sissy. Said he was going to teach him to be a man if he had to beat it into him." She shuddered again, then looked straight at Toni. "There wasn't any . . . sexual abuse, if that's what you're thinking. With Jenny and me, it was mostly a control thing. He wouldn't let us date, have friends over, that sort of thing. He was always accusing us of stuff too. Said he knew we were sleeping around, even when we hardly knew what that meant." She rolled her eyes. "Jenny and I couldn't wait to get out of there. We talked about it all the time — planned it for years. We each left the day after we graduated from high school — me first, of course, then Jenny two years later. We never regretted it — except for worrying about Tom. Things got a lot worse for him once we left. I really don't know how he stood it all these years."

Toni's heart ached as she listened to Megan's recounting of Tom Blevins's childhood. She'd already sensed it had been bad, but she had no idea how bad until now. Abe finally spoke up.

"What about your mother? Where was she when all this was going on? Was she involved in the abuse too?"

Megan dropped her eyes. "She was there. That's all — just there. She didn't ever beat Tom, if that's what you mean, but she never tried to stop it either. At least, not after the one time . . ."

Her voice trailed off, and they waited. When Megan spoke again, her words seemed to come from somewhere far away, detached from the present but frightening in their almost monotone matter-of-factness. "Tommy — Tom — wasn't much older than my own Tommy." She glanced at her son again. "Just a little boy . . . That was the first time — at least, the first time I remember. Tom was crying, and he just wouldn't stop. Sam kept yelling at him to shut up. Finally he picked him up and shook him till he stopped crying. Mama was screaming by then, telling Sam he was going to kill her little boy. Sam just ignored Mama and threw Tom down on the bed. I think that must have helped Tom catch his breath because he started crying again, only this time it was just a little whimper. Mama tried to go to him and pick him up, but Sam wouldn't let her. In fact, he lit into her and beat her so badly she lost two teeth and had a black eye for nearly two weeks. After that, she never got in his way or tried to stop him again when he went after Tom. Seeing what happened to Mama when she tried to stand up to him, Jenny and I learned to keep quiet too. But now . . . with all that's happened with Tom and the school shootings and all, I sure wish we hadn't. If we'd just said something . . ."

She buried her face in her hands then, but the sobs Toni expected to hear never materialized. She finally looked up, dry-eyed, and shrugged. "It's too late now, isn't it? I mean, maybe — if Tom was sticking with his not guilty plea — I could say something and the jury might feel sorry for him and let him off a little easier. But now . . ." She shrugged again. "Like I said, it's too late. . . ."

"Not necessarily," Abe answered, kicking into his police detective mode. "Megan, would you be willing to testify to what you've just told us? Do you think Jenny would back up your story?"

"I . . . don't know — about either one of us testifying, I mean. I don't think my husband would want me to get involved. And Jenny — no, probably not. She just wants to forget about the whole thing. She's so paranoid about the media hounding her that when I talked to her a couple of days ago, she told me she's thinking of moving again and even changing her name."

Abe's jaws twitched. "At least consider it," he urged. "Please, Megan. If not for Tom, then what about your mom? She's still caught in that situation. You might be able to help her."

"She's there because she wants to be," Megan answered flatly. "I tried to talk her into leaving and coming here to live with us, but she won't do it. So that's that." She fixed her eyes on Abe. "I don't want to discuss my mother anymore. Sorry, but that's just the way it is."

Abe nodded in resignation, his lips pressed together as if to prevent himself from saying anything further. Toni answered for him then, her voice soft in an effort to maintain a sense of camaraderie between them. "We understand, Megan. Really. And for now, anyway, we'll leave your mom out of it." She wanted to say so much more, but thought better of it. She was anxious to keep Megan on their side, as she had no idea where all of this would lead, and they might very well need to talk with her again later. "We really appreciate what you've told us about Tom," she went on. "It doesn't excuse what he's done, but it certainly helps us understand him better. He's had a really hard life."

Megan nodded. "Really hard. You're right. I can't remember a time when he was happy. Never. Except . . . well, maybe that was just because he was already planning . . . the shooting. I don't know. It just seemed like, when I called him a few weeks before he . . . did what he did, he seemed happy, excited or . . . I don't know. It was something I wasn't used to hearing in Tom's voice, so I'm really not sure. The strange thing was, when I told him — like I always did when I called him over the years after I'd left home — when I told him how badly I felt about leaving him there alone, he laughed. Seriously. He laughed, and then he said, 'What makes you think I'm alone? I used to be, but I'm not anymore, and I'll never be alone again.' When I asked him what he was talking about, he said, 'You wouldn't believe it if I told you.' Then he hung up. That was the last time I talked to him. That's why, when you said maybe there was more to Tom's story than he was telling, I thought maybe you were right. Maybe someone else was involved. Who knows?" She shrugged. "He's always told me more than anyone else in the family, but that isn't much. It wouldn't do any good to try to get anything out of Jenny — she hasn't talked to Tom in a couple of years. Mama wouldn't be any help either. For the most part, Tom quit trying to talk to her years ago. I think he always loved her — a lot — but . . . he felt betrayed by her, you know?" She dropped her eyes. "We all did. I know I should go visit Tom. I've thought about it every day since I first heard what happened, but . . . my husband, the baby . . . I just can't bring myself to do it." She looked up, her eyes pleading for understanding. "Can you see why I can't go? Can you?"

Toni nodded and turned to Abe. He was already gazing at her, his dark eyebrows raised questioningly. Toni knew what he was thinking because she was thinking the same thing. Someone else *was* involved in the shootings, but who was it? If the police hadn't been able to come up with anything, how would they ever discover that person's identity?

CHAPTER 10

"You're up early," Toni observed, smiling at her younger sister who sat at the kitchen table bleary-eyed, munching on a bowl of cereal. Melissa was already dressed in jeans and a sweatshirt, her hair combed, looking very much as she did on school mornings. But it was Saturday, and Melissa never got up early unless she had somewhere to go.

"Mmm," Melissa grunted, nodding slightly as she swallowed. "Babysitting today. Mrs. Johnson called me last night while you and Abe were out. She needs to run some errands and doesn't want to take Tyler with her because he's just getting over a cold. So she wondered if I could come over and stay with him." She tucked a strand of long hair behind her ear. "I told her I'd be glad to. I haven't seen Tyler much since school started anyway. I've missed him."

Toni sat down at the table next to her,

pleased that Melissa had something constructive to do, something that would help keep her mind off the many issues she was juggling at the moment — and something that did not include Brad Anderson. As much as Toni knew she could trust Brad with just about anything — including her younger sister — she still felt it was unhealthy for Melissa to restrict her spare time and confidences to one person, particularly an attractive, older male. Melissa had always been so close to her father, considering him — along with Carrie Bosworth — her best friend. Having lost him so recently, it would be natural for Melissa to gravitate toward a father figure. Toni's concern was that her sister might misconstrue her attraction to Brad and his attentiveness to her as something other than what it was. Spending the day with Tyler Johnson might be just what Melissa needed to get her mind off her problems and on to something constructive.

"I know you've missed Tyler," she said. "You're so good with him. He really loves you, you know. I'll never forget his seventh birthday party. Wasn't that a great surprise when his dad showed up?"

Melissa smiled. "It sure was — and a relief too. That's all I heard all summer while I was taking care of him — how he wanted his dad to come back in time for his birthday in September. He sure missed him when he and Tyler's mom split up. Tyler used to pray every day that God would bring his daddy back from Texas, and he never doubted that God would answer either. Sometimes that used to worry me. . . ."

"I know. Me too. But it all worked out, didn't it? The last I heard, Mr. Johnson had called off his new relationship and he and Tyler's mom were back together again. Sure hope things continue to go well for them."

"That's one of the reasons she called me," Melissa explained. "She said her husband could stay home with Tyler today, but they felt like it was more important for them to spend a little time away together. They're just going to run some errands, have lunch out, stuff like that. Cool, huh?" She took another bite of cereal.

Toni nodded. "Cool, yes. I wish everyone's relationships could work out so well."

Melissa frowned inquisitively, still chewing her breakfast.

"I guess I've been thinking about Tom Blevins and his situation," Toni said, purposely failing to mention that a couple of her own relationships had also flashed through her mind. She couldn't do much to make up to Brad for having hurt him, but she certainly hoped things with Abe would be better from now on. "I haven't really had a chance to talk to you since Abe and I went to see Tom's sister Megan yesterday morning," she said. "We actually learned quite a bit about the Blevins family while we were there. Nothing very good, I'm afraid . . . although his sister is very nice, and quite helpful too." She smiled. "Megan has a two-year-old named Tommy. He's a cute little guy . . . and *very* busy."

Melissa swallowed and put her spoon down. "Named after Tom, huh?"

Toni nodded again. "Yes, and after their father, too, since that was also his name. Tom's sisters don't remember much about him, and Tom never really knew him because he left home almost immediately after Tom was born. Not long after that, their mother married Sam Blevins, the only father Tom has ever really known. And it sure doesn't sound like that's a very positive relationship, to say the least."

"I'm not surprised. Even though I didn't know Tom or his family much, I always heard his dad — or stepdad, whatever you want to call him — was pretty mean. A real drunk too."

Toni hesitated. April hadn't come out of her room yet, and Melissa seemed willing to talk, which wasn't always the case lately. Maybe this was the perfect time to ask her about the things Megan had told her during their visit. "Melissa, I need to talk to you about something. This may sound a little strange, but . . . do you remember a time in grammar school when some of the boys were picking on Tom — out on the playground, I think it was, and —"

Melissa interrupted her. "That would have been every day. Seriously, I used to get so sick of seeing it. Sometimes the teachers broke it up, but sometimes they didn't even bother. I really hated that. I felt sorry for Tom."

"I know you did, but I was talking about a specific instance. According to Megan, when you saw these two boys picking on Tom, you jumped right in to defend him. She said Tom told her you knocked one of them to the ground and then went after the other one, who ran away. Megan said Tom talked about it a lot after that. In fact, that's the main reason Megan decided to return my phone call. She said she felt she owed it to me because I was your older sister and you were the only one she could remember who ever stuck up for Tom."

Melissa looked confused. "I don't remember that," she said. "I'm sorry, but I really don't. I always wished someone would help Tom whenever I saw him in trouble like that, but I can't remember anyone ever doing it, including me. Doesn't that seem strange to you? I mean, if something like that had really happened, I'm sure I'd remember it."

Toni nodded. It seemed strange indeed. Yet, it had happened quite a few years ago, if indeed it did happen. Maybe the more recent incident would still be fresh in Melissa's mind. "Megan also mentioned another instance, a year or so ago. She said that Tom asked you for a date and you turned him down. Do you remember that?"

The look of confusion on Melissa's face turned to incredulity. "A date! You've got to be kidding. No way did Tom Blevins ever ask me out on a date. I mean, he tried to talk to me a few times, but that was it. Nothing about a date, that's for sure. That I would remember, I guarantee you. Of course, if he had asked me, I would definitely have turned him down. I felt sorry for him, sure, but he was way too weird. What I can't figure out is why in the world Tom's sister is saying these things happened when they didn't. It just doesn't make any sense."

"It doesn't make much sense to me either. I wondered, even when she was telling me, why you wouldn't have at least mentioned these things after the shooting. I can see where you might have neglected to do so before, but in light of what happened —"

Melissa got up from the table and carried her now empty cereal bowl to the sink. "Well like I said, those things just did not happen. I have no idea why Tom or his sister would make something like that up, but it's not true. Period." She rinsed her bowl and then glanced at her watch as she dried her hands on the dishtowel. "Gotta run," she announced, heading out of the kitchen toward the front door. "I'll see you sometime this afternoon."

"Do you want a ride?" Toni called after her.

"No thanks. It's not raining right now, and it's just a short walk."

Toni heard the front door slam. Almost immediately afterward she heard April's bedroom door open and her footsteps in the hallway. As Toni sat at the kitchen table, her thoughts were racing. If the stories Tom had told Megan about Melissa were lies — and she was sure now that they were — maybe his talk about not being alone anymore, about having someone else in his life, was also untrue. Was it possible she was on a major wild goose chase, trying to track down an accomplice who simply didn't exist? Had Tom Blevins, in his desperate need for companionship, invented a friend, a partner of some sort, just as he'd invented the stories of Melissa's coming to his aid and then turning down his invitation for a date? Furthermore, if the friend was a figment of Tom's imagination, did Tom realize that . . . or had he honestly come to believe this person existed? Abe was now leaning toward believing in the reality of this coconspirator, and Tom's lawyer had seemed quite interested and pleased in the results of their visit to Megan. For the first time, however, Toni was beginning to have her doubts.

She forced herself to smile as April entered the room. The situation was becoming more complex by the day, and she certainly wasn't going to solve it by sitting at her kitchen table and worrying about it. And at this point, she saw no reason to burden April with anything further.

Abe and Toni were once again sitting side by side in the front of his Honda, but this time they were headed north to Centralia to attempt a visit with Abe's aunt. It was Wednesday morning, and a light mist sprinkled their windshield as they drove along under the gray Washington skies. Abe had hoped to make the trip on a sunny day, but Toni had been called to substitute at the local grammar school on Monday and Tuesday, so today was her first free day of the week. The evening before, as they sat talking over takeout Chinese food in Toni's kitchen, they decided that rather than wait for the weather to clear — which could take a while in this part of the country — they would just make the best of whatever weather the morning brought them. And if that included rain, they hoped the dampness would keep Sophie home until they arrived.

In some ways Abe envied what he considered Toni's ideal schedule. Technically, she had a job — that of substitute teacher for the River View School District — but it left her with enough free time to pursue the many other issues in her life that now demanded her attention — not the least of which was her new obsession with uncovering the entire truth about the Tom Blevins case.

Abe had to admit that Toni's previous obsession with discovering the truth about her father's death had been a worthwhile one. Now that she'd transferred her inherited private detective instincts to the Tom Blevins case, Abe was suddenly almost as obsessed with the case as Toni had been from the beginning. Their visit with Megan Browning had sparked more than an idle curiosity within him. Whereas before he'd been involved primarily to placate Toni and to try to keep her out of trouble as she went about what she saw as her quest for truth, he now believed as she did — that there was something more to the River View High School shootings than one lone gunman suddenly going berserk and firing randomly into a group of students and faculty.

The funny thing was, now that Abe was almost sure there had been an accomplice to Tom's crime, Toni had begun to believe that the accomplice might be an imaginary companion invented by Tom to quell his loneliness and boost his courage. Abe supposed that was possible, but he'd been a detective long enough not to confuse possibilities with reality.

And that was the true problem. While Toni had something constructive to do — subbing every now and then for the River View School District — Abe was still on paid leave from the police force and would be for a while yet. He missed being on active duty, even though he enjoyed the extra time it afforded him to spend with Toni. Today was no exception. He glanced over at her.

Her eyes were closed, but he was sure she wasn't asleep. She had a slight smile on her lips. Abe smiled, too, relieved that their relationship was once more on track. Turning his eyes back to the road, he prayed that nothing else would come along to derail it.

"I'm not asleep," Toni murmured.

"I know."

"I could feel you watching me."

He turned to her again. Her blue eyes were open now, and she was staring at him. His heart raced as he spoke. "Do you blame me? I happen to think you're very beautiful."

She smiled. "I'm glad to hear it, but unless you can see in two places at once, you'd better keep your eyes on the road, detective."

Abe's sigh was exaggerated as he did his best to suppress a smile. "OK, OK. I can take a hint. Drive now, gaze at your beauty later."

They arrived in Centralia at about ten-thirty, the light drizzle still steadily coming down. As they neared the street where Sophie's home sat nestled against a hillside, Abe pulled to the curb. "Can we pray before we head up there?" he asked, taking Toni's hand. "I think we're going to need all the help we can get on this one."

Toni nodded. "You're probably right. If your aunt considers you dead, we're going to need a major miracle just to get her to acknowledge you."

Bowing their heads, they asked for God's blessing on their visit, his wisdom and guidance in what they should do and say, and his love to go ahead of them and soften Sophie's heart. It was a big order, but in the short time Abe had known Yeshua as his Savior, he'd come to understand that they served a very big God.

When they finished praying, Abe kissed Toni, tenderly and gently, wishing it could be so much more. *Patience,* he told himself. *All in good time.* Then he pulled away from the curb and rounded the corner that led to Sophie's house. They were stunned to see her walking across the street from her neighbor's house, the hood of her raincoat pulled over her head.

"Is that her?" Toni asked. "Is that Aunt Sophie?"

"It is," Abe confirmed. "You see how God has already begun to answer our prayers? I was afraid she'd be locked away in the house and wouldn't even answer the door once she realized who was standing on her front porch. But there she is, and she can't make it into the house before we get to her."

It wasn't until Abe had parked the car at the curb in front of Sophie's house that she turned and saw them. By that time she was halfway across her yard, headed for the door. As always, Abe's heart caught at the familiar face peering at him from beneath her hood — a slightly older version of his mother, whom he'd lost a few years earlier, killed in the same car accident that took his father. Sophie's brown eyes, which were usually so bright and full of life, registered only shock, then a brief flash of regret before going hard. Anticipating that she would turn and hurry to the house, Abe and Toni jumped out of the car and headed straight for her.

As Abe reached out to her, hoping for the warm, welcoming hug he was so accustomed to receiving from his only aunt, he glimpsed the weakening resolve in her eyes, and he almost dared to believe she would open her arms and receive him. However, as quickly as the sign of weakness had come, it disappeared, replaced by a steely-eyed stare and a clenched jaw.

"Aunt Sophie," he said softly. "Please . . . I've come to talk to you, to try to explain . . ." The woman squared her shoulders but did not speak a word. She cut her eyes briefly toward Toni, as if sizing up the *goy* who had so bewitched this son of *Avraham* as to make him turn from the God of their fathers. Her eyes returned to her nephew in obvious disgust. Then she turned on her heel and started toward her house.

"Aunt Sophie, please . . ." Abe tried to take her arm, but she shook him off, her eyes focused only on the door in front of her. Abe looked helplessly at Toni. Things were not going well, and he really had no idea what to do next.

Toni moved quickly, immediately placing herself between Sophie and her intended refuge, forcing the elderly woman to look at her. "Mrs. Jacobson, please. I know we haven't met, and I had hoped we would long before this. But . . . Mrs. Jacobson, your nephew loves you very much, and I know you love him —"

Sophie raised her hand and pointed a long finger in Toni's face. "My nephew is dead. I sat *shivah* for him. He is dead." She glared at Toni for a moment as Abe watched Toni's short blonde curls begin to frizz in the mist that settled upon them. It seemed odd that he should notice something so trivial when his only close living relative was proclaiming him dead, but that seemed to be the one thing that stood out in his mind at that particular moment.

Toni tried again. "But, Mrs. Jacobson —"

"Please, leave me alone, young lady. I have nothing more to say to you." Pushing past her, she hurried to her front door, fumbling at the handle as Abe and Toni stared after her.

"Aren't you going to try to stop her?" Toni asked, taking a step in Sophie's direction.

Abe reached out to stop her. "Let her go. She won't even talk to me, don't you see? I'm dead to her. We're not going to accomplish anything standing in the rain pounding on her door. We might as well just go."

"But —"

"Give it up, Toni. She's made up her mind, and we're not going to change it. We'll just have to leave it with God and let him work on changing her heart."

Toni nodded in resignation and accompanied Abe to the car. He opened the door and let her in, then closed it and turned for one last look at Sophie's house. For a brief instant he saw her drawn face peering at them from behind a curtain. Then it quickly vanished, the curtain falling back into place, but not before Abe felt a spark of renewed hope that God truly would answer their prayers and change Aunt Sophie's heart.

■ ■ ■ ■

Oh, Avraham, why? Why did you come here? And why did you bring her, the goy who stole you away from your people and your God? Did you come to torture me? To twist the knife?

Choking back tears, she dared another peek out the window. This time they were gone, the taillights of Abe's car disappearing around the corner. *Adonai, God of my fathers, why? Why must it be this way? You know he's all I have left. Everyone else is gone. My darling David, the love of my life — gone, these many years. My sister, gone — giving up her life in a car accident with that goy husband of hers. Then Sol, my only brother, shaming the family name with those awful women and then . . . then becoming involved in criminal activities. Who would ever have thought? Now he's gone too, killed in a gunfight, trying to save . . . Avraham. And for what? So he, too, could shame the family name and abandon the law of Moshe to become a . . .* She could hardly bring herself to think the word, let alone say it. *To become a . . .* Christian. My beloved Avraham, a Christian. *Oh, Adonai, have mercy on this daughter of yours. I have tried to serve you faithfully all these years, to live up to the Shema, loving you first, above all else, but this — to have to give up the only family I have left . . .*

She stared out onto the now empty street, shrouded in gray, slick from the cold drizzle that continued to fall from the heavens. "It is too much," she whispered, "too much to ask of me. Too much to demand from me in order to prove my love for you. You gave me no children of my own. Must you also take away the one who has been like a son to me? I know I am commanded to love you with all my heart and soul and strength — and I have tried. Oh, how I have tried! But this . . . *Adonai,* the price of loving you — must it be so great?"

Lorraine's trial was over, the first member of the baby-selling ring to be convicted. The verdict had just come in, and Melissa had heard it on television. Everyone else was gone, and she sat on the couch in the living room, rehearsing the reporter's announcement. Guilty. Guilty of kidnapping, murder . . . the list went on. All that was left was for the jury to determine Lorraine's sentence. Given the seriousness of the crime, the reporter had ventured the opinion that once Lorraine entered those prison doors, she would undoubtedly never see daylight again. And that, Melissa was sure, was exactly how it should be.

Yet, at the same time, what little kindness — and it was very little — had been shown to Melissa during her kidnapping ordeal had come from Lorraine, the woman who, for a brief time, had served as Melissa's father's secretary. Of course, Melissa now knew that Paul Matthews had given Lorraine that position as a favor to his friend, Dr. Bruce Jensen, not knowing that she was being planted in his office to monitor his investigation into Julie Greene's disappearance and to make sure he didn't get too close to the truth. When it looked as if he was about to do that, Lorraine had alerted Bruce, who ultimately betrayed and killed Melissa's father. That betrayal had haunted the grief-stricken teen since the day she'd first learned of it. Would Bruce Jensen's trial, which would begin in a matter of days, give her some sort of closure? Or would she forever be haunted by the horror of her father's death at the hands of a man he'd loved and trusted?

The reporter's words faded as Melissa closed her eyes and allowed her mind to drift back to the day when she had naïvely climbed into the car with Carlo, believing he was some sort of talent scout from Hollywood looking for extras in an upcoming film. The next thing she knew she'd been tied up and blindfolded and taken to a cabin in the woods where she was held for several days while her captors discussed her fate. Lying helplessly on an old cot in the back room of the cabin, unable to see or move, and terrified of what was to become of her, Melissa had soon been approached by a drunken Carlo with threats of rape — and worse — when he suddenly fell forward and landed across her body, his life ended by a single gunshot to the back of his head. He'd been killed by Raymond, another member of the ring, who felt Carlo was more of a liability than an asset to their illegal but lucrative enterprise. Raymond and Lorraine had then removed Carlo's body, leaving Melissa to wonder if she'd be the next one dragged out of the room feet first.

Yet all of that, despite its horrors, was not the worst of it, because it had all taken place before she knew of Dr. Jensen's involvement with her father's death and her kidnapping. When, in the next room, she'd heard the doctor's voice, haggling with the others over whether they should ship her out of the country and sell her as a sex slave or just kill her, she had thought things couldn't get any worse. But she was wrong. Before it was over, she'd witnessed another killing — that of Abe's uncle, Sol Levitz — during the shootout that accompanied her rescue. Soon after that she found out that Bruce Jensen had killed her father.

How could she ever forgive him for that? Why should she even have to? Just because Carrie forgave Tom Blevins for shooting her and causing her to be stuck in a wheelchair, did that mean Melissa had to follow her example? She just didn't think she could do it. What Bruce Jensen had done to their family was simply too awful to forgive.

Even as those thoughts ran through her mind, she heard a distant, quiet voice calling to her, telling her that if she would just take the first step, he would carry her the rest of the way.

"No," she cried, tears brimming in her eyes. "I can't! I just can't! Please don't ask me to do this. It's impossible. Bruce Jensen is a terrible man. He murdered my father. How can you expect me to forgive him for that? He doesn't deserve it, God. He doesn't deserve to be forgiven."

No one does, whispered the voice. *But I offer forgiveness anyway . . . because of my Son.*

Melissa felt a chill pass down her spine.

She knew that no one had spoken, but she also knew what she'd heard. The voice had come from inside her, and yet she realized it was God's voice, speaking truth to her as only God can — truth that penetrates the lies, the fears, even the pain. . . .

"I know," she said softly. "I know that's true, but . . ."

I'll carry you, said the voice. *When you're ready. And I will carry Bruce Jensen as well . . . if he will let me.*

Melissa cried softly. She had no arguments left inside her. They'd all been demolished by the truth of God's love — for Bruce Jensen as well as for herself. Is that how Carrie had been able to forgive Tom? Had God spoken to her too? Had he told her of his love for Tom Blevins? If so, why did it seem so much easier for Carrie to accept God's message of unconditional love than it was for Melissa — especially when that message included extending God's love to the one who'd almost single-handedly devastated her life?

Grabbing a tissue from the end table beside the couch, Melissa wiped her eyes and blew her nose. She knew exactly what God was calling her to do, but where would she ever find the strength to follow through on that calling?

CHAPTER 11

Toni had scarcely been able to think of anything all weekend other than Tom Blevins's fabrications about Melissa. Her curiosity had finally gotten the best of her, and after discussing it with Abe on Sunday evening, she'd decided to go to the jail first thing Monday morning and try once again to talk with Tom. Unless Tom had specifically requested that her name be removed from his visitors list, she should still be able to get in — assuming, of course, that he would come and talk with her again.

A native Washingtonian, Toni had long since become accustomed to the seemingly interminable gray, wet winters of the Pacific Northwest. This morning, however, the gloom was getting to her. As she drove the short distance to the jail, her windshield wipers sloshing steadily, she found herself longing for spring. *Less than a week,* she thought, *and January will finally be over.*

February may not be much better, but at least we can start looking for the first crocuses to pop up — maybe even a few blossoms on the trees. It would certainly be a welcome change from all this dreariness.

She sighed as she parked the car and prepared to make the dash to the jail's main entrance. Times like these made her wonder what it would be like to live in a sunny climate, somewhere that didn't require an umbrella at least 75 percent of the year. She smiled crookedly as she thought of the bumper sticker that was so prevalent in her part of the world: "Celebrate the Seattle Rain Festival — September through June." It would be funny, she thought, if it weren't so close to the truth.

By the time Toni made it inside and was signing in for her visit, she'd shaken out her very wet umbrella and was trying not to drip her way through the building any more than necessary. Of course, everyone else was in the same position, and most seemed hardly to notice. Sitting down in the waiting room, she opened the book she'd brought along and hoped it wouldn't be long until her name was called. It wasn't.

Now she sat, once again, in the sole chair on her side of the divider, watching the metal door through which Tom Blevins would soon appear, relieved that he'd agreed to the visit. How she prayed things would go more smoothly than they had the time before.

I need to plan my strategy, she thought. *Figure out ahead of time what I'm going to say, how I'm going to approach him. . . .*

Before she could get any further in her thoughts, the door creaked open and Tom was there, dressed in jailhouse orange as before. Just as he had done at the last visit, he fixed his eyes upon his visitor the moment he walked through the door, his face a mixture of defiance and hostile indifference.

Still, he sat down opposite her, and following her lead, picked up the phone. Toni fought the discouragement that threatened to overwhelm her as she looked into his hard, pale eyes. How could someone so young appear so determined to shut out all human contact? Was there someone, somewhere, whom he so desired to see that he simply had no room for anyone else?

"Tom? How are you?"

The boy shrugged but didn't answer.

"You remember me, don't you? Toni Matthews."

Tom smirked. "Sure, I remember you. Melissa's big sister, the do-gooder that claims she wants to help me. How could I forget?"

"I . . ." This was not starting off well. She took a deep breath. Determined to plow ahead, she refused to be put on the defensive as she attempted to connect with this dangerously lonely young man. She decided the direct approach was the safest. Who knew how much time Tom would give her? She'd better get to the heart of her visit before he decided the interview was over and walked out on her as he had the last time. "Tom, I went to see your sister last week — Megan." She paused, waiting for a response. His eyes narrowed slightly, but otherwise his expression was unchanged. "She's a . . . very nice young lady. And her son, Tommy, is adorable. You must be proud to have a nephew named after you."

As she continued to watch Tom closely, she sensed he was wavering between acknowledging a sense of pride and emotional attachment to his little namesake and an angry outburst at her intrusion on the forbidden terrain of the Blevins family. Unblinking, she refused to break eye contact with Tom. Finally he spoke, his voice as cold and hard as his eyes. "So that's where my lawyer got his so-called information about

242

my sister. You shouldn't have gone to see her. You had no right."

She conceded that perhaps Tom was correct in his assessment, but she also sensed it would be a mistake to admit it at this point. "You gave me no choice, Tom. You wouldn't talk to me, and I haven't been able to see your mother —"

Tom's face reddened, and he pounded the narrow counter on which he leaned. "I told you to stay away from my mother. Leave her out of this, you hear me?"

Before he could get up and walk out on her as he had on their previous visit when she'd referred to his mother, Toni apologized. "I'm sorry, Tom. I shouldn't have mentioned your mother. I won't do it again. Please . . . stay and talk with me. I think you'll be interested in what I learned from Megan. Or has your lawyer already filled you in?"

Tom glared at her, leaving her to wonder just how much Harold Barnett had told him about Megan. Since he didn't get up and walk out, Toni thought that perhaps Mr. Barnett hadn't told him everything or Tom thought there might be more than he'd already learned. Whatever the reason, Toni was grateful. Unspeaking — but, to Toni's relief, still unmoving — Tom remained where he was, watching her . . . and waiting.

"It was about Melissa," she began, eyeing him warily. "Megan told me that she . . . came to your rescue once. Some kids were picking on you during recess and —"

"Megan's lying. That never happened." Although his facial expression scarcely changed as he spoke, Toni saw him clench his fists as he leaned forward, his nose inches from the Plexiglas that separated them. "Any fights I got into, I took care of myself, OK? I sure didn't need some stupid girl helping me. So just forget that story, got it? It's a lie. Period."

"But —" She caught herself. It was obvious she'd already pushed Tom to the limit, and she still had one more question for him. There was no sense antagonizing him any more than she'd already done. She only wished she could figure out a way to appease him before approaching him with the rest of Megan's information. It certainly would help if she knew whether or not Tom's lawyer had already passed the story on to him. Regardless, she had to know his reaction, so she plunged ahead.

"OK," she said. "I guess I can understand how stories get confused sometimes. Details get changed or misunderstood. It's happened to me — many times."

Tom raised an eyebrow. "Oh, yeah? Like when?"

Toni opened her mouth to answer, then closed it again. She suddenly realized that Tom was challenging her to give him an example that mattered — nothing insipid or inconsequential, but something he could relate to, something on a par with the drastic situation in his own life.

"Like . . . when my father died." For the first time since she'd arrived, Toni saw Tom's face soften. It was brief but enough to encourage her to continue. "I was devastated, of course, but something didn't seem right to me — one little detail that just didn't seem to fit. No matter who I tried to talk to about it, I kept being told to let it go, that I was just imagining things. . . ."

The temporary softening Toni had observed in Tom's countenance had been replaced by a growing tension. It was obvious he now knew she was attempting to make a connection between her suspicions about her father's death and her suspicions about Tom's crime — an inference that there was something more than the generally accepted consensus in either case. She had to stay focused and be careful, or she was going to lose him completely.

"I guess what I'm really trying to say is . . . I understand how details and facts can be misconstrued or misinterpreted. I misinterpreted a note I found in a file in my father's office, but in the end it led me to the truth I was looking for. Maybe I misunderstood or misinterpreted what Megan said to me — not only with the story about the bullies on the playground, but also with the other story she told me."

Tom's eyebrow went up again, but he didn't speak.

"It was something that happened about a year ago, I guess. Megan wasn't real sure of the time, but it was fairly recent. Anyway, she said that you asked Melissa for a date, and that . . . she turned you down." Toni swallowed before going on. "Is that true, Tom? Do you remember that?"

Tom's eyes narrowed once more, but there was no angry eruption this time. He simply leaned back in his chair and stared at her. "You're one crazy broad, you know that? What makes you think I'd ask your loser sister for a date? And what makes you so sure she'd turn me down if I did?" He shook his head. "You people are all alike, aren't you? Including that lying sister of mine. All of you — you're all the same. You disgust me." He calmly placed the receiver back on the hook, then stood up, turned his back, and walked to the door, where he pounded once and called, "Guard, I'm ready to go back now."

Toni sighed. As sure as she was that it was Tom and not Megan who was lying, she was no closer to learning the truth of why Tom had invented such stories or how his vivid imagination about Melissa tied in with his suspected partner in crime than she'd been when she'd first arrived at the facility. If only she could let her suspicions go. Certainly she had no responsibility to help Tom Blevins — if indeed learning the truth would even help him. Yet she felt compelled to continue — as if God himself was calling her to do so — and so she would. If only she knew what to do next. . . .

Tom lay stretched out on his bunk, his feet crossed at the ankles, his arms under his head, staring at the ceiling. What was it with this crazy woman anyway? It was weird enough when she'd showed up the first time, but now she'd been here again, claiming to want to help him, when all the time he knew she just wanted to dig up some juicy information for some exclusive story somewhere. Why else would she have gone to see Megan? This Toni Matthews didn't fool him one bit. Why would she care what happened to him? No one had ever cared before. He had no reason to think it would be any different now.

And that stuff about Melissa. . . . What had Megan been thinking when she told that nosy Matthews woman about that? Megan had always been the only one — until this last year, of course — he'd ever confided in. He thought she knew that everything he told her was private. If he'd known she was going to go blabbing it to someone else, he never would have told her.

He winced when he thought of what Melissa must think of him now that she'd heard the stories he'd told about her — and he knew that she'd heard them by now. He might be able to fool everyone else, but Melissa knew his stories were just that — stories, with absolutely no truth to them except that Tom had once wished they were true. Well, at least the part about Melissa helping him when those bullies were picking on him on the playground so many years ago.

Tom remembered that day as if it were yesterday — even though he'd had countless other experiences just like it. Being picked on by bullies had been an almost everyday occurrence for Tom Blevins, but that particular day was different. That day he'd noticed Melissa standing nearby, watching, and he was sure he'd seen tears in her eyes. Even as his tormentors gleefully landed their punches and vocalized their taunts and insults, he'd ignored them, wondering throughout the entire ordeal if Melissa cared for him as it appeared she did. If so, why didn't she do something to help? Call a teacher, or . . . ? Yet, he'd reasoned, she was probably scared, and he didn't blame her for that. Fear had already become an almost constant companion in his few short years of life, and he understood how it sometimes paralyzed its victims into inaction. Still, he couldn't help but wonder if Melissa would come to his aid if she could. . . .

That had become the focus of his day-dreams, his place of escape for years. When the tormentors attacked — whether at school or at home — he retreated to his make-believe world, where Melissa came to his rescue whenever he needed her. By the time he was in his teens, he was convinced she loved him, but each time he worked up the courage to talk with her, he retreated before actually asking her for a date. The last time had been when he'd seen her standing alone at her locker — and Toni was right, it had been about a year ago, just before her father died — and Tom had resolved to tell Melissa of his feelings for her and to convince her to become his girlfriend. But before he could get through more than a faltering hello, another boy — one of the popular guys from the football team — came up and whisked her away. Melissa hadn't even bothered to say good-bye. In fact, Tom realized she'd forgotten he was even standing there. Shamed and rejected yet again, he'd turned and walked away, feeling more alone than he had in years.

That's when Tom had decided he'd been wrong about Melissa. She didn't care about him any more than anyone else. He'd written her off then and told Megan the story of Melissa's turning him down for a date. He never dreamed that story would go beyond his older sister and reach the ears of Melissa and Toni Matthews and probably everyone else in their circle of family and friends. Now — once again — Tom Blevins imagined himself the laughingstock of River View. Even his own lawyer knew. Toni's recounting of Megan's stories wasn't the first time Tom had become aware of them. Harold Barnett had already confronted Tom with them, and he'd vehemently denied them, passing the blame to his sister, just as he had when Toni talked with him. He felt bad about that, but he'd had no choice. He certainly couldn't admit to making up anything so pathetic and humiliating.

Tom closed his eyes. Why did it always have to be him? No one else got picked on *all* the time. No one else was rejected by *everyone* — well, not everyone, he reminded himself quickly. Still, even that one exception had not yet contacted him, and he was becoming more worried by the day. Surely the one person who'd cared for and appreciated him, who'd taken away his aching loneliness and given him the companionship he'd so longed for, wouldn't abandon him now. He closed his eyes, refusing to give in to the tears that stung his eyelids. He would be patient. He would wait. Sooner or later, he'd hear, and then —

"Mail call."

The guard's voice, passing down the hall in front of his cell, brought Tom back to the present — to the jail, the loneliness, the fear, and the uncertainty. Tom sensed he wouldn't have any mail today. The only letter he'd received so far had been from that crazy girl, Carrie Bosworth, the one he'd shot and who was now in a wheelchair, the one who wrote to him, telling him such off-the-wall things as God loved him and forgave him — and so did she. Tom wondered if the bullet from his gun had somehow affected the girl's brain, since the things she claimed to believe sounded a lot more bizarre than any of the stories he'd ever invented. He sure didn't need any more letters from a nutcase like that.

It was midmorning on Thursday when Toni entered Valerie Myers's office. She greeted the assistant principal, thanked her for taking the time to see her, and then quickly took in her surroundings as she sat down in the straight-backed chair on the visitor's side of the slightly cluttered desk. The less than spacious room was warm and welcoming, yet clearly defined in its no-nonsense décor. Toni knew without asking that Valerie had decorated it herself.

"So this is where you hang out," Toni observed.

Valerie smiled. "It is indeed — more often than I should, I'm told, but since I have no family . . ." She hesitated briefly, then went on. "It's my home away from home, I suppose. Other than occasional days off — such as the time I ran into you at the park — this is where I live during the daylight hours."

Toni nodded, her mind snatching at a

distant memory of someone telling her about Valerie's brief marriage while she was still in college. It had ended in divorce — no children — with her husband leaving town and never being heard from again. From what Toni understood, Valerie never talked about it, and since it bore no relevance to Toni's reason for visiting the attractive, middle-aged assistant principal, she dismissed it and moved on.

"I appreciate your taking the time to see me on such short notice," Toni said. "I debated with myself for several days before calling you. . . ."

"I'm so glad you did." Valerie's smile was genuine, erasing years from her countenance. "How is Melissa? I see her quite often here at school, and she's always polite, of course, but . . . something's not the same, is it?" She sighed and arched her eyebrows. "Of course, I could say that of most of our students lately, and few of them have experienced the level of trauma that Melissa has endured in the last year."

"Melissa's . . . fine. At least, I hope she is. I pray she's beginning to cope with the many issues she's been thrown into lately, but . . . sometimes I worry. The outcome of that first trial last week didn't seem to affect her as deeply as I thought it would. If it did, she's not telling me about it, and that's certainly a possibility. However, this next trial — the one for Bruce Jensen — will be even more difficult for her. I'll be so glad when it's finally over."

Valerie nodded slowly. "Yes. It seems our little town has suddenly been inundated with spectacular court cases, doesn't it? Of course, with Tom Blevins changing his plea to guilty, at least we'll be spared the emotional upheaval and financial cost — not to mention the media circus — of another major trial. I suppose we can all be thankful for that. Although . . ."

Toni frowned. "Although . . . what?"

"Oh, it's probably nothing. But sometimes I wonder about Tom, about the shooting, and . . ."

Her voice trailed off again, and Toni leaned forward in her chair, trying to keep her voice calm. "Valerie, is there . . . something about Tom that puzzles you, something that doesn't ring true about his case?"

Tilting her head slightly, she eyed Toni and said, "That's why you came here, isn't it? You suspect something too."

"Yes." Excitement leapt in Toni's heart. Someone else shared her suspicions — someone who'd been around Tom Blevins a lot more than she had. Maybe Valerie was the one who could help her after all. "Yes, I do suspect something, but I have to tell you, Valerie, I have no idea what that something is. The more I think about it, the more I talk with people about it, the more confused and uncertain I become. But —"

"But it's there. That much you know for certain."

"As certain as I can be about anything regarding Tom Blevins. He's a hard one to investigate. I can't get near his mother, Tom certainly isn't giving out any information, and the only one I've been able to talk to — Tom's oldest sister, Megan — told me a couple of stories that made no sense at all. Still, she did corroborate what we already suspected about Tom's horrible home life."

Valerie nodded. "I'm afraid that's a given. What did Megan tell you that didn't make sense? Or are you not free to share that information?"

"I wouldn't share it with just anyone," Toni admitted, "but I certainly see no harm in telling you about it. Maybe you can even shed some light on why Tom would lie about Melissa as he did." Toni then re-counted to Valerie the stories she'd heard from Megan of Melissa's involvement in Tom's life and Melissa's very believable denials of those stories. In addition, she told her how Tom had denied ever telling those stories to Megan in the first place, instead accusing his sister of being the one who was lying. As she spoke, Valerie listened intently, her dark eyes expressing her sadness as the tale unfolded. When Toni finished, Valerie sighed deeply.

"It's so tragic, isn't it? That someone like Tom Blevins — a young man who, under different circumstances, could undoubtedly have made some sort of positive contribution to society — has instead chosen to live in a fantasy world, eventually acting out his pain by taking the lives of innocent bystanders. How is it that none of us saw it coming, that we didn't try to intervene in some way?" Her mouth tensed, and her eyes closed briefly. "I've asked myself that question a million times, but I always come up empty. Yes, we knew he was a loner, an underachiever with little or no social contact. Yet, he wasn't the only one who fell into that category. Every school has them — several of them — but the vast majority of them don't go off the deep end and murder people. So why Tom? What happened that suddenly set him off? Or was it more than a random, almost spontaneous act? Was it planned? If so, how carefully and for how long? And . . ." She leaned forward and looked intently at Toni. "Did he plan it alone . . . or was someone else involved? That's what I *really* want to know."

Toni's heart raced. Valerie was voicing the exact questions she'd asked herself dozens of times. Suddenly her suspicions seemed more credible, and she wondered if she was finally going to get the break she'd been searching for. Did Valerie Myers somehow hold the key to the truth about Tom Blevins's crime? Or was she, like Toni, just one more frustrated amateur detective, searching for answers that might not even exist?

"That's what I want to know too," she told Valerie. "*Exactly* what I want to know. So far, I've learned nothing. I've talked to Tom and Megan, but what I really want is to talk to their mother. I don't know why I'm so sure she can shed some light on this case, or even if she'd be willing to, but she's the key. I'm almost sure of it."

Valerie pressed her lips together and nodded. "You're probably right, but getting to Cora Blevins won't be easy. Still . . . there must be a way. Maybe, if we put our heads together . . ."

The phone rang then, and Valerie smiled apologetically. "I'm sorry, Toni. I wish I had a secretary to screen my calls, but I'm afraid it's not in the budget."

Toni started to stand. "Do you want me to leave?"

Valerie motioned her back to her seat. "Stay," she said. "I'm sure it won't take long."

Toni tried to busy herself with studying the pictures on the walls: group shots of soccer teams and graduating classes; photos of several individuals unknown to Toni, possibly Valerie's friends or family members; and various plaques and certificates interspersed among the smiling faces. But she couldn't help overhearing enough to know that Valerie's caller was upset about something. Apparently Valerie was finally able to bring some semblance of calm to the situation before hanging up, sighing heavily as she did so.

"One of the less positive aspects of this job," Valerie explained as Toni turned back to face her. "Angry parents — even some angry faculty members — almost always get referred to me rather than to Mr. Duffield. I suppose I'm here to run interference for the principal, and I don't mind, but . . ." She sighed again and looked at Toni knowingly. "It isn't always easy."

"I can imagine. With all you do around here, it must seem a thankless job at times."

Valerie shrugged. "Oh, I don't know. The many great people I meet — parents and faculty, and especially the students — far outweigh the occasional whiners. Mostly I just listen, try to placate them, and hope for the best." She smiled. "I remember Jeff — Mr. Duffield — telling me that's exactly what he does when any of those difficult people get past me and get hold of him. I remember one situation last year, some former teacher he'd had to let go for some reason — I never was sure exactly what happened in that situation, but she just wouldn't leave him alone. I'm not even sure if she was trying to get him to hire her back, or what. I still don't know how he finally got rid of her, but apparently he did because she finally quit calling. That's when he told me that we just have to outlast them. I suppose he's right. Anyway, enough of that. Where were we?"

"You were saying that maybe if we put our heads together . . ."

Valerie brightened. "Of course. Maybe between the two of us we can find a way to get through to Cora Blevins — without that husband of hers around. Any ideas?"

Toni shook her head. "Believe me, if I had any, I would have acted on them by now. The more I try to come up with a way, the more impossible it seems."

"Ah, but there's the challenge." Valerie's dark eyes twinkled. "Things may seem impossible, but if I've learned one thing in life, it's that things are seldom as they seem. Don't you agree?"

Toni nodded again. She may not have lived as many years as Valerie Myers, but she too had learned — many times over — that things were indeed seldom as they seemed. "You're right. Getting to Mrs. Blevins may seem impossible, but it's not. We just haven't gone about it in the right way yet. So, what do you suggest? What's the best way of getting a chance to talk with her . . . alone?"

Brad tried to tell himself that his visit was all about Melissa and not about Toni. He tried, but he wasn't buying it. What were the odds that anyone else would?

Still, that was his story, and he was sticking to it as he walked the few blocks from his office to the Matthews's home. It was Thursday afternoon, two days before the last weekend in January, and the weather had improved almost overnight. The entire week, prior to and including yesterday, had been another soggy one, boringly typical for this time of year. This morning, however, had dawned as a sneak peek at spring, a promise of long days of sunlight and flowers and outdoor activities. All Pacific Northwesterners knew the nice weather could be over before nightfall, but they also knew enough to enjoy it while it lasted.

That's exactly what Brad was doing. He'd scarcely taken a day off from his legal practice since Christmas. And when his father, one of two senior partners in the firm, suggested that Brad take a long weekend and get away from the office for a change, his thoughts had immediately turned to Toni. Just one year earlier, any spare moment either of them had was spent together, so it was only natural that Brad's first reaction to some time off work was to wonder how he and Toni would spend it. Now, of course, all that had changed. Any time he spent with Toni these days was strictly because of Melissa — not that he was using Melissa for that reason, but he had to admit that it was an added perk to their relationship.

Is it a perk at all? he wondered. Maybe he would be better off severing all ties with the Matthews's family, including Melissa. Toni seemed to think the two of them spent too much time together anyway; maybe she was right. Yet Melissa needed someone to talk to, and Brad truly did care for the girl. Besides, he had an absolutely legitimate reason for going to see her today. Just last night, as he was going through some old pictures, he'd come across a snapshot of himself with Melissa on one side and Paul Matthews on the other. The picture was less than two years old, taken when the three of them, along with Toni, had gone on a picnic. Brad remembered the day distinctly, including the way Toni's blonde hair had shone in the early summer sun as she took that very picture. His heart ached at the memory, and he reminded himself that he was bringing the picture to Melissa, not Toni.

Turning the corner onto their street, he marveled at the almost warm breeze that greeted his change of direction. Of course, it was after three, and he knew it wouldn't be long before the temperature would drop, along with the winter sun. With his jacket slung over one arm, he was ready to make the trip back home after his visit — whatever time that might be.

As he neared the walkway that led to the Matthews's home, his heart rate increased. He wished it wouldn't. He had, in fact, tried repeatedly — and unsuccessfully — over the last several months to put Toni Matthews out of his mind, but it never seemed to work for more than a few moments. Before long a word, a sound, or a color would tug at his heart, and he'd be right back where he'd always been — in love with the girl who'd promised to spend the rest of her life with him and had then moved on to someone else. Even now, recognizing the futility of his longing, he couldn't help but hope that she'd answer the door when he arrived.

She did. His heart seemed to stop as she stood in the doorway, a surprised look on her face, hesitating for a moment before greeting him and inviting him in.

"I should have called," he said apologetically, stepping inside. She was close enough that he could detect the familiar scent of her cologne. It was the same fragrance she'd used since they were high school sweethearts. Pushing the memory aside, he realized he hadn't yet explained himself.

"It . . . was such a beautiful day that I walked to work this morning, and then my dad suggested I take some time off, so I started walking and ended up here, and . . . I have this picture for Melissa, so . . ." Brad's voice trailed off as he realized he was rambling. He realized, too, that Toni knew him well enough to recognize his discomfort. She smiled and invited him to sit down in the living room. He appreciated her graciousness but sensed she was uneasy with his unplanned visit.

"Can I . . . get you something?" she asked. "Some tea or . . . ?"

Brad shook his head, carefully settling down on one end of the couch. "No, I'm fine. Thanks." Hoping to break the tension, he asked, "So, where's April?"

"She's at her church. She's become quite involved in the last few months and volunteers as much time as possible. I imagine she'll be home in time for dinner."

Brad nodded, and Toni smiled again, sitting down on the opposite end of the couch, leaving an invisible yet purposely drawn line between them. "So," she said, "what picture did you bring?"

"Excuse me?"

"You said you brought a picture for Melissa."

Brad felt the hot flush of embarrassment creep up his neck and face. Why was he blushing like a schoolboy? He was an attorney, he reminded himself, a longtime family friend who had every right to be here. He forced a smile as he reached into his pocket. The snapshot was surrounded by tissue paper. He unwrapped it and extended it to Toni across the great divide of couch that separated them. "It's this one," he explained. "Taken a couple of summers ago when the four of us — you and Melissa and your dad and I — went on a picnic up at the lake. Remember?"

He tried to appear nonchalant as she took the picture from him, but he was disappointed that she carefully avoided his fingers as she did so. He wondered what memories the picture would stir up in her heart. Apparently they were emotional ones, as she stared at the picture for several moments before looking up. When she did, her sky blue eyes shone with tears.

"That was a wonderful day, wasn't it?" she asked, her voice husky. She swallowed. "Who would ever have dreamed there would be so many changes in such a short time? That Dad would be . . . gone . . . less than a year later. Murdered . . ." She choked on the final word, and a tear spilled over onto her cheek. For a moment Brad forgot how many other things had changed — primarily that he was no longer Toni's fiancé and that he had no right to take her in his arms and comfort her. Forgetting all that, in one fluid movement he reached over and pulled her toward him, wanting only to hold and comfort the woman he loved, to take away her pain and make her smile again. It wasn't until she'd laid her head against his shoulder, allowing him to hold her as the tears slipped down her face, that he realized she hadn't pushed him away. He knew her compliance was due to her grief over the loss of her father, but still he couldn't convince himself not to take advantage of the situation. If only he could hold her in his arms like this forever. . . .

Then the front door opened, and the voices invaded their moment together. It was Melissa whom Brad saw first as he raised his eyes and looked toward the entryway, his arms still encircling Toni. At the same instant he felt Toni pull back slightly from him, and he knew that she, too, had heard the voices. As the two of them stared in surprise at the shocked look on Melissa's face, they were even more surprised to see Abe Matthews walk up behind her. The expectant smile that had been on Abe's face as he and Melissa entered the house quickly faded to disbelief as he stood, statuelike, his eyes fixed on the compromising scene in front of him.

Suddenly the feel of Toni in his arms brought a flush of chagrin to Brad's face, and he released her in defeat, simultaneously wondering at the repercussions of his untimely visit. It was obvious this episode would not endear him to anyone now present in the room.

CHAPTER 12

It had been the longest weekend of Toni's life, and it wasn't over quite yet. Although it was close to midnight on Sunday, Toni sat alone in the darkened living room, her heart aching and her mind almost numb from the many times she'd rehearsed in detail the events of the last few days.

It all started that Thursday afternoon when Brad Anderson unexpectedly showed up with the picture for Melissa, which stirred up fresh memories of grief and loss that Toni had thought she had under control. The photograph had been her undoing. Seeing her father's face, so youthful and handsome — and alive — had suddenly and inexplicably made his death that much more unbelievable.

Toni just couldn't understand why the picture had affected her that way. It wasn't as if she hadn't already seen countless pictures of her father since his death. In fact, several pictures of her father were displayed throughout the house. This particular snapshot, however, had somehow struck a nerve that had unleashed a fresh torrent of grief and tears. In response, Toni had instinctively leaned on the nearest shoulder available. Unfortunately, that shoulder had belonged to her former fiancé, and the next thing she knew, her present fiancé — not to mention her sister — had walked in on the innocent yet suspiciously compromising scene.

Toni sighed, raking her fingers through her tousled blonde curls. Could the timing possibly have been worse? She doubted it. Now she was left to deal with the fallout, which was extensive. She wanted, first and foremost, to explain to Abe and Melissa her reasons for allowing Brad to hold her while she cried. She wanted to make them understand that the scene they'd witnessed had absolutely nothing to do with Brad and everything to do with her father. She wanted to tell them that, despite the fact that it would soon be a year since Paul Matthews's murder, Melissa wasn't the only one who still grieved his passing. On some days Toni actually found herself expecting her father to come walking into the room, his cheerful voice arriving ahead of him to announce his entrance. When he didn't, the pain would start all over again.

Oh, how she missed his smile! And how that smile had tugged at her heart from the snapshot Brad had laid in her hand. As she'd gazed at the photo, it was obvious that her father had been enjoying the outing that day with his two daughters and the man he'd watched grow into manhood and whom he believed would someday become his son-in-law. Even now, Toni couldn't help but wonder what her father would have thought of Brad being replaced by Abe.

And he had been, she reminded herself — fully and completely. Despite the respect and affection she had for Brad Anderson, she had no regrets about no longer being engaged to him. The depth of love she felt for Abe dispelled any thoughts she ever had that marriage to Brad would have been the better choice. Abe was the only man she wanted to share her life with, and yet the two of them seemed to be running into all sorts of bumps in their relationship lately. Then, just when she thought they'd smoothed out those bumps, along came another one. This one was the biggest so far. Toni was painfully aware that it was going to take a lot of explaining on her part — and a lot of understanding on Abe's — if ever they were to work through it and get on with their wedding plans.

All of that, of course, didn't even begin to address the issue of Melissa's reaction to coming home and finding Toni in Brad's arms. Even after Abe excused himself and walked out the front door — which was almost immediately upon seeing Toni and Brad together — Melissa had stood rooted to the spot, staring in disbelief. When Toni got up and tried to go to her, Melissa had turned and run to her room, slamming the door behind her. They'd had virtually no communication since. Melissa had spent the entire weekend at Carrie's house, even going to church and sitting with the Bosworth family on Sunday, then leaving with them again as soon as the service was over.

Toni sighed and got up from her perch on the couch. Walking to the window, she stood staring out at the deserted neighborhood, the wet pavement glistening under the streetlights. The rain had returned, quelling the brief respite from winter weather. It was only the end of January, and yet Toni couldn't remember a winter that had seemed longer. Would spring ever arrive? Would she and Abe — not to mention Melissa and April and Carrie, and all the other residents of River View so recently affected by so much crime and devastation — ever be able to rejoice over the spring thaw and find hope and promise once again?

As she had so many times before, Toni thought back to how simple her life had seemed only one year earlier. She was finishing her master's degree, planning her wedding to Brad, looking forward to teaching in the very school system she'd grown up in, staying near to her father and her sister. . . .

All that had changed, however. So much upheaval. So much tragedy. Wouldn't it be easier if she could just drop the Tom Blevins case and deal with the many issues she already had on her plate? Was it really necessary to complicate her life further with this incessant tilting at windmills, searching for a coconspirator who might not even exist? Why couldn't she leave things alone and trust that the police were doing their homework and would root out any information necessary to clear up the entire school shooting incident? Why should she think she could find clues that trained professionals had overlooked? She had yet to find a way to get to Tom Blevins's mother, even with Valerie Myers's help, let alone discover anything that would shed new light on Tom's crime. Maybe she should just abandon the whole cause. . . .

I am your Father. . . .

Toni jumped, turning from the window as if she actually expected to find someone standing behind her. Yet she knew better . . . because she knew the voice. She even recognized the words. God had spoken them to her heart months earlier when she was first grieving over the death of her father and had been in so much emotional turmoil over the shifting relationships and circumstances in her life. She'd understood then that her heavenly Father was calling her to his heart, reassuring her of his great love for her and that he — and only he — would work everything out in the end. Certainly that was the message he was reinforcing with her now.

"Thank you," Toni whispered into the darkness as a sense of warmth crept over her. "I didn't realize how much I needed to be reminded of that. *Father.* Thank you, Lord. That reminder puts everything into perspective again. And . . . if you really are calling me to look into the Tom Blevins situation, then I will — whatever the consequences."

Comforted, she made her way back to her room, confident that despite all the unknowns of tomorrow, she would finally be able to sleep.

■ ■ ■ ■

Melissa shivered in the damp chill of the Monday morning gloom that hung over her parents' gravesites like an omen, threatening to descend upon her and squeeze the very air from her lungs. It was a school holiday — an in-service day for the teachers — and Melissa was grateful that the rain had finally stopped for a while. She'd left the house early, hoping to avoid Toni, and hadn't bothered to take an umbrella. As a result, she'd gotten pretty wet along the way, but her rainproof down parka was warm, and she had it zipped to her chin. Her long hair hung in damp strands down her back, occasionally falling over her shoulder and onto her face when she bowed her head to write in her journal. Sitting on a bench a few feet from the graves, ignoring the chill that seemed intent on settling into her bones, she stared at the grassy area that covered the remains of the two people she wished more than anything could be sitting beside her, helping her to walk through the almost impossible crises that had invaded her life.

It was bad enough, she thought, closing her eyes, *to grow up without a mother, but now I don't have a father either. I'm sorry, God. I know you're my Father, but . . . I need someone right now, someone I can see and hear. I thought I at least had Brad, but . . . Why, God? Why is Toni doing this? She has Abe. Why is she going after Brad too? Does she really want me away from him so much that she'd stoop that low to interfere in our relationship? And why would she risk what she has with Abe? I thought they were so happy. I just don't understand, God. I don't understand any of this. . . .*

Sighing, she opened her eyes and gazed once again at her parents' graves, still praying silently. *I know what you've been telling me, God — that I need to forgive Bruce Jensen — and in some ways I want to, but I have to admit, I'm just not there yet. And now all this with Toni . . . and Tom and Carrie and . . . sometimes I wonder if I'll ever be able to understand any of the things that are going on, let alone forgive. . . .*

Large, fat drops of rain began to fall then, intermittently plopping onto Melissa's open journal and smudging the ink. She took a deep breath and closed what she considered her only remaining confidante, then tucked it under her parka, stood up, whispered good-bye to her parents, and walked slowly out of the cemetery and into the steadily increasing downpour.

The tiny Italian eatery was more of a hole-in-the-wall than it was a restaurant, but it had long been one of Abe's favorites. Apparently Harold Barnett felt the same way, because when Abe called him earlier that morning and asked if they could meet for lunch, Sal's was the first suggestion out of Harold's mouth.

Abe arrived first, parking directly in front of the little diner, which enabled him to duck inside without getting soaked. Before settling down on an old red-cushioned stool at the long counter — the only seating area in the entire establishment — he removed his raincoat and tossed it across the stool next to him, saving a place for Harold. He knew how crowded Sal's could get at lunchtime, so he'd suggested they arrive a few minutes ahead of the noontime rush. Harold had never been known for his punctuality, though, being easily sidetracked by even the slightest lead that he thought might in any way be beneficial to one of his clients. It appeared today was to be no different. As the old "Drink Coca-Cola" clock on the wall behind the counter slowly edged toward noon and the remaining seats filled up quickly, Abe hoped Harold was circling the block, looking for a parking place, and not off on another quest for justice that might keep him occupied right through lunch and possibly into dinner. Of course, Abe couldn't say too much as he, too, had worked through many meals when he was on a case.

Abe sipped his water and surveyed the menu. At one time or another, he'd sampled almost everything Sal's had to offer and had yet to find anything he didn't like. The tempting fragrances of tomatoes, onions, and garlic wafting from the closet-sized kitchen adjacent to the counter had his mouth watering and his stomach growling as he periodically checked the clock and the front door. With the lunch crowd continuing to arrive, he wondered how long he could get away with holding on to an empty seat.

Still, he decided, even if Harold didn't show, he was glad he'd come. It was the first time he'd really felt hungry since showing up at Toni's house the previous Thursday evening, walking in with Melissa, who'd also just arrived, only to find his fiancée in the arms of Brad Anderson, the man she'd almost married. Abe had tried for days to convince himself that there was a logical and innocent explanation for what he'd seen, but so far he hadn't been able to come up with one. He'd also tried to persuade himself to return Toni's calls and give her a chance to offer that explanation, but he just wasn't ready for that yet. Perhaps he was afraid that the explanation she'd give him would be one he didn't want to hear.

No, he couldn't let himself think that way. He truly loved Toni, and he believed she loved him. Or, at least, he'd believed it until Thursday afternoon. Now, he had to admit, he had his doubts, and he wondered if the best thing was just to back off and let her work through her feelings for him — and for Brad — once and for all.

Forgetting the clock on the wall, Abe glanced at his watch. It was almost 12:15. Where was Harold? Was he even on his way? Abe decided that if his attorney friend hadn't arrived by 12:30, he would go ahead and order without him. The ravioli at this place was better than any he'd ever tasted, and he was anxious to sink his teeth into a plate of it.

Then he realized what else he'd seen when he glanced at his watch: the date. Until this very moment Abe hadn't remembered that it was Tuesday, the first day of February, the very month Abe had hoped Toni would become his wife. *Only two weeks until Valen-*

tine's Day, he thought. *Just a month ago I tried to persuade her to make that our wedding date. It seemed so romantic at the time, but the way things stand now, with the wedding itself in jeopardy, I'd just as soon sleep right through Valentine's Day.* . . .

"Hey, Matthews," Harold boomed, clapping Abe on the back. "What kept you? Can't you ever be on time for anything?"

Abe jerked his head toward the right, where Harold was picking up Abe's coat and availing himself of the now empty stool. He handed the coat to Abe, who draped it across his lap for lack of anything else to do with it. He was amazed that he'd been so absorbed in his thoughts about Toni that he'd actually missed his friend's arrival. Seeing the big man's grin and his shining eyes, apparently waiting for a reaction to his tongue-in-cheek greeting, Abe smiled. It was obvious the attorney had been forced to park quite a distance away, as his nearly bald head was wet and shiny, and his coat was soaked.

"Yeah, you know how I am," Abe said, swallowing his smile. "Never mastered your kind of promptness."

Harold's laugh was hearty. "That's right, pal, and don't forget it. You could learn a thing or two from me." He picked up a menu and glanced at it, then tossed it back down. "Don't know why I bother to look at that thing. I always order the lasagna. It's my one weakness." He patted his slight paunch. "A weakness I indulge regularly, I might add."

Abe laughed too — for the first time, he realized, in several days. "Why not?" he asked. "Life's too short to spend it eating health food, right?"

Harold nodded in agreement, still laughing, as Sal's only waitress — a short, dark-haired, middle-aged woman Abe had always assumed was Sal's wife and who looked as if she'd sampled entirely too much of her husband's cooking — came up to take their order.

When she'd gone, Harold looked at Abe, his jovial mood seeming to have evaporated. "So," he said, his voice subdued, "what's up? I sure hope you have something new to report about your girlfriend's investigation because mine is sure coming up empty. I mean, I've got nothing. Zero. Zilch. I'll take anything you can give me. The sentencing is in two weeks, you know. If the kid hadn't already agreed to go with a guilty plea and avoid a trial, I'd be trying to defend him with both hands tied behind my back, hoping for a few softhearted jury members who'd vote against putting my client to death. I'm as convinced as ever that he didn't plan this alone, but the police haven't come up with anything else, and neither have I. That, my friend, is where it stands."

Abe raised his eyebrows. Harold had laid out his feelings in one brief speech, and that was that. Nothing new, nowhere else to go, and Abe had nothing to offer him in the way of encouragement.

"I'm afraid I don't have anything for you either," he said. "Not since we last talked and I told you what we'd learned from Tom's sister. But nothing came out of that, as you know. Tom says his sister's lying, and Melissa says Tom's lying. Of course, we believe Melissa. . . ." He paused as the waitress set their salads and a basket of breadsticks in front of them. "I think Toni still has it in her mind to talk with Tom's mother, but so far that hasn't panned out. I see it as a dead-end street myself, but I know Toni. She won't quit until she's exhausted every possible opportunity, productive or not." Abe stabbed at a cherry tomato, but it got away from him. He gave up, deciding it wasn't worth the effort, then fixed his eyes intently on his companion. "To tell you the truth, Harold, now that Tom's pleaded guilty and isn't even going to trial, what's the point? I'm sorry to say that, I really am, but . . . honestly, is there any sense in even trying to unearth a coconspirator at this stage of the game? If the police haven't found anything, what are the odds that Toni will? Personally, I think she's just spinning her wheels."

Harold picked up a breadstick and appeared to be studying it carefully. It looked small in his beefy hands, and Abe wondered if he'd sounded as worried about Toni's involvement as he actually was. When Harold turned to him, Abe knew he'd seen right through him. He felt his face flush.

"The point is getting to the truth," Harold answered slowly, "and as a cop, you know it. Whether finding a conspirator changes anything for my client or not, I still want the truth, the whole truth, and nothing but the truth. And that's more than a cliché, Matthews. I mean it. I may not get it, but I have to keep trying. I was really hoping that's why you called and asked me to meet you for lunch." He smiled woodenly. "Or did you just get so frustrated trying to convince Toni to drop out that you needed me to tell you she's crazy? If that's the case, pal, you're definitely talking to the wrong guy."

Abe hesitated, stung by the man's honesty

and the depth of his dedication. "You're right, and that's what Toni keeps telling me too. I'm afraid I've been burning most of my energy trying to get her to back off this thing, but when that lady of mine —" He swallowed the lump that seemed to have come from nowhere. "When Toni puts her mind to something, there's no stopping her. She hasn't learned much of anything since she started this quest — nothing I haven't already told you about — but I don't think she's any closer to quitting than when she first decided to get involved."

"Sounds like quite a crusader."

Abe nodded. "She is. And I have to admit, it's one of the things I love about her . . . even though it's also one of the things that drives me crazy at times."

Harold's smile was slightly more natural this time. "That's what love is all about, isn't it? You can't live with them, you can't live without them, so if you're going to love them, then you do it no matter what. Am I right?"

"Right again." Abe's chest felt tight and the lump was trying to return to his throat. It was time to change the subject if he didn't want to completely ruin his masculine image, although he was sure he'd already done some serious damage to his image as a dedicated yet impartial detective. "Actually, I just wanted to touch base with you and see if maybe you'd come up with anything new. That and . . . it was a good excuse to get together for lunch."

Harold's grin spread across his face now as the waitress set their steaming entrees in front of them. "Well, then, what are we waiting for? Neither one of us has any good news to report, but the food looks great. One out of two ain't bad, Matthews, so let's just drop the shop talk and dig in."

Abe picked up his fork, eyeing his ravioli and wondering why he'd thought he was actually hungry enough to eat it. As much as he liked Harold, if it were Toni sitting here next to him, he imagined he could devour his entire meal and part of hers as well. Right now, however, his heart hurt too much to even think about eating — no matter how good the food might be. Still, he would have to eat or do an awful lot of explaining to his obviously ravenous companion. That was something — no matter how good a friend Harold might be — that Abe was not willing to do. So he took a bite of ravioli and marveled that for the first time in all the years he'd been coming here, Sal's food tasted like sawdust.

■ ■ ■ ■

As Abe was choking down his lunch at the Italian diner, Toni sat at the kitchen table with April, trying to work her way through a bowl of soup and a warm roll, fresh from the oven. She appreciated April's efforts at preparing such a delicious lunch, but she was having a hard time making small talk and acting as if nothing was wrong. Still, she had to try.

"This soup is delicious, April. The rolls too. But you really didn't have to go to so much trouble. I could have made a quick sandwich or —"

"Don't be silly, my dear. Cooking for you and Melissa is no trouble at all. Actually, I enjoy it. It's been so long since I've had someone to cook for. . . ."

Toni nodded. She knew April's husband had been dead for many years, but she also knew that the elderly widow still missed him immensely. And, of course, April missed cooking for her granddaughter, Julie, who'd always been so close to her and had stopped by to visit with her regularly before leaving Colorado and running off with Carlo.

Toni shivered, and her skin crawled at the thought of the despicable man who'd not only murdered Julie but had kidnapped Melissa as well. Thank God her sister hadn't suffered the same fate as poor Julie Greene. . . .

"Are you all right?" April's question caught Toni off guard. She hadn't realized her mind had wandered, and her mood must have been reflected on her face.

"I'm . . . fine," she answered, wondering why she was lying to the kind, white-haired lady who sat across from her. "I just . . ."

April reached over and laid her hand on Toni's. "I don't believe you're fine at all," she said, her voice tender and her eyes narrowed with concern. "I know it's none of my business, but things haven't been 'fine' around this house in days. We've scarcely seen Melissa. She's either gone or locked away in her room, and Abe hasn't been around since . . . I don't know when. Sometime last week, wasn't it? And you . . . Toni, I know you've sustained a lot of loss in your life, particularly lately, but the last few days you seem unusually depressed and worried. Please, if there's anything I can do to help . . ."

Tears spilled over from Toni's eyes onto her cheeks before she could stop them, and her hand trembled even as April covered it with her own. "You're right," she whispered.

"Nothing's fine. Not me, not Melissa, not Abe, not anything. And it's all my fault. . . ."

April got up and went around to sit beside her, once again taking Toni's hand. "Do you want to talk about it?"

Toni nodded. "I didn't think I did, but . . . yes, I do. I need to. I feel so . . . confused. So alone. I thought I was doing better the other night when . . . when I heard God speak to me, reminding me that he's my Father, but the next morning things still looked as dismal and hopeless as ever."

"Circumstances often look that way, my dear. But you must remember, things aren't always as they seem."

Things aren't always as they seem. For a brief moment April's words illuminated the memory of Valerie Myers making the very same statement. But April was still talking, so Toni dismissed the memory and tried to refocus on what she was saying.

"God is bigger than circumstances, Toni. You know that. So nothing is hopeless. What happened to precipitate all this? Everything seemed to be going as well as could be expected — under the circumstances, of course — up until a few days ago."

Toni sighed, brushing away her tears with her free hand. "That's true," she said. "Even with Bruce Jensen's trial coming up and all the repercussions from the school shooting, things were going along pretty well. But . . ." She hesitated, then took a deep breath and continued. "Oh, April, it was such a foolish thing I did. I wasn't thinking. . . . I didn't mean for it to happen, and it wasn't at all the way it looked. . . ."

April frowned. "I'm sorry, my dear. I'm not following you. What exactly was it that you did?"

"I . . . I opened the door Thursday afternoon, and Brad was standing on the front porch. He said he'd come to bring something to Melissa, but she wasn't home, so I invited him in. We sat down on the couch and he showed me a picture he'd found of . . . of the three of them: Brad, Melissa, and . . . Dad. I just stared at it, remembering the day I'd taken that picture and how happy we'd all been — especially Dad. I just missed him so much. . . ."

Her voice trailed off, and she was fighting tears again. Steeling herself, she went on. "Seeing Dad's smile and remembering . . . I just broke down. Brad's reaction was so natural, so understanding. He put his arms around me and let me cry. Then . . . then Abe and Melissa walked in and saw us, and . . . oh, April, I can only imagine what they must have thought. But there was nothing to it . . . nothing, honestly . . . except that I miss Dad and . . ." She sighed and shook her head. "Now they're both upset with me. I've called Abe several times and left messages on his machine, but he hasn't returned my calls. Not that I blame him — or Melissa either. She's hardly spoken to me since it happened. And now . . . I just don't know what to do. I truly don't."

April patted her hand. "Don't try to do anything," she said, her voice as gentle as the compassion in her eyes. "Some things we just can't fix. Be open to talk with them when they're ready — and they will be, I promise you — but leave the rest of it with God. He's the only one who can work it all out anyway. You've got to trust him to do that, you know."

"I know. That's what he reminded me of the other night. There really isn't any other answer, is there?"

"None. At least none that I've found in my many years on this earth." She patted Toni's hand again. "Now, do you think you can finish your lunch, or would you like to talk some more?"

Before Toni could answer, the phone rang.

"Do you want me to get it?" April asked, her eyebrows arched questioningly.

"No, I'll get it. Thank you, April . . . for

everything."

April smiled, and Toni picked up the phone, her heart pounding as she prayed she would hear Abe's voice on the other end.

"Toni? It's Valerie Myers. How are you?"

"I'm . . . fine," she answered, fighting the disappointment that swept over her when she realized it wasn't Abe. *There I go, lying again. I'm not fine at all, but I can't very well tell her that.* She took a deep breath. "And how are you?"

"Excited. Can we get together and talk?" Her voice was animated, almost conspiratorial as she continued. "Toni, I think I've found a way to get to Cora Blevins without that bodyguard husband of hers around. Interested?"

Toni sat up straight. *Was she interested? Now that was an understatement.* "Where and when? You name the place, and I'll be there."

"Would tomorrow work for you? If you can swing by my office around one o'clock or so, I should be free for about an hour. How does that sound?"

"That sounds wonderful," Toni answered. "I'll be there."

By the time she hung up the phone, Toni was beginning to feel hopeful once again. Things were far from "fine," but at least one

of the many complicated issues she was juggling might finally begin to unravel and lead
her to the truth.

CHAPTER 13

Dear Tom:

I hadn't really planned to write to you again after the first letter, especially since I haven't had any response from you yet, but I wanted to say that . . .

What? What do I want to say? Frustrated, Carrie, propped up against the pillows on her bed, crumpled the paper and tossed it toward the wastebasket in the corner. She missed, but it didn't matter. It wasn't the first discarded correspondence to Tom Blevins she'd sent sailing in the direction of the trash that night, and from the looks of things, it wouldn't be the last.

Why don't I just give it up? I can't figure out what I really want to say anyway. Why do I feel like it's so important to write to him again? I've already told him I forgive him. Why can't I just leave it at that? What more can I possibly say to him?

Yet somehow she knew there was more, something more that God wanted her to write to Tom and to send to him quickly. But she'd agonized most of the afternoon and evening over what it might be, and she still hadn't come up with anything.

Her shoulders ached as she sat on her bed, propped up on pillows, her pajama-covered legs lying uselessly in front of her as if they were some sort of foreign objects. The pain had actually started earlier that day while she was still at school. Carrie had been so excited about returning to River View High this semester, and most of the time she was glad she'd been able to do so, despite the media's attempt to broadcast her every move. That had finally slowed down, but she had days — like today — when she wondered if returning to school had been such a good idea.

Carrie had been steering her wheelchair down the hallway past the gym when the shouts and laughter of the cheerleaders, practicing their routine for the upcoming basketball game, had assailed her ears. That's when the first twinge of pain had hit her shoulders. A cheerleader herself — until Tom's bullet had cut her down in the hallway — Carrie had felt freshly wounded all over again. Would she ever again be able to participate in any of the normal activities she'd so taken for granted before the shooting?

The sudden pinpricks at the back of her eyelids warned her of another approaching bout with self-pity, but she closed her eyes and clenched her fists, determined not to give in. *Help me, God,* she prayed silently. *You know I don't want to fall into the trap of feeling sorry for myself, but you also know that I don't always do too well at avoiding it. Everybody thinks I'm so strong, but I'm really not. You know that better than anybody. Oh, Father, I'm sorry, but sometimes I still want to scream at Tom and tell him how angry I am at him for doing this to me. I know it wouldn't help me walk again, and it sure wouldn't bring Tom closer to you. But I have to admit, I think it would make me feel better — at least for a little while.*

Opening her eyes, she stared down at the pad of paper in her lap. *OK, God, I won't scream at Tom or tell him that sometimes I think he's a creep. I'll write whatever you tell me to write, but I don't have a clue what that is. So I'm listening, OK? In the meantime, it sure would be nice if you'd take away this pain in my shoulders. . . . .*

The knock on the door startled her. "Come in," she called.

Donna Bosworth entered the room, her wide gray eyes smiling at her only child. "How are you, honey? I was on my way to bed when I noticed your light was still on. Do you need anything?"

Carrie returned her mother's smile. "I'm fine, Mom. Thanks. I'm just . . . trying to write a letter."

"Really?" Donna raised her eyebrows and sat down on the edge of Carrie's bed. "To whom?"

"Tom Blevins. I've already written to him once."

Donna looked surprised. "I didn't know that. Did he . . . write back?"

"No. No response, I'm afraid."

"So you've decided to write to him again."

"Not really. I mean, it wasn't my idea. . . ." Carrie sighed and tried to readjust her weight in an effort to ease the pain in her shoulders. Before she could say another word, her mother was on her feet, reaching for Carrie's shoulders. "Here, honey. Let me help turn you, and I'll give you a back and neck rub. Would you like that?"

"I'd love it," Carrie admitted, "if you're sure you don't mind."

Donna was already turning Carrie over as she answered. "Now, why in the world would I mind? I'm your mother, and I happen to love you very much, remember?"

"How could I forget?" Carrie murmured, settling down on her stomach as her mother began to rub the tension from her shoulders. "You're the best mom in the world, you know."

Donna laughed. "Well, I'm certainly glad you think so. Now, while I have you nice and relaxed, why don't you tell me about this letter that wasn't your idea to write."

"Actually, I wrote the first letter because I'd been feeling for some time that God wanted me to write to Tom and tell him that I forgave him, and, of course, to tell him about God's forgiveness too. So I did. I thought that was the end of it, but ever since I got home from school today, I've been sensing that I need to write him another letter. The problem is, I don't know what I'm supposed to say to him."

"I assume," said Mrs. Bosworth, "that you believe God is directing you to write this second letter."

"Yes. But —"

"Then don't worry about what to say, sweetheart. If God wants you to write to Tom, all you have to do is be willing. Don't try to force it. He'll give you the right words at the right time. You'll see."

"Thanks." Carrie sighed contentedly.

"Even my shoulders feel better. Like I said, you're the best."

Donna laughed. "And don't you ever forget it, young lady. OK, I'm off to bed. You'd better do the same. Do you want me to help you turn back over?"

"No, thanks. I'm fine like this for now, and I can turn myself if I need to. It takes a while, but I can do it."

Donna bent over and kissed her daughter's cheek. "I know you can, honey. You're a lot stronger than most people would be in your situation. Now get some sleep. Tomorrow's a school day."

"I know, Mom. Goodnight."

As her mother left the room, turning out the light as she went, Carrie felt herself drifting off, the frustration and tension seeming to have drained from her body. Maybe now she could relax enough to hear from God. If she did, she'd write that letter to Tom first thing in the morning.

Despite the sadness that had hung over Toni for almost a week now, she could feel a tingle of anticipation rising up within her as she parked her car in front of the high school administration office. It didn't hurt that the sun was finally breaking through the early afternoon clouds, promising at least a few hours of clear skies and slightly warmer temperatures. As she approached Valerie's office, she tried to keep her feelings in check. Any excitement she might be experiencing was premature, she reminded herself, since a meeting with Cora Blevins didn't assure her of any new information about Tom or his crime. However, the possibility of seeing the woman gave Toni a glimmer of hope. Besides, she'd sensed all along that the key to tracking down Tom's accomplice — assuming he had one — was in talking with the young man's mother.

Valerie's door was open, and Toni peeked inside. The assistant principal was sitting at her desk, her head bent over a file. When Toni rapped on the door, Valerie looked up, a slight frown creasing her brow. Her look of concern and surprise changed quickly when she recognized Toni.

"Come in," she said, her voice warm and her smile wide. She gestured toward the empty chair on the visitor's side of her desk. "Sit down. Let me put this away and we'll get right down to business, unless, of course, you'd like a cup of coffee first." She slid the closed file into the bottom drawer of her desk. "Although I have to warn you, it's half a day old and very potent."

Toni laughed. "No, thanks. I hardly ever

drink the stuff, even when it's fresh."

Valerie smiled again, then folded her hands in front of her. "How are you, Toni? And how is Melissa?"

Toni flinched. Melissa was as well as could be expected, she supposed — at least, she hoped so — but it had been days since they'd spoken to one another. Toni doubted, however, that sharing that information with Valerie was necessary or even wise at this point. "We're . . . fine," she answered, hoping to get through the pleasantries quickly and get on to Valerie's plan to meet with Cora Blevins. "How about you?"

"Hanging in there. Busy, as always, but I like it that way." Valerie's smile faded and her dark eyes looked serious. "So, are you still intent on meeting with Tom's mother?"

Toni nodded. "Absolutely. I have no idea what I may — or may not — learn from talking with her, but I know I have to try."

"Good." Valerie seemed both pleased and relieved. "I've given this a lot of thought, and I talked to a couple of people I know I can trust who know the Blevins family. Here's what I found out. Cora Blevins never — and I mean *never* — leaves that house without her husband. And he almost never leaves her at home alone, especially since he can't seem to hold a regular job for any length of time. How they manage financially is beyond me. One of my contacts seemed to think he receives some sort of permanent disability payments. Could be, I suppose. The bottom line is, the man wants total control, and she's obviously too intimidated to buck him on it. But I found out that there's one time almost every week . . ."

Toni's eyes opened wide. This was what she'd been waiting for.

"It seems Sam Blevins plays poker with some of his buddies on Sunday afternoons. They rotate meeting at each other's homes, so we'd have to make sure it wasn't the Blevinses' turn to host the game. When it's not at his place, Sam is gone for three or four hours, and he usually leaves his wife at home. Now, there's no guarantee Cora would talk to us, even if we manage to catch her at home without Sam. But if we find out the poker game is at someone else's house this Sunday afternoon, are you willing to give it a try? I'll certainly go with you, if you'd like, unless, of course, you'd rather take your fiancé along instead. I'd certainly understand if you would, since he's a policeman. . . ."

Toni was already shaking her head. "No. I don't want Abe to come with me. I don't know Cora Blevins well at all, but I imagine she'd open up better without a man present — particularly a detective. She's already talked to the police and the lawyers several times, I'm sure — although, undoubtedly with her husband present. I think we should make this as comfortable and informal for her as possible, don't you?" Toni didn't tell Valerie that even if she thought it would be a good idea to bring Abe along, she couldn't ask him because she hadn't talked to him in almost a week. But she couldn't let herself think about that right now. This might be her only opportunity to talk with Tom's mother, and she wasn't about to miss it.

"I agree completely," Valerie said. "Women tend to open up better with other women, and we're going to have a hard enough time getting her to trust us as it is. She's obviously lived in fear of her husband for so many years, and she's been so isolated. Still, I'd like to think that if she knows anything at all about an accomplice or anything else that might help Tom, the welfare of her son will win out in the end and she'll tell us what she knows. That's a best-case scenario, of course."

Toni nodded again. "That's exactly what I'm counting on. I know we may not learn anything from her, and even if we do, it probably won't make a bit of difference at this late date, since Tom is due to be sentenced in less than two weeks. However, if someone else is involved, the judge who's handing down the sentence should at least know about it before making his decision."

"Agreed. OK, then. We're on for Sunday, right? Assuming, of course, that I can find out for sure that Sam Blevins will be playing his weekly poker game at someone else's house. I'll call you as soon as I know. Should we just meet here and drive over together?"

"Sounds good to me," Toni said, anxious to get on with the meeting but wishing she could find a way to talk to Abe before going to the Blevins home. Maybe she'd try calling him one more time.

It was Wednesday afternoon, and Melissa had gone to Carrie's home after school. The two of them now sat in the Bosworths' backyard, enjoying a few minutes of rare winter sunshine before the pale yellow orb sank in the west. The girls basked in the welcome warmth, though it was still far from shirtsleeve weather. In sweaters and jeans, Carrie sat in her wheelchair with Melissa beside her on a webbed patio seat. They had put their homework on hold so they could spend some time outdoors.

"It's peaceful back here," Melissa commented. "I've always loved your backyard."

"Me too. I can't imagine ever living anywhere else." She turned to Melissa and smiled. "I can't wait for spring. I love sitting out here, listening to the birds and watching for the first crocuses to come up, and then the tulips. . . ."

"We should have some blossoms on the apple and cherry trees pretty soon too. The streets always look so pretty when they burst into bloom." Melissa sighed. "It's been a long winter."

Carrie's smile faded. "That's for sure, and it's not over yet." She leaned her head back and closed her eyes, and the girls were silent for a moment. Then Carrie asked, "Have Abe and Toni set a wedding date?"

Melissa hesitated. This was a topic she'd made a point to avoid with Carrie recently, but it had been bound to come up sooner or later. "I'm . . . not sure," she answered, hedging and trying not to lie at the same time.

"What do you mean, you're not sure?" Carrie asked, her eyes still closed but a teasing tone in her voice. "I thought you were going to be the maid of honor. Don't you think they should let you in on these little details, just to make sure you don't miss the big event?"

When Melissa didn't answer, Carrie opened her eyes and turned again to her friend, who was staring down at her hands, clasped tightly in her lap. "What's wrong?" Carrie asked. "You look like you're about to cry."

"I'm trying not to," Melissa answered, swallowing hard as she blinked back tears. "But you're not making it easy, you know."

"Sorry, but isn't that what friends are for? To talk to when things are bothering us? We've been doing it for years, Melissa."

Melissa sighed, her voice soft and resigned as the first tears spilled over onto her cheeks. "I know, and I really do need to talk to someone about it. I just . . ." She looked up at Carrie. "I'm . . . not so sure they'll be getting married after all."

Carrie's brown eyes opened wide. "You're kidding. I thought everything was so perfect between them."

"I thought so too. But after what I saw last week . . ."

Carrie waited, and Melissa appreciated her friend's sensitivity. She also appreciated that Carrie knew her well enough to realize she needed a moment to collect herself and that she would go on with her story when she was ready.

"It was Thursday afternoon," she began,

"right after I left your place. I got home the same time Abe arrived, so we went in together. And . . . Toni was there."

Carrie raised her eyebrows as if to say, "And . . . ?"

"She wasn't alone."

This time Carrie spoke. "You mean, Mrs. Lippincott was there with her."

"No, April was still at her church." Melissa paused again. "Toni was with . . . Brad."

"Brad Anderson? What was he doing there?"

"That's what I wanted to know. So did Abe. They — Toni and Brad — tried to convince us that Brad had come to see me, but —"

"But what? That sounds like a logical explanation. You told me yourself that you've been spending time with him lately."

Melissa's green eyes were brimming with fresh tears as she fixed them on her friend. "He wasn't there to see me, Carrie. That was just an excuse. He was there to see Toni."

"How do you know that?"

"Because . . . when we walked in on them, they were sitting on the couch together, and . . . Brad had his arms around Toni." Melissa's voice took on a hard edge. "And you should have seen the guilty looks on their faces when they saw us."

Carrie closed her eyes and turned away from Melissa, resting her head on the back of her chair again. "Wow. I don't know what to say."

"Now you know why I didn't say anything sooner, but it's all I've thought about since it happened. And no matter how much I try to figure it out, none of it makes any sense. Toni had Brad, but she gave him up to marry Abe. I got used to that idea, I really did. I like Abe a lot, and I think — I *thought* — he and Toni were perfect for each other. But now . . ."

As Melissa's voice trailed off, the girls were silent once again. Melissa knew that Carrie was groping for something to say, but what could she, or anyone else, possibly say to make everything all right again? Melissa hadn't talked to either Abe or Toni since Thursday, and she hadn't seen Abe around the house during that time. Of course, she hadn't seen or talked to Brad either. Melissa assumed he was embarrassed and avoiding them all. *Which he should be,* she reminded herself. She'd always thought she could trust Brad. Now she wasn't sure she could trust anyone.

"I really don't know why I'm going to tell you this," Carrie said, interrupting Melissa's thoughts as she turned to her once more. "I'm not even sure it has anything at all to do with what you just told me about last Thursday, but . . . somehow I sense I'm supposed to tell you anyway. If not for now, then maybe for later."

Melissa was puzzled. Carrie often said things that didn't make a lot of sense to her at the time, but somewhere down the road the words always seemed to come back to her, suddenly becoming clear. Melissa was sure it was because Carrie was so close to God and he often spoke to her. Melissa resolved to listen and to tuck away her friend's words for future reference if, indeed, she didn't understand their meaning or application at the moment.

"Actually, I want to tell you a couple of things," Carrie said. "First, remember that things aren't always as they seem. There could very well be a logical and innocent explanation for what happened. And you owe it to Toni — and Brad — to give them a chance to share that explanation. The second thing is even more important. It's about . . . the price of love. I think what I'm trying to say is, it costs something to love someone. That may sound strange, but Melissa, you already know there's a price; you paid it when you lost your dad. Your mom, too, even though that was a long time ago. Still . . . I feel like I need to remind you that loving someone can hurt, and it involves risks. But if you aren't willing to take those risks, to pay the price of love, your life is meaningless." Carrie paused before continuing. Melissa was staring at her lap again, her fingers lacing and unlacing as Carrie spoke.

"That's about it," Carrie said. "You already know what it cost God to give us a chance to return his love. Maybe . . . maybe he's challenging you to follow his example in some way. . . ."

Melissa nodded, a fresh batch of tears brewing as she realized that even if she didn't understand the entire relevance or application of Carrie's words to her current situation, her friend was definitely right about God's challenging her to follow his example. But how was she to do that? And where was she to get the strength — and even the willingness — to do so?

She looked up when she felt Carrie's hand on her arm. "Will you take me back inside?" Carrie asked. "I think it's time for me to write another letter to Tom Blevins. I've been thinking since yesterday that God wanted me to do that, but I couldn't figure out what I was supposed to say. Suddenly, while I was talking to you, it all seemed to fall into place."

Friday. Another week almost gone, and Tom still hadn't heard anything. The sentencing was drawing closer, and for the first time he was beginning to wonder if he'd made a terrible mistake by taking the entire rap himself. Even though his lawyer continued to assure him that by changing his plea to guilty and foregoing a jury trial he'd avoided the death penalty, he was terrified at the thought of what might happen to him if he ended up spending the rest of his life in jail. Which, at this point, was exactly what he expected to do. Even if the district attorney recommended and the judge agreed to a twenty-five-year-to-life sentence rather than life without parole, Tom Blevins was sure he'd spend the rest of his natural life in prison simply because he would never live long enough to walk back out those prison doors once he'd been placed in the general population.

Tom's skin crawled and his heart raced at the thought of what would happen to him when the older, larger, stronger inmates got hold of him. And he knew they would. Lying on his back on his cot, Tom closed his eyes, trying in vain to block out the hideous images that tormented his every waking moment, tempting him to give in to the thought that suicide seemed, more each day, the best way out. If only he'd never let himself get caught up in all this, talked into committing murder in the hope that they would then be able to be together. . . .

It would have been different, of course, if things had worked out as planned. They hadn't, though, and now, completely alone and facing a future he'd been promised he would never have to deal with but that now seemed inevitable, he finally asked himself the question he'd been avoiding for weeks: With things having turned out so badly, was it really worth it? Were those few months they'd had together worth what he was going through now? If he'd known things were going to turn out like this, would he have ever tucked Sam's assault rifle under his coat, walked into River View High, and started shooting?

For the first time since he'd been hauled out of the school, wounded and handcuffed, Tom Blevins was honest with himself. No, he would not have done it had he known what would happen to him, but now it was too late. People had been killed, wounded, paralyzed, and he was going to have to pay the price alone.

Before he could begin to search for a practical way to carry out the suicide that now seemed a welcome release, he heard a voice yell, "Blevins. Mail call." Startled, he jumped up from his bed and hurried to the door where an envelope protruded through the slot. Snatching it up, he returned to his prone position on the bunk, wondering fleetingly if anyone ever got bedsores from lying around so much in jail. *The least of my worries,* he reminded himself, pulling the letter from the already opened envelope. He hadn't even bothered to read the return address. Surely this would be the letter he'd been waiting for.

It wasn't. It began with the familiar, neat script of the only other piece of mail he'd received since he'd been there. *Carrie Bosworth. What did that crazy girl want this time?*

Dear Tom:

Hello again. I hadn't really planned on writing to you a second time, especially since you didn't respond to my first letter. I truly thought I'd already covered everything that needed to be said. But then, yesterday, I could sense the Lord urging me to write to you once more, even though I wasn't sure what I was supposed to say. . . .

Oh, man, there she goes again with that God stuff. Does she really expect me to believe that he talks to her, that he gives her messages to deliver to me? Even if he did talk to her, why would he tell her to pass something on to me? God's never cared about me before. If he had, I wouldn't be here right now, and I wouldn't have had to put up with that old man slapping me around all those years. If God didn't help me then, I sure don't want to hear from him now.

But he couldn't stop himself. Tom read on.

This afternoon I was sitting out in the backyard with a friend of mine — Melissa Matthews. You know her, right?

Tom smirked. *Oh yeah, I know her, but I might as well be invisible as far as she's concerned.*

Well, Melissa and I were talking about some personal situations, and I suddenly found myself telling her about the price of love. Even as I was saying it, I knew that's what I was supposed to tell you about.

Tom, I don't know any of the details about what you did. I don't know why you did it or what led up to it, but you know — and God knows. Whatever it was, God wants you to know that there is always a price to pay for loving someone. I'm not sure how that applies to you, but I assume it has something to do with what you're going through right now.

Tom swallowed, resisting the impulse to toss this second letter from Carrie Bosworth right into the toilet where he'd disposed of the first one. He couldn't, though — not until he'd finished reading it. Then, he promised himself, he would get rid of it and never think about it again.

There's something else, Tom. And it's a lot more important than the price you're paying. And that's the price God paid for loving you.

Tom was fighting tears now, but he blinked them away and continued to read.

I told you in my last letter that God loves you. It's true, Tom. That's why he sent his only Son, Jesus, to die for you. You see, Tom, you and I — and everyone who ever lived — are sinners, and sin is what separates us from God. It started with Adam and Eve; we have all followed in their footsteps and chosen to go our own ways instead of God's way. Because of that, we have a price to pay. The Bible says that price is death and eternal separation from God. That's justice, just like the term someone serves in jail for committing a crime.

Tom was getting angry now, but still he read on.

But there's another side to God besides justice, and that's his mercy. Because he loves us all so very much, he took it upon himself to pay for our sin. He sent his Son to take our place. Jesus lived his entire life on this earth without ever sinning — the only one who has ever done that — and then he died on a cross, shedding innocent blood as the price for our guilt. When God raised him again after three days, it proved that even death couldn't separate us from God any longer, if we would personally accept the sacrifice Jesus made in our place. In other words, Tom, he took the rap for you, and for me. The price was great — but his love was greater. That doesn't mean you won't have to pay for your crime here on this earth, but it does mean that you don't have to allow your sins to continue to separate you from God for all eternity. I pray you will ask him to forgive you, Tom, and then receive his love and allow him to heal your broken heart.

Carrie

The tears were flowing by then as Tom crushed the letter in his hands and held it to his chest, then rolled over on his stomach and sobbed into his pillow.

CHAPTER 14

Toni and Valerie had chatted anxiously from the moment they left the school until they arrived at the Blevins home. Suddenly they were silent as Toni slowed the car to a stop at the end of the long dirt driveway. The run-down old house sat back from the street, barely visible from their vantage point. As the "liquid sunshine" that had been falling all weekend drummed a steady beat on the car's roof, Toni glanced over at Valerie and asked, "Are we ready for this?"

Valerie's smile was noncommittal. "As ready as we'll ever be, I suppose."

Toni nodded in agreement and started forward once again. As glad as she was to have Valerie beside her, she couldn't help but think how much more at ease she would feel if Abe were with her instead. That was impossible, of course. Not only would his presence have hurt her chances of persuading Mrs. Blevins to talk about Tom's situation, but Abe hadn't yet returned any of Toni's calls, including the one she'd made after her meeting with Valerie on Wednesday. She'd so hoped she could talk with him before going to the Blevins' home, but even as she'd left her message on his answering machine, she'd doubted he'd call her back.

What did Abe's continued silence mean? Was their relationship really over? Would he end it just like that, call off their engagement without even giving her a chance to explain what had happened? Surely what they shared together was too important to dismiss so easily. He was probably just thinking things through, she reassured herself, praying about what to do.

Toni's heart ached as she thought of the opportunities Abe had given her in the preceding months to agree to an earlier wedding date. If she'd listened to him, they'd be getting married in a matter of days. Instead, no date had been set, and she now wondered if it ever would be. In addition, Melissa was still giving her the silent treatment, and Brad had seemingly disappeared into thin air, undoubtedly too embarrassed to talk with any of them, at least for a while.

As they pulled up in front of the dilapidated house, two skinny, snarling German shepherds greeted them menacingly, their ruckus alerting anyone within earshot of the intrusion on their privacy. A lazy bloodhound, sprawled out on the front porch, opened his eyes and raised his head just enough to evaluate the trespassers but apparently didn't feel they appeared dangerous enough to warrant getting up from his nap. He closed his eyes and didn't move again. Toni and Valerie waited in the car for a moment, watching the front door and windows for any sign of life.

"Do you think we should get out?" Valerie asked. "The only other time I've been here, those dogs were in the house, but then, so was Sam Blevins. Maybe he leaves them outside to guard the place when he's gone."

"You're probably right," Toni agreed. "They were inside the one time I came too." She raised her eyebrows. "They don't look any too friendly, do they?"

Before Valerie could answer, the front door of the house creaked open just enough to allow Cora Blevins to poke her head through and give them a wary glance. "I think maybe she's more scared than we are," Toni observed. "Shall we get out and see what happens?"

"I'm game if you are. I just hope those sweet little dogs had their breakfast this morning."

Toni gave Valerie a dubious half-smile, and opening her door gingerly, stepped out into the rain, as Valerie did the same. The dogs' barking and growling increased in intensity, but they held their ground as Cora ordered them to stay.

"What do you want?" Mrs. Blevins asked, her voice more forceful than Toni remembered it when she was in her husband's presence. "If you're here to see Sam, you'll have to come back later."

Toni and Valerie followed the dogs' cue and stood still beside their respective car doors, the cold rain dripping from their hair and down their faces. "We're not here to see Sam," Toni explained. "We're here to talk with you, Mrs. Blevins . . . about your son, Tom."

The frail woman, wrinkled beyond her age, flinched slightly as a wave of fear crossed her face. "What's happened to my boy?" Her voice wasn't nearly as firm now. "Is he OK?"

"Tom's fine," Toni assured her. "We just want to talk with you for a few moments. Please, Mrs. Blevins."

The woman hesitated. "I don't know . . . Sam's not here, and he don't much like me havin' company when he's gone."

Valerie spoke up then. "We won't take much of your time. We just want to ask you a few questions."

"Questions about what?" Cora was frowning now. "Are you reporters?"

"No," Valerie answered. "I'm Valerie Myers, the assistant principal at the high school. I've been here before. Don't you remember?"

A slight look of recognition flickered across Cora's face, but she still looked puzzled. "I . . . guess I do. But that was a long time ago, before my boy quit school. What are you doin' here now?" She cut her eyes toward Toni. "And who are you? I think I've seen you before too."

"Yes," Toni said. "I'm Toni Matthews. I was here a few weeks ago, hoping to talk to you about Tom. Your . . . husband . . . was home at the time."

The look of fear returned to Mrs. Blevins's eyes as she began to shake her head from side to side. "Sam wouldn't like this. He really wouldn't . . ."

Toni took a step forward, but the dogs bared their teeth and she stopped. "Please, Mrs. Blevins, we won't take long. We're just trying to help Tom, and we can't do it alone."

The door to the house opened another

crack. "You . . . want to help my Tom? Why? What can you do for him that his lawyer can't?"

Toni glanced at Valerie. They were both soaked by this time. Their eyes met briefly, then Toni turned back to Tom's mother. "I honestly don't know, Mrs. Blevins. I don't know if we can help Tom at all, but we want to try. We . . . think you might have some information that could at least point us in the right direction."

The wait seemed interminable as Cora Blevins stood framed in the doorway, the dogs growled their warnings, and Toni and Valerie tried not to shiver as the cold and dampness seeped through their clothes and into their bones. Finally Mrs. Blevins called to the dogs, "Jake, Bruno, come."

The dogs turned and immediately went to the porch, stationing themselves on either side of the snoozing bloodhound.

"All right," said Cora, opening the door the rest of the way. "Come on in, but just for a few minutes." She glanced nervously down the driveway past Toni and Valerie as they climbed the steps to the front porch. "I don't know what I can tell you that could help my Tom," Mrs. Blevins said, "but I'll try." She was fighting tears now. "I surely don't want to see my boy die, even though I know what he done was wrong. I also know he ain't supposed to get the death penalty now, since he pleaded guilty, but . . . I hate to think of what'll happen to him in prison."

As Cora Blevins continued to hold the front door open, Toni and Valerie stepped past her into the dingy front room of the house, the temperature only slightly warmer inside than out. Toni's heart constricted as the three baby pictures on the far wall caught her eye. The photo in the middle, portraying a happy infant in blue, was obviously Tom, showing off what Toni imagined was one of the few smiles of his young life.

Cora, wearing a faded housedress and sweater, led them to a lumpy couch draped with a faded yellow bedspread. As Toni and Valerie sat down, Cora pulled up a straight-backed chair from the kitchen table and sat down on it, then pulled her sweater tight across her chest, clutching the edges until her knuckles turned white. Toni, trying not to shiver, couldn't help but notice that the house, though small and in sore need of repair, was neat and tidy. It was obvious that Cora Blevins had tried to decorate it as best she could, with a few modest macramé decorations and planters scattered through-out the room. Toni wondered if the woman had done the macramé herself but didn't ask.

When Mrs. Blevins failed to invite them to take off their coats, Toni wondered if it meant she simply hadn't thought of it, being as unaccustomed as she was to company, or if she was intending to hold them to their word to keep the meeting brief. Either way, Toni resolved to find out all she could but not to take advantage of the rare audience they had gained with this fearful, beaten-down woman. Toni would have felt better if she and Valerie weren't dripping all over the couch and the threadbare rug under their feet. Tom's mother seemed not to notice.

"Mrs. Blevins," Toni began, praying silently even as she spoke, "I'm going to get right to the point. From the moment I heard that your son was the prime suspect in the school shootings, I couldn't believe he'd done such a thing alone. I didn't know Tom well over the years, but I'd seen him enough to sense that he just wasn't the type to mastermind something like that on his own."

Cora's demeanor became defensive. "You sayin' my boy's dumb?"

Toni caught her breath and glanced at Valerie before looking back to Cora. "Not at all. I just —"

" 'Cause he's not, you know. Tom could've been somebody important if he just hadn't dropped out of school. Least, that's what I always thought. Seems that teacher friend of his thought the same thing —"

Cora Blevins's soft brown eyes grew wide with fear, and she put her hand over her mouth as if to stop herself from saying another word. It was obvious she hadn't meant to say as much as she had.

"What teacher is that?" Valerie asked. "Was it someone who came here to talk with you when Tom was having problems before he dropped out of school?"

Cora's eyes darted back and forth from Toni to Valerie. "No. Not really. I . . . I didn't mean . . ."

"It's OK," Toni said, her voice soothing. "You haven't said anything you shouldn't. Really. We just need all the information we can get if we're going to help Tom. Knowing the identity of this teacher might be exactly what we're looking for. Please, Mrs. Blevins. If you know anything — anything at all — please tell us. Help us help your son."

Tears were forming in Cora's eyes now, the fear beginning to be replaced with a deep sadness that seemed to emanate from her entire being. "I . . . I don't know her name. Truly, I don't. Tom wouldn't tell me, and I never met her, but . . . he mentioned her to me once. We — Tom and I — didn't talk much, especially these last years. But every now and then we'd try, you know? And this one time, when I told him I wished he'd stayed in school, he said . . . he didn't need school, that he was smarter than most people there anyway. Said he knew that was true 'cause one of the teachers told him. I asked him which teacher, but he wouldn't say. Made me promise I'd never tell a single soul about her, and I didn't — till now. Tom said he saw her every week, and she understood him like nobody else ever did." She stopped, looking helplessly at her two guests. "That's all I know. He wouldn't say nothin' else, and he never talked about it again. Do you think — whoever this teacher is — she might be able to help my Tom?"

"I don't know," Toni answered. "Valerie and I will have to see if we can find out who she is. You're . . . sure Tom said this teacher was a woman?"

Cora nodded. "Positive. I . . . I didn't tell nobody else about this," she said, wringing her hands absently. "Not the police, not Tom's lawyer, not the reporters, nobody. I promised Tom, and besides, I . . . I didn't want Sam to know about it. He didn't like it much when Tom and I talked, just the two of us. Thought we was talkin' 'bout him . . . keepin' secrets from him, you know?" Her eyes were pleading now. "Was I wrong not to tell before?"

Toni smiled reassuringly. "Don't worry about that, Mrs. Blevins. You've told us, and now we'll see what we can find out. If we're able to learn anything at all, we'll let you know."

The fear grew in Cora's eyes.

"Don't worry," said Toni. "We'll wait until you're alone again to talk to you about it."

Cora nodded, her relief obvious. "Thank you," she said. "Please, if you can help my boy at all, please try. I . . ." She choked back a sob. "I love him very much, you know. I just . . ."

"It's OK, Mrs. Blevins," Toni said, as she and Valerie rose to go. "We understand. We'll do whatever we can."

Abe held the phone to his ear, listening to it ring. When the answering machine clicked on, he hesitated, then hung up. He had no idea what he wanted to say to her, especially in a recorded message. He wasn't even sure why he'd finally decided to return her call. Maybe it was the urgency in her voice when she'd left her last message, saying she needed to talk with him about a possible visit to Cora Blevins. Or maybe it was because he just plain missed her. Whatever the reason, he berated himself for having waited so long to contact her.

It was Sunday afternoon, and for the first time since becoming a believer several months earlier, Abe had purposely stayed home from church. He just wasn't up to seeing Toni yet, at least not in that particular setting. It had been difficult enough the week before, trying to focus on worship and listening to the sermon when his heart and mind were absorbed with the curly-haired blonde sitting two rows in front and across the aisle from him. Never once during the entire service had she turned to look at him; yet he couldn't keep his eyes off her for more than a few seconds at a time. Abe certainly didn't want a repeat of that painful ordeal, and somehow he sensed it had been as difficult for Toni as it had been for him. At least he hoped it had. Staying home from church today had convinced him that he was going to have to see her again — and soon — but he'd decided it would be at a time and place when he knew they could be alone, not in public where he had to worry about keeping his emotions in check. This was no time to hold anything back.

Honesty would have to win out over pride. He'd put it off as long as he could; they needed to talk.

So, he'd finally decided to return her call, having waited until he was sure she'd be home from church and finished with lunch. No one answered, though, not even April or Melissa. He assumed April had stayed for something at her own church, as she often did, while Melissa had probably gone to Carrie's. But where was Toni?

As he leaned back in his recliner, refusing to allow himself to speculate on her whereabouts, he closed his eyes and listened to the rain pattering gently but regularly on the overhang of his front stoop. *Should I go somewhere?* he wondered. *But where?* The weather wasn't very inviting, and besides, he really wasn't in the mood. Maybe he'd just stay put and try calling Toni again later. . . .

He had no idea he'd dozed off until the ringing phone woke him from a sound sleep. Before reaching for the receiver, he glanced at his watch. It was four o'clock in the afternoon. Abe could hardly believe he'd slept so long, but then again, he hadn't been sleeping well at night lately. Without checking his caller ID or even considering letting the call go onto the answering machine, he cleared his throat as he put the receiver to his ear. "Hello?"

"Abe?"

Her voice was hesitant, but it touched his heart the moment he heard it. He spoke only one word in response: "Toni."

"I . . . I hope I didn't bother you, but . . . I just got home from the Blevinses' house, and I was so hoping that you'd be home and that you'd answer. I —"

Abe sat up straight. "You were at the Blevinses' place? Just now?"

"Yes. With Valerie Myers. We went over there together. We had a chance to talk with Cora Blevins without her husband being there, and . . . Abe, please, can we get together and discuss it? Please . . ."

Abe's heart ached as he nodded. "Of course. Where and when? Do you want me to come over there?"

"Could you? April and Melissa will both be gone for a while yet, so it would give us a good chance to talk."

"I'll be there in fifteen minutes."

It had been a long day for April, having stayed after the service for a potluck meal and then to help to decorate for an upcoming event. However, even as everyone else had drifted home — some having offered her a ride, which she declined — she'd stayed behind, sensing the need to go back into the sanctuary and pray for Toni. She'd decided to stay there as long as necessary, then take a bus or call a cab to take her home. She'd already phoned and left a message for Toni and Melissa, letting them know not to expect her until later that evening.

As she sat quietly in a rear pew, alternately praying softly and reading passages from her Bible, she wondered what lay ahead and why God had called her to pray for Toni's protection. She was sure of only one thing, though she had no idea of the details: Toni was in danger — maybe not right at the moment, but soon.

She'd had to fight her first instinct to hurry home and warn Toni, but it was as if God had lovingly placed his hand on her shoulder and told her that it was much more important for her to stay where she was and to pray. If she would do that, he'd assured her, he would take care of the rest.

So she'd stayed, wondering every now and then why God had wanted her to pray here at the church rather than in her room at the Matthews's home where she already spent many hours in prayer each day. She knew God had his reasons and purposes, though, and she had learned through the years that it was best to align herself with them as quickly as possible.

You are my hiding place;
You will protect me from trouble
and surround me with songs of deliverance. . . .

As April read the familiar verse from Psalm 32, she suddenly sensed the need to write it down. Not knowing why but knowing full well the importance of obeying God, she pulled a tiny notebook and a pen from her purse. When she'd copied down the words and the Scripture reference, she tucked the paper back into her purse and then continued to pray, confident that God would show her what to do with the inscribed verse when he was ready. Meanwhile, she fought the occasional sense of panic that tried to invade her heart, submitting her fears to God and wondering just exactly what he had in mind.

By the time Abe arrived, Toni was trembling. Hurrying to the door to let him in, she took a deep breath and tried to calm the racing of her heart, but it was hopeless. *Oh, please, God, help us to work through our differences and straighten out our misunderstandings! Heal our relationship, Father, please . . .*

Opening the door, Toni fought the tears that threatened to overwhelm her. Abe stood there on the front porch, looking broad-shouldered, handsome . . . and very vulnerable. It was obvious he was feeling every bit as bad as she was. Wordlessly, responding only to the pain she saw mirrored in his face, Toni reached out her hand. When Abe took it in his own, she gently pulled him inside.

"I'm so sorry," she whispered as he stood looking down at her. "I can only imagine what you've been going through these past days, what you must have thought when —"

With his free hand, he placed a finger on her lips. His voice was soft but firm, his dark eyes serious. "It doesn't matter what I thought when I walked in here that afternoon. What matters is the truth — what really happened. Can we sit down and talk about it?"

Toni nodded. They released hands and walked to the couch in the living room, sitting down next to one another but not quite touching.

"Do you want to tell me first what happened at the Blevinses' place today?" Abe asked gently. "Did you actually get to talk to Tom's mother without his stepfather being there?"

Hesitantly at first, then with a gathering confidence, Toni told him of the visit. Abe listened intently, not commenting until she was finished. "A woman teacher," he said finally. "Neither you nor Valerie have any idea who she might be?"

"No, but Valerie said she'd look into it, ask around a little, try to narrow down the list of possibilities."

"Good. Meanwhile, you know we have to tell Harold Barnett about this. The police too."

"I was afraid of that. Poor Cora Blevins was so worried about what was going to happen as a result of her breaking her promise to Tom not to tell. Do you think she'll get in trouble over that?"

"I doubt it. She had no reason to think that little tidbit of information might be important to the investigation. Who knows? It might not be, but it's sure worth looking into." He paused. "Don't worry. I'll try to see that things are handled as diplomatically as possible where her husband is concerned."

Toni nodded again, relieved for Cora Blevins's sake and grateful for Abe's sensitivity. The temporary break in tension she'd felt while relating her story to Abe was quickly waning, however, and her heart began to race as she clasped her clammy hands in her lap. *Where do we go from here, God? What do I say now?*

"I love you, Abe," were the words that sprang from her mouth, surprising even her with their suddenness and intensity. When Abe's eyes softened, she went on, her speech gaining speed along the way. "I had no idea Brad was coming over that day. I guess it was a spur-of-the-moment decision on his part. He said he'd found a picture he wanted to give to Melissa, and it was such a nice day, and his father told him to take the afternoon off, so he started walking, and ended up here. At least, that's what he said. So I invited him in to wait for Melissa. When he . . ." She paused, taking a deep breath. "When he showed me the picture of my dad standing between him and Melissa, smiling and looking so youthful and alive, I just broke down. I . . . I miss him so much sometimes, and that day, when I saw his face . . ."

The tears were threatening again, and she hesitated, trying to get her emotions under control. Before she could say another word, Abe took her hand in his. "You started to cry, and he put his arms around you to comfort you. Is that what you're trying to tell me?"

Toni swallowed. "Yes. That's all. That's all it was. I wasn't even thinking about Brad . . . just my father, and how very much I miss him. The next thing I knew, I heard Melissa's voice, and I looked up, and . . . oh, Abe, how can I ever tell you how sorry I am for hurting the both of you, even though I had no intention . . ." Her voice trailed off, and she waited, knowing that Abe was wrestling with his own flood of emotions.

"I'm the one who's sorry," he said finally. "I let my own jealousies and insecurities take over. I should have stayed and confronted the situation head-on, but I ran away. I didn't want to deal with it. Maybe I was afraid you might tell me you were still in love with Brad, even though deep down I knew that wasn't true. I know the kind of person you are. There had to be a logical explanation, and I should have let you give it sooner, but . . . I suppose I just wanted to nurse my hurt feelings and wounded ego for a while." He raised her hand to his lips and kissed it gently. "I was miserable without you, Toni. I'm so sorry for dragging this thing out and putting you through so much unnecessary guilt and pain. Can you ever forgive me for being so immature and self-ish?"

She could hold back her tears no longer. "Oh, Abe, I'm the one who needs your forgiveness. I should have handled the situation with Brad differently. I —"

Before she could speak another word, Abe had pulled her against him and lifted her chin, pressing his lips against hers. Toni thought her heart would burst with joy as she melted in the arms of the man she loved — and whom she planned to marry at the very first opportunity. Now if something would only happen to bring healing between her and Melissa. . . .

As the cab pulled up in front of the Matthews's home, April Lippincott paid the driver, and holding her umbrella over her head, started up the walkway toward the house, smiling at the sight of Abe's car parked in the driveway. Maybe this was why God had kept her at the church to pray rather than sending her home to do so. Maybe Toni and Abe just needed some time alone.

April had no way of knowing how long the detective had been there, of course, but she hoped that things were finally being worked out between him and Toni. If so, she was very glad — and very relieved. If what she'd sensed about Toni being in some sort of danger was true — and she had no doubt it was or God wouldn't have called her to pray for the young woman's protection — then Abe's presence was a welcome one indeed.

CHAPTER 15

Valerie was so far behind on her paperwork that she despaired of ever catching up. She was making a valiant effort, though, as she sat at her desk on Friday morning, poring over student files even as she wondered if the police had made any progress in discovering the identity of the teacher who supposedly had befriended Tom Blevins. Although she'd discreetly asked around a bit herself, she'd learned nothing and had decided it was best to leave it to the professionals. If they came up empty as well, she would conclude that Tom had fabricated the story to impress his mother, as it was obvious Cora Blevins believed it to be true. Valerie, however, wasn't too sure about the woman's grip on reality.

"Valerie?" She startled at the male voice that interrupted her reverie. Looking up, she saw Jeff Duffield standing in front of her desk. She hadn't heard him knock, which he usually did before entering. "Got a minute?" he asked, his hazel eyes moving from Valerie to the work on her desk and back again.

"Sure," she answered. "What's up?"

Jeff settled his tall, husky frame into the chair opposite her. As she watched him, she marveled at how well the man carried his age. She knew he was fifty because she'd attended his office birthday party the previous year, but his dark wavy hair was still thick and untouched with gray, his complexion clear and unwrinkled. It was common knowledge that he worked out at a gym regularly, and everyone agreed he looked much younger than his wife, to whom he'd been married for almost twenty-five years. Valerie had often wondered if the appearance of age difference might have something to do with the fact that they'd separated for a few months last spring. She would never know, of course, and she was glad they'd patched things up. She remembered how attentive his wife had been when he'd been injured in the November shooting — how she'd picked up his messages almost daily and shielded him as much as possible from phone calls and visits, particularly from prying media members. Jeff had recovered from his injury with no obvious ill effects, and his marriage now appeared stronger than ever. Valerie knew all this not so much from the principal himself, but from the office gossip that swirled around her. She'd learned long ago that it was impossible to avoid the wagging tongues, but she did her best not to join in.

Jeff leaned back in the chair and crossed one leg over the other in what seemed to Valerie as an attempt to appear relaxed, smiling as if his visit were less important than she sensed it really was. Not buying his feigned nonchalance, she waited for him to speak, wondering why she felt the need to be on guard. She'd known Jeff Duffield for years and had never before experienced this sensation with him.

"So," he began, "how's everything? Getting caught up, are you?"

"Not really," she answered honestly, "but I'm keeping my head above water. How about you?"

He shrugged. "Oh, the same, I suppose. Clear up one problem, three more turn up to take its place."

Valerie nodded. *Where was he going with this? And how long was he going to take to get there?*

"My wife keeps trying to convince me to take a vacation and get away for a while, just the two of us — a sort of second honeymoon, I suppose. I told her things were just too hectic around here right now, especially with the police coming around again."

Was this what he'd come to talk with her about, the investigation into a possible connection between Tom Blevins and a teacher at River View High? Was he just making idle conversation, or was there a point to all this? And why did he avert his eyes when she looked directly at him?

"Things were just beginning to settle down to a manageable routine," he went on. "The initial investigation was a nightmare, I know, and I wasn't even here for most of it. You took the lion's share of that burden, and I appreciate it more than I can ever tell you." He flashed her a thin smile, then continued. "I understand from several sources that the police were here daily, digging into records, talking to anyone and everyone who ever knew Tom, and yet coming up with nothing except that he just finally snapped and came in here shooting. Of course, we know he must have planned it for some time, but who would have thought he actually had the ability to pull it off?" He raised his eyebrows and shook his head slowly, then let out a somewhat exaggerated sigh. "All that's history now, isn't it? He did it, and that's that. One dead, several wounded . . . It surely would have been a lot worse if those two officers hadn't been here for an assembly that day." He smiled once more, his lips tight, his teeth hidden, as Valerie wondered at his somewhat methodical recitation of the commonly known event. "When he pleaded guilty, I thought that was the end of it. Here we are today, though, with police detectives interviewing the entire staff and even some of the students all over again. Sometimes I wonder if we'll ever get back to normal."

Valerie was sure now that this was what he'd come to say to her, but she couldn't imagine why. Surely he didn't resent the fact that she and Toni had gone to see Mrs. Blevins and subsequently passed along the information about Tom's alleged teacher-friend to the police, initiating the renewed investigation. The way Toni and Abe had explained it to her, they really had no choice but to pass on the information to the authorities. And, although the police presence was a bit of a disruption to the school's daily activities, it wasn't nearly as intense as it had been immediately following the shooting.

"I sometimes wonder if I know what

normal is anymore," Valerie said, feeling the need to respond to Jeff's somewhat stilted and almost nonstop commentary. "I used to think I did, when the biggest problems we faced around here were failing students, budget cuts, and irate parents. But this — what happened in November — changes everything. You never look at things the same after something like that."

Jeff's nod was curt, his lips tight once again. "True, but I thought the disruptions were finally over and we could all work together to try to get things back on track, as much as possible anyway. The students need that. But now, with police crawling the halls again, interrogating everyone —"

"They're just trying to find out if there's anything to what Mrs. Blevins said about a teacher befriending Tom."

The principal's forehead drew together in a frown. "Ridiculous. You know as well as I do that the boy never got close to anyone, and if he *was* involved in a friendship with someone on the faculty, I surely would have known about it. The teacher involved would have come forward long ago and talked to me — or at least to the police. I have confidence in my staff, Valerie. They're honest, straightforward people. No one would have held back information that might have proved pertinent to Tom's case, and I, for one, resent any implication otherwise."

Valerie was puzzled. She understood and appreciated Jeff's loyalty to the school's faculty and agreed with his overall assessment of their character, but surely he could see the need for the police to follow up on even the most improbable lead. She wondered briefly if his seeming overreaction was a result of somehow feeling personally responsible for the life that had been lost, not to mention those that had been permanently scarred and changed.

"I'm sure that's true," she said, "but —"

Mr. Duffield waved away her comment. "I know what you're going to say, and you're right, of course. The police are only doing what they have to do — just as you did when you reported to them what Mrs. Blevins said. But . . ." He paused, his eyes narrowing as he observed her, holding her gaze for the first time since he'd entered her office. "I still can't quite figure out why you went to see Tom's mother. And how in the world did you get involved with Toni Matthews? I didn't realize the two of you were such good friends."

Valerie had always liked and respected Jeff Duffield, but for the first time she felt herself becoming angry with him. What was he trying to say? Was he blaming her for the renewed police presence on campus?

"Mr. Duffield — Jeff — I've only recently gotten to know Toni beyond a casual acquaintance. Much of that was due to Melissa's being with Carrie when she was shot. However, when Toni first told me she suspected that someone else was involved in the shooting, I have to admit, it made sense to me. I'd thought the same thing myself, and I was more than slightly surprised when the police didn't turn up anything on an accomplice. I know Tom fits the profile of the lone gunman, but I just couldn't shake the feeling that there was more to it. When Toni and I discovered we both felt the same way, even after the police investigation showed nothing to support our suspicions, it was only natural that we would pursue our hunch together. That's how we ended up at Cora Blevins's home and learned about Tom's supposed friendship with a teacher."

"Ah. That's the keyword, isn't it? *Supposed* friendship. The kid was lonely — not to mention mentally unbalanced, even if the court-ordered psychiatric evaluation says he's capable of understanding what he did. He obviously made up this relationship, for whatever reasons. Wishful thinking, maybe. Who knows? The point is, the friendship never existed, and now we've got the police back here, disrupting things and making people uneasy, especially the students."

"I would think their presence here does more to reassure the students and faculty than to make them uneasy. Besides, from what I've seen, they've been very discreet in their questioning. I haven't yet heard anyone express any concern over their being here."

"Well, you have now," Jeff said, glancing at his watch and rising abruptly. "I'd better get going. I've got a meeting in a few minutes. Personally, I'll be glad when this thing is settled once and for all." He strode to the door, then turned back, his hand on the knob. His irritation of a moment earlier had disappeared, replaced by an almost disinterested smile, which Valerie wasn't buying. "By the way, did Mrs. Blevins say anything else about this teacher — other than that she was a woman?"

"Not a thing. As I already explained to the detective, Mrs. Blevins never met her, and Tom refused to discuss the relationship after his initial mention of it. Why do you ask?"

Jeff's smile broadened and he shrugged again. "Just curious. I can't help but think that if he did have some sort of friendship with one of our faculty members, he would have been more specific about who she was. Just goes to prove my theory that it's nothing more than the figment of a lonely, emotionally disturbed boy's wild imagination. Well, I've got to run. It was nice talking with you."

He closed the door behind him, and Valerie sat in her chair, stunned, wondering why she felt as if she'd just been reprimanded — or worse yet, threatened. Maybe she, too, had a wild imagination. Maybe her boss had just wanted to bounce his feelings off her and see if she could shed any new light on the subject. Or maybe there was more to Jeff Duffield than she'd previously realized.

"Going out with Abe again?"

April's question caught Toni mid-stride as she walked out of the kitchen, heading for the entryway closet to retrieve her parka. Friday had dawned crisp and clear, without a cloud in sight, but definitely not a day to go coatless. Toni turned to April, who sat on the living room couch, working her way through a pile of mending.

"Not yet," Toni answered, smiling. "Although we are planning to go out to dinner this evening."

April returned the smile. "I'm so glad you and Abe were able to work through your differences. Now to work things out with Melissa . . ."

Toni nodded, her smile fading. "Yes. I keep praying, and trying to break through that barrier she's put up around herself, but . . ."

"Give it time, my dear. She loves you very much. She'll come around, especially now that she sees you and Abe back together again."

Toni wanted to believe that April was right, but she'd feel a lot better if she could just see some signs that Melissa was wearing down. To date, she'd noticed nothing. She sighed. "I pray that happens soon. She seems to be withdrawing further and further inside herself, especially now that she no longer feels free to confide in Brad. I thought about calling him and encouraging him to contact her and try to explain what happened, but . . . I think it's best if I leave that situation alone."

"A wise decision," April agreed, laying her mending beside her on the couch. "My eyes are beginning to hurt a bit. I believe I'll take a break and go start lunch. Will you join me, or do you have other plans?"

"Actually, I just made a date with Valerie Myers, the assistant principal at the high school. She called a few minutes ago and said she wanted to talk with me, so we're meeting for a quick bite at the diner. I should be home in an hour or so. Maybe Melissa will be here in time to have lunch with you, since this is an early dismissal day. I doubt it though. She'll probably go over to Carrie's. Seems she spends more time there lately than at home." Refusing to allow herself to once again get caught up in worry over Melissa, she pulled her keys from her purse, which was slung over her shoulder, then turned to leave. She stopped when April spoke again.

"Toni . . ." Her voice was hesitant. "I . . ."

Toni took a step toward the elderly woman. "Are you all right?"

"I'm . . . fine, my dear. Truly. But . . ." April's brow creased slightly, and Toni thought she looked agitated. Concerned, she sat down beside her on the couch.

"What is it, April? What's wrong?"

"I . . . don't know. Possibly nothing." She took a deep breath and fixed her pale blue eyes on Toni. "It's just . . ." Then she took another breath and tried again. "Do you remember Sunday evening, when I came home late from church? You were here with Abe when I returned."

"Of course, I remember," Toni answered, her heart warmed by the memory. "That's when Abe and I made up. I meant to ask you how your day was, but you'd already gone to bed by the time Abe left."

"Yes. I wanted to give you two some time alone. But . . . right now I want to talk to you about something else — about the reason I was so late coming home that evening."

"I assumed you were staying to help out with something at church. At least that's the conclusion I drew from your phone message."

April nodded. "That's true. That's exactly what I did. But even after we finished, which was long before suppertime, I felt compelled to stay . . . to go into the sanctuary and pray."

Toni smiled. "Nothing wrong with that."

"Of course not. But it's what I was praying about that I wanted to discuss with you. The time just never seemed right . . . until now . . . when you said you were going to meet Valerie Myers for lunch. I suddenly sensed that I was supposed to tell you what has been on my heart these last days."

Toni waited, as April seemed to be regrouping in order to complete her story.

"I was praying for you, Toni. For your safety. I have no idea why, but I feel that you are — or will be — in danger. I didn't

sense the need to tell you about it until now
— although I've continued to pray all week.
I certainly won't stop now that I've told you
about it, but . . ."

Toni's heart skipped a beat. *Could April's
warning be in some way connected to Valerie's phone call?* The assistant principal had
said she had something she wanted to
discuss with her in private, something she
couldn't quite pinpoint, but important
nonetheless — important enough not to
verbalize it on the phone. She'd sounded
quite anxious.

"That's all you can tell me?" Toni asked.
"You don't have any idea what sort of
danger, when or where, or . . . ?"

"None," April admitted. "I wish I did. I
only know I was to pray for your safety,
which I've done, and to tell you about it at
this particular moment."

Toni nodded. "Thank you, April. I appreciate it. I don't really understand it
either, but . . . God certainly knows the
details, so we'll just have to leave that part
with him."

April took Toni's hands. "May I pray with
you before you leave?"

"Of course," Toni answered as they closed
their eyes and bowed their heads.

"Heavenly Father," April prayed. "I don't

know why you've called me to pray for Toni's protection, but I know most certainly that you have. We don't know what danger lies ahead, Lord, but you do. So, once again I ask for your covering and protection over Toni. Lead and guide her, Father, according to your purposes. We place this situation in your loving hands, and we thank you that we know you hear us . . . and you will answer. In Jesus' name, amen."

"Amen." Toni looked up. "Thank you, April . . . for praying, of course, but also for caring . . . and for being here with us."

April smiled. "It's I who should be thanking you, my dear — you and Melissa — for opening your home to me. You've made me feel so welcome, as if I'm part of the family."

Toni leaned toward April and kissed her cheek. "That's exactly what you are," she said, then rose to go. "I'd better run. Valerie is expecting me."

April's forehead creased once again. "There's something else," she said. "Can you wait one more moment?"

Before Toni could answer, April was up and hurrying toward the hallway. "I'll only be a minute," she called back. "I need to get something out of my purse."

Toni went to the entryway closet and

pulled out her parka, donning it as she waited. When April returned, she handed Toni a tiny slip of paper. "Something the Lord impressed me to write down," she explained. "I'm sure it's for you."

Opening the paper, Toni read the familiar words from Psalm 32: "You are my hiding place; you will protect me from trouble and surround me with songs of deliverance."

Smiling, she tucked the paper in her pocket and gave April's cheek another peck. "Thank you," she said softly. "One of my favorite Scriptures." Then she turned and went out the door.

It had been a long time since Melissa had stood at Brad's front door. Her heart hammered in her chest as she wondered what he'd say when he saw her. She hadn't spoken to him since the day she and Abe had walked into the house and found Toni in Brad's arms. At the time Melissa had thought she could never forgive either of them, nor would she ever trust them again. However, the many hours she'd spent meditating on Carrie's words to her concerning the price of love, as well as things not always being as they seem, were starting to make sense. It was her growing understanding of those words that had convinced her to walk up to Brad's front door and ring the bell.

She waited. When she'd just about decided he wasn't home, she heard his approaching footsteps from inside. Then the door opened, and there he stood, dressed in gray sweats and looking somewhat sleepy — and very surprised.

"Melissa?" He blinked as if trying to clear his vision. "I . . . certainly didn't expect to see you here."

Melissa's heart raced, and her hands felt sweaty, despite the cold weather. The sun had been out when she got out of school at noon, so she hadn't bothered to put on her mittens before walking the six blocks to Brad's apartment. She was glad she'd worn her parka. The air outside was frigid. "Can I . . . come in?"

Brad stepped back and held the door open. "Of course, but . . . how did you know I was here?"

Melissa unbuttoned her jacket. "I called your office before I left school and found out you had the day off."

"Oh. Guess I should have known. Seems that Matthews detective blood runs deep."

Melissa smiled at his obvious attempt at humor. She knew Brad had no clue why she'd come. Wanting to put him at ease as quickly as possible, she plunked down on the couch, laid her parka beside her, and smiled up at him. "I . . . thought maybe we could talk. About what happened with Toni. About . . . a lot of things."

Brad nodded and sat down beside her, running his fingers through his sandy blond hair. "I certainly owe you that much," he began, then hesitated. "Can I get you anything first? A soda, some hot chocolate . . . ?"

Melissa shook her head, reaching up and tucking her long auburn hair behind her ears. "I'm fine. We got out of school early today, and when I found out you'd taken the day off, I thought I'd come by and try to catch you before going home for lunch. I hope that's OK." She smiled shyly. "I didn't wake you or anything, did I? I know you're always up early and you're always so neat and . . ."

Brad's smile was apologetic. "I don't usually look like a slob. Is that what you're trying to say? And I almost never take days off, but I've been putting in so many hours lately, and I just needed some time to . . . think things through. In answer to your question, no, you didn't wake me. I've just been sitting here, drinking some coffee and going over everything that's happened. . . ."

Melissa nodded. "So much has happened, hasn't it? Sometimes I just wish I could turn the clock back to a year ago when Dad was still alive, and . . ." Her voice caught, and she found herself fighting tears. She dropped her eyes, then felt Brad's hand on hers and looked back up at him. "I've missed you," she said softly, glad for the warmth of his touch. "I tried to stay away, but —"

"I am so sorry," Brad said, interrupting her the moment she paused. "What you saw in your living room that afternoon was all my fault. It wasn't Toni's, I promise. I went there to bring you a picture, and you weren't home. So Toni let me in and . . . when I showed her the picture — it was of your dad, along with you and me — she was overwhelmed and ended up crying on my shoulder. That's all there was to it. I hope you can believe that. Although . . . I have to admit, I . . . was hoping something like that might happen. I'm afraid I haven't gotten over your sister yet, but it was so unfair of me to take advantage of the situation the way I did. Please forgive me, Melissa."

Melissa nodded. "Of course, I forgive you, and I do believe you. I haven't really talked to Toni much since that day, but I did see the picture sitting on the mantel. It made me cry too. I should have known it was something like that. I know Toni loves Abe. In fact, they finally made up, and I'm really glad — even though I know it hurts you. But . . . what really made me come here today was something my friend Carrie said. First, she said that things aren't always as they seem. That was obviously the case when Abe and I walked in on you and Toni last week. She also said something about the price of love. That it costs something to love someone. That we have to take risks when we love, or life is meaningless — especially when we think of the price God paid to give us a chance to love him. . . ."

Her voice trailed off once again, and when she looked at Brad, there were tears in his eyes. "You've had to do a lot of growing up in this last year, haven't you?" he asked. "Sometimes I think you're way ahead of me."

"I doubt it. I still have a long way to go before I can understand all that's happened, but . . . I'm trying, Brad. I really am."

"I know you are, and as your big brother, I'm very proud of you."

Brad's smile reassured her that she'd done the right thing in coming to see him, but she wasn't finished yet.

"There's . . . something else," she said,

trying to calm her heart and praying she wouldn't blush with embarrassment at the confession she was about to make. "I . . . I think I got a little jealous when I saw Toni with you. I felt like she had Abe, so why did she need you too? Then I started wondering if I was having the . . . wrong feelings . . . toward you." She swallowed, willing herself to continue. "You've always been the big brother I never had. But suddenly, with Dad gone and you paying attention to me instead of Toni, I think I . . ." She closed her eyes and took a deep breath. "I'm afraid I was developing a crush on you," she said, her voice barely above a whisper. "I needed someone so much. I needed my dad, but he was gone, and . . . I knew it was wrong. I knew I didn't really feel that way about you and that you thought of me as your little sister, nothing more, but . . ." Tears spilled over onto her cheeks then. "I'm so sorry. I just —"

Brad took Melissa in his arms and pulled her against his chest. "Go ahead and cry," he whispered. "I can never replace your dad, but if it's a big brother you need, then I'm here for you. You have nothing to be sorry about."

Relief washed over Melissa as her heart felt cleansed by the truth she'd spoken.

She'd taken the risk. She had been willing to be rejected and hurt, but she'd said what needed to be said. And she was glad she did. She had her big brother back. Now she would concentrate on working things out with her sister.

As Toni drove away from her lunch meeting with Valerie, she was more confused than ever. For more than two months now, she'd been *almost* convinced that there was more to the school shooting than a lonely, disturbed young man going over the edge and gunning down innocent people. Despite her best efforts, however, she hadn't been able to prove a thing. She still had nothing more to go on than a hunch, a gut feeling that there was a conspirator out there somewhere, and a nagging suspicion that this unknown teacher-friend of Tom's — whoever and wherever she might be — had something to do with it. Valerie was in agreement with her, although she, too, was at a loss as to the identity of the teacher. What disturbed Toni the most, though, was Valerie's story of her visit from Jeff Duffield.

"I have no idea why I'm telling you this," Valerie had said as she and Toni sipped hot tea and waited for their turkey sandwiches.

"And I'm asking you, please, not to say a word about this to anyone — not even your fiancé, at least not at this point. To tell you the truth, Toni, this is probably totally irrelevant to Tom's situation, but . . . then again . . ." Then she'd proceeded to tell Toni, almost verbatim, about her conversation with Mr. Duffield just a few hours earlier — including his strange behavior and the odd feelings it had stirred within her.

More suspicions, Toni thought. *More hunches and more vague feelings . . . When are we ever going to come up with something solid?* She glanced at her cell phone, tucked into the outside pocket of her purse. *Why did I promise Valerie to keep this information to myself and not share it with Abe? I wish I could call him. I really need to talk about it, to bounce it off someone who knows and understands the situation and see if we can make some sense out of it all. . . .*

Turning the corner a couple of blocks from the diner, Toni spotted her church in the distance. She knew the pastor and his secretary had both gone home by this time, as they always closed the office early on Friday afternoons. Still, she felt a sudden urge to stop and . . . and what? Pray, as April had done the previous Sunday evening? That certainly seemed to be the impression she was getting as she neared the parking lot.

The sanctuary is unlocked, I'm sure, she thought. *Every weekday, even when the office is closed, the sanctuary is open for prayer. . . .*

Making her decision, she steered her car into the driveway and then into the parking space nearest the sanctuary entrance. Shutting off the engine and pocketing the keys, she grabbed her purse and stepped into the cold afternoon air. As she headed up the steps toward the double wooden doors, her mind full of the many issues she wanted to discuss with her heavenly Father, she didn't even notice the dark sedan slow to a stop across the street, nor the lone figure that slipped silently out of the car and across the deserted street to follow her inside.

CHAPTER 16

Another Friday. Less than two weeks until his eighteenth birthday. It was a wonder he could keep track of the days, locked up in this tiny, windowless cell, spending the majority of his time lying on his back, staring at the ceiling. It would be over soon, his lawyer had told him — the sentencing, the move from the local jail to the state prison, the placement into the general population. Only days earlier that prospect had left him contemplating suicide. Since his last letter from Carrie, however, Tom Blevins had been having second thoughts about ending his life, despite the fact that his logic screamed at him that it was the only sane solution to the impossible future he now faced.

A lifetime in prison. Locked up with men who will hurt and abuse me . . . maybe even kill me. What kind of life is that? Why am I hanging on when that's all I have to look forward to? Yet something was holding him back. . . .

It was the letter, he was sure — the things Carrie had said to him about paying the price of love. How had she known? Who'd told her? More important, whom had she told? If Carrie knew, then other people were bound to know too. But why hadn't his lawyer said anything? Was that Harold guy holding out on him, waiting to see if he'd finally break and squeal on the only person who'd ever really loved him?

Or had she? Was he just kidding himself, believing what he wanted to believe because she'd made him feel so good about himself when they were together, so hopeful about their future? The suspicion that he'd been set up, that everything she'd ever said to him was a lie — that their entire relationship had been a lie — was growing inside him daily. It hurt worse than any pain he'd experienced in his not quite eighteen miserable years of life.

Still lying on his back, he reached under his pillow and drew out the crumpled, worn letter. He'd committed the words to memory, and yet he read it daily — sometimes hourly — trying to figure out how this girl knew so much about him.

Tom, I don't know any of the details about what you did. I don't know why you did it or what led up to it. But you know — and God knows. . . .

God knows. God knows. . . . Why did she have to say that? Why did those words keep echoing in his mind? Before the shooting, Tom had sworn he didn't even believe God existed. Now he had someone writing him letters, telling him not only that God knew all the details of his life, but that he loved him anyway. That was the hardest part to believe. He could just about accept the part about there being a God who knew all about him, and he definitely understood what Carrie had said about there being a price to pay for loving someone. But God loving him — *him,* Tom Blevins — so much that he sent his Son to die in his place, to take the rap for his sin, to pay the price for him. . . . How could that be?

Tom realized that he wanted, more than he'd ever wanted anything in his life, to believe that everything Carrie said was true. Because if it was, if God himself knew and loved him that much, then maybe there was still hope for him.

Oh, God, he prayed silently. *If you're there — if you're real — please show me. I don't*

*know how, but somehow let me know that
those things Carrie said are true. That you
love me. That you sent your Son to die for
me. That you can somehow . . . forgive me
for . . . everything. Please, God, I need
you. . . .*

Even as hot tears stung the inside of his
eyelids, squeezing out and over onto his face
and dripping down into his hair and onto
his thin, flat pillow, a sense of love and peace
unlike anything he'd ever known or even
dreamed of seemed to wrap around him like
a warm blanket, assuring him that he was
not now — nor would he ever again be —
alone. As he basked in that sweet reassur-
ance, a voice drifted slowly into his con-
sciousness.

"Blevins. Blevins! You got a visitor. Get
up, boy. The chaplain's here to see you."

It had been awhile since Toni had been in
the sanctuary when it was entirely empty.
How different it seemed from the Sunday
morning capacity-crowd services they'd
been having lately. Yet, for her purposes, the
quiet and solitude was just what she needed
at the moment.

As she settled into a pew toward the front
of the sanctuary, she suddenly appreciated
the many hours April spent in sweet com-

munion with God. No wonder the dear lady's faith was so strong. No wonder she seemed to sense things before they happened. . . .

She shivered slightly, not so much from the fact that the thermostat in the relatively large building was set fairly low, but because she remembered April's words before she'd left the house earlier that day: "I was praying for you, Toni — for your safety. I have no idea why, but I feel that you are — or will be — in danger. . . ."

Reaching her hand into her coat pocket, she pulled out the slip of paper April had handed her just before she'd walked out the door to go to her meeting with Valerie. "You are my hiding place; You will protect me from trouble and surround me with songs of deliverance." As she read the words April had penned the previous Sunday while sitting and praying in her own church just a few blocks away, Toni smiled. *God has such a sweet way of reassuring us just when we need it,* she thought, returning the paper to her pocket. She had nothing to fear. God had called April to pray, and she'd answered the call. God would surely respond and protect Toni, whatever the danger. Quite possibly, she reasoned, due to April's intercession and God's faithfulness, that danger had already been defused. Now if only the other situations in her life could be cleared up as easily. . . .

God, she prayed silently, *I'm so grateful that things have worked out between Abe and me, and I have to believe you're already working in Melissa's heart as well. Oh, Father, our family has had so much loss, so much pain. Please bring healing and unity to those of us who are left. . . .*

Her mind drifted then to Tom Blevins and to the horrific day in late November when he'd unleashed his pent-up anger on the unsuspecting students and faculty at River View High. She knew things would never be the same in their small community, but she prayed that the entire truth of the incident would somehow come to light — and soon — so that healing might also come and everyone involved could move on with their lives.

So many have been hurt, Lord. So many! And yet . . . I know you're concerned not only with them but also with Tom, even after the awful thing he did. I know you love him, and I know that if someone else was involved in this crime, you know who it is. Please, Father, show us. Lead us to anyone who might have conspired with Tom, or . . . She bowed her head and closed her eyes. *Oh, God, if we're wrong — if there really isn't anyone else — please show us that, too, so we can finally let it go. . . .*

Quieting her thoughts, she sat in silence a few moments, her head still bowed and eyes closed, hoping God would speak something to her heart. She had no idea that someone had come in and sat down beside her until she felt the hard metal pressing against her side and heard the voice say, "You'd better hope God is listening to your prayers, Miss Toni Matthews, because you're just about to meet him face-to-face."

When Abe pulled up in front of Toni's house and didn't see her car, he scolded himself for not having called first; but his visit had been a last-minute decision, and besides, he'd wanted to surprise her. The weather was cold, but the winter sun was shining, and the air was crisp and clear. When he'd found himself with a few spare hours on his hands before picking her up for dinner, he'd thought it would be nice if they could go for a drive in the mountains before they ate. So he'd jumped in his car, and here he was. He considered calling her on the cell phone before knocking at the door, but then he decided that maybe April had borrowed Toni's car to run an errand, which she did on occasion.

Climbing the steps to the Matthews's home, Abe smiled. It was so good to have things worked out between them, and Toni had even agreed that they'd pick a wedding date over dinner this evening. She'd also agreed that the date would be soon. The sooner the better as far as Abe was concerned.

April answered the door and invited him in, explaining that Toni had gone to lunch with Valerie Myers but that she expected her home any minute. "I'm sure she won't be long," April explained, her eyes twinkling. "She mentioned that the two of you are going out to dinner tonight, and it was obvious she's looking forward to it."

"She's not the only one," Abe said, grinning. "Maybe that's why I'm here five hours early."

April laughed. "Why don't you come sit down and wait for her? I've just finished the lunch dishes, and I'm getting back to work on my mending."

Abe followed her to the living room. "Wow," he teased, taking off his jacket and laying it on the couch. "I didn't know anyone besides Aunt Sophie did mending anymore. If I lose a button off my shirt, I just throw the shirt away and go buy a new one."

"Why do I find that hard to believe?" April asked, smiling as the two of them sat down.

"OK, you're right. I don't throw them away. Actually, I put them in a huge pile and tell myself that someday I'll take them all somewhere and have them fixed. But some of those clothes have been sitting in that pile for years. Aunt Sophie has offered several times to do things like that for me, but I never think of it when I'm going up to visit her." Abe's smile faded. "Of course, I haven't been up there since that day Toni and I went, and I'm sure she told you how badly that turned out."

"Yes, she did. And you haven't heard from her since?"

Abe shook his head. "No. And I really miss her. She's all the family I have left, but she's written me off as dead. Says I've betrayed my family and my faith — not to mention the one true God, of course."

"How sad that she doesn't yet understand that her God and ours is one and the same. Almost all first-century Christians were Jews, you know."

"True. But she isn't open to hearing that. According to her, you're either one or the other. If I've accepted the Jesus of Christian-

370

ity — Yeshua — as my Savior, then in her eyes, I'm no longer a Jew."

April sighed. "I'm afraid your aunt isn't the only one with that mistaken idea. Many in the church believe the same way. Maybe if we started referring to our Savior by his given name of Yeshua, rather than Jesus, it might be a reminder to us all that he was born to Jewish parents, raised in the Jewish temple with Jewish traditions and teachings, and publicly declared many times that his mission was to the Jewish people first."

"I couldn't agree more," Abe said, grinning. "In fact, Toni and I have decided to incorporate some of the Jewish traditions into our wedding ceremony."

"Really? Oh, Abe, that's wonderful! Have you decided on a date yet?"

"We're going to discuss that over dinner tonight. That's probably why I'm here so early. I can't wait to get that date picked out and marked on the calendar. Just between you and me, I'm still pushing for Valentine's Day."

April laughed. "Oh my, you are in a hurry, aren't you? That's only a couple of days away."

"Why do you think I'm pushing so hard?"

The phone rang then, and April reached for it. "Probably Toni, calling to let us know what time she'll be here."

It wasn't Toni, however. Before April had ended her brief conversation, Abe had surmised that it was Melissa who'd called, but he couldn't quite figure out why April seemed so surprised by what the girl had to say.

"That was Melissa," April announced, hanging up the receiver.

"I gathered that. Everything OK?"

"I think so. Actually, she sounded quite happy." She looked into Abe's eyes. "She's with Brad. She said they had a long talk and that everything is fine, and he'll bring her home in a little while." She raised her eyebrows. "What do you think of that?"

"Interesting. I'm . . . not quite sure what else to say. I'm curious to see what Toni's reaction will be."

"So am I. In fact, I'd expected to hear her voice when I answered the phone, so Melissa caught me by surprise — particularly when she told me she was with Brad." She paused, her brow wrinkled slightly. "Abe . . . I don't mean to alarm you, but have you talked to Toni today?"

"Not since this morning. Why? Is something wrong?"

"Not really. At least I hope not. But . . ." As April told him how she'd been praying

372

for Toni's safety over the past week, Abe felt his jaws tense. He trusted April enough to know that if she said she'd heard from God, then indeed she had. The fact that Toni was even slightly late in returning from her lunch date with Valerie suddenly made him uneasy.

"I'm going to call her," he said, pulling his cell phone from his jacket pocket and punching her preprogrammed number. After several rings, the call went through to voice mail and he was asked to leave a message.

"Toni? Hey, sweetheart, it's me. Call me as soon as you get this message, will you? I'm here at your house with April, and we're concerned that you're not home yet. I came early so we could go for a ride before dinner. Hurry home, OK? But be careful. I love you."

He clicked off and laid the phone down on the couch beside his jacket. "It's not like her not to have her phone turned on," he said. "If she hasn't called in a few minutes, I'm going to go look for her. Meantime, I think I'll call the school and see if Valerie Myers is back from lunch yet. If she's still out, maybe the two of them just got to talking and forgot the time."

April handed him the phone book, and he

quickly found the number of the high school office. Trying Toni's cell phone again and getting no answer, he quickly dialed the school. He was put through to Valerie right away, who seemed more than slightly surprised to hear from him. When he told her he was waiting for Toni at her home, she sounded even more surprised.

"She's not there yet? It's been almost an hour since we left the diner, and she said she was going straight home. She even mentioned that the two of you have a very important date this evening."

"That's true, and I'm here early, but . . . Did she say anything to you about being in any sort of . . . danger?"

"Danger?" Valerie's voice took on a nervous edge. "What do you mean? Is Toni in some kind of trouble?"

"I don't know. It's a long story, and I don't have time to go into it now, but I think it's possible that —"

Valerie cut in before he could finish his sentence. "I knew I should never have asked her not to say anything to you about our conversation at lunch today. I'm so sorry. I just —"

"Sorry about what? What conversation? What did you two talk about?"

By the time Valerie had finished giving

Abe a summary of her concerns about her visit from Jeff Duffield and her subsequent relaying of that visit to Toni during lunch, Abe was pacing, cell phone in hand. When he hung up, he tossed it back on the couch and looked at April, who was watching him anxiously. "Are you sure you don't know where else she might have gone?" he asked. "Did she say anything at all about stopping somewhere? An errand maybe, or . . ."

April shook her head slowly. "No. Nothing. I wish I could help. . . ." She hesitated, frowning slightly. "There is . . . one thing. . . ."

Abe caught his breath. "What? Anything, April, no matter how unimportant it might seem."

"It's not that it's . . . unimportant. It's just . . . When I was praying for Toni on Sunday, I felt compelled to write down a Scripture, which I did, and then I felt strongly that I needed to give it to her just before she left today."

"A Scripture? Do you remember what it was?"

"Certainly. It was Psalm 32:7: 'You are my hiding place; You will protect me from trouble and surround me with songs of deliverance.' I gave her the slip of paper I'd written it on; she read it, smiled, and tucked it into her pocket, then left. Do you think it has any relevance to Toni's not being home yet?"

Abe paused, trying to recall why that particular Scripture had special meaning. Then he remembered. That Sunday, several weeks ago in church, Toni had said something. . . .

Grabbing his jacket and phone from the couch, he headed for the front door, calling out to April as he went, "I'm not sure if there's any connection or not, but there just might be. At least it gives me a starting place. I'm going to the church to look for her. If she calls, tell her to call me on my cell phone. I'll keep trying to call her, and I'll check in with you periodically."

If it hadn't been for the gun pressed against her side, Toni might have thought she was dreaming, particularly since the woman holding that gun seemed so soft and pretty — until Toni looked into her eyes. Hard and ice-blue, they stared at her, daring her to move. Wisely, she didn't, though she was desperately tempted to bolt and run. But her P.I. training kept her still, watching and waiting for the right moment.

"Do I know you?" she asked, forcing herself to keep her voice steady. "I'm sorry, but I don't recognize you. . . ."

The woman's smile was as cold as her eyes. "Of course you don't recognize me. I wasn't at the school or even in this town long enough for the two of us to meet. But I know you. You're famous around here for poking your nose in where it doesn't belong. A lot of people are on trial right now because you just couldn't accept the coroner's report that your father died of natural causes. Now you can't leave the Tom Blevins thing alone. Your father's case I can understand. But Tom? What's he to you? Why do you care if someone else was involved or not? He pleaded guilty, so you know he won't get the death penalty. What's the big deal?"

Toni studied the woman closely as she talked. She'd said she hadn't been at the school long. Did that mean she'd taught at the high school for a short time? Could this be the teacher-friend that Tom had mentioned to his mother? Was it possible that they'd had some sort of relationship? It was obvious, even with the makeup and skillfully styled red hair, that this woman, though attractive, was at least in her midthirties, possibly older. Surely she and Tom had not been romantically involved. . . .

"I asked you a question," the woman said,

jabbing the gun into Toni's ribs. "Why are you going around stirring up more trouble over something that's already been settled?"

Toni focused on her breathing, determined not to give in to panic. "I . . . didn't mean to stir up trouble, but . . . my younger sister, Melissa, was with her best friend, Carrie, when Tom opened fire in the school hallway. Carrie was partially paralyzed by one of his bullets, and Melissa took it pretty hard —"

"So you decided to climb on your white horse and go looking for bad guys," the woman said, interrupting Toni and jabbing her again with the gun. "Well, maybe that was your mistake. Maybe you should have been looking for a bad *girl* instead." She sneered. "If you really want to know who the bad guy is, I'll tell you. You're not going to be around long enough to pass the information along anyway."

Toni sat perfectly still, glad the woman seemed anxious to talk. It would buy Toni a little time and possibly a chance to disarm her. *Help me, Lord,* she prayed silently. *This must be the danger you warned April about. Please help me to stay calm, and show me what to do.*

"The bad guy," the woman continued, "is one Mr. Jeff Duffield, illustrious principal of River View High, respected family man and upstanding leader of our fine community." She laughed when she saw Toni's reaction. "Shocked, are you? Well, let me tell you a little more about dear Mr. Duffield. When he hired me, he was so attentive and caring, so thoughtful. At first I thought he was just a nice person, a great boss, but then I noticed that he gave me a lot more attention than anyone else on staff — mostly when we were alone, of course. Then I met that wife of his. What an old hag." She smiled and lifted her chin. "How could she expect to hold on to a man like Jeff when he was seeing *me* every day?"

Toni had met Mrs. Duffield only a couple of times, but she had to admit that the woman's assessment of their comparative looks was accurate. Still, she couldn't imagine how anyone could be attracted to someone so cold and calculating as the woman who now sat next to her, threatening to take her life.

"Before long Jeff and I were a real item," the woman went on, her voice laced with bitterness and sarcasm. "He said he was going to dump his wife and marry me as soon as the school year ended. But the closer it got to the end of the year, the more he kept saying it would never work as long as I was teaching at the high school. He wanted me to move to a nearby town so we could still see each other but not to let anyone know about us until he had his divorce. I wanted to believe him, but when I had trouble finding another job, he fired me. Can you believe it? He just flat-out fired me. Oh, he did it in a nice way, of course. Gave me a glowing letter of recommendation, even found me another job — but not in a nearby town. It was over a hundred miles away. He said he was doing it for us, to save our relationship and our future together." She laughed. "I still tried to believe him, but when he stopped coming to see me and wouldn't return my calls — he even changed his home number so I wouldn't call there — that's when I knew he'd used me." Her cold eyes narrowed. "And I don't like being used."

Toni suppressed a shudder. She sensed it was important not to show any fear, but it was becoming more difficult all the time. Still, if she could just keep the woman talking, somehow gain her confidence and buy more time. . . .

"That's . . . really too bad," she said. "About Mr. Duffield, I mean. I had no idea that —"

"You had no idea he cheated on his wife?"

The woman had interrupted Toni again, but at least she was still talking. Toni wondered if she planned to shoot her there, in the sanctuary, or take her somewhere else. If they went outside, she might have a better chance to make a move. She decided to wait for an opening in the conversation and then suggest they go somewhere other than the sanctuary, using the excuse that someone might walk in on them, and then see how the woman reacted. Meanwhile, Toni tried to concentrate on the woman's words, hoping she might say something that would give Toni an opening to turn the conversation around — and maybe even get her to put the gun away.

"Not only did your good old high school principal cheat on his wife with me," the woman said, "but I've since found out that he cheated with half of River View — and who knows how many in surrounding towns. Oh, yes, Mr. Duffield is quite the respectable citizen, isn't he?" She smiled wickedly. "You know, at first I thought about telling my story to anyone who would listen, but then I decided that ruining his reputation wasn't enough. That's when I came up with the perfect plan to repay Jeff for his 'kindness' to me. And that plan was named Tom Blevins." She laughed again.

"What a sap that kid was! Do you have any idea how easy it was to seduce him and make him believe I loved him? He actually thought we were going to run away together after he proved his love for me by killing the man who'd supposedly fired me for no reason. If others got hurt at the same time, so what? I convinced him that they deserved it after the way they'd treated him. The dumb kid bought that story hook, line, and sinker. Too bad he didn't finish the job and get rid of Jeff Duffield once and for all."

Toni felt herself breaking into a cold sweat as the reality of the woman's confession became clear. This teacher, who'd been hired to serve in a position of trust to the students, had seduced one of them in order to get back at the married man who'd ended their affair. Obviously she'd meant for Mr. Duffield to die, so that part of her plan had failed. Sadly, other lives had been sacrificed to carry out her plan. How cold-blooded did someone have to be to entice a teenager to kill someone and to risk killing and maiming others in the process? If Toni had previously had any doubts that this woman would carry out her threat to kill her, those doubts were gone. She now knew that she was fighting for her life.

"Like I said," the woman continued, pressing the gun harder against Toni's side, "it was the perfect plan, the perfect crime — until you came along. No one knew about my relationship with Tom. No one. With all the school shootings in the news and with Tom being such a loner and such a creep, most people just assumed he acted alone. Oh, sure, the police checked out the conspirator theory, but I'd planned everything perfectly, and I knew they wouldn't find anything. Even if Jeff didn't die — which, unfortunately, he didn't — he couldn't voice any suspicions about me, even if he had any. And I don't think he did — not until you stirred the pot with this so-called relationship between Tom and some mystery teacher." She narrowed her eyes again, glaring at Toni. "If you'd just left things alone. But no, you had to go snooping around and drag the police back into it. Well, I'll tell you something, Miss Private Detective. They're not going to find out anything, OK? Nothing. I left River View before the relationship with Tom started, so no one can put us together — no one but Tom, of course, and he'll never tell." She laughed again. "He loves me, you know, and he actually thinks I love him."

Toni was sickened at the thought of this woman, who undoubtedly was old enough to be Tom's mother, seducing the vulnerable teen and using him to commit murder. Yet, according to the woman's confession, that's exactly what had happened. And although nothing the woman had told Toni lessened Tom's responsibility for the horrible crime, it certainly did explain his motives for committing it.

Once again, Toni found herself praying for God to help her. Now that the woman had completed her story, it was going to be difficult to keep her talking. Toni sought desperately for a diversion, anything to force the woman off guard even for a split second so Toni could make her move. However, before she could come up with a plan, her cell phone rang.

Startled, Toni jumped. She'd forgotten her phone was in her purse on the pew beside her. And she knew, even on the first ring, that it was Abe trying to reach her. She hadn't talked to him since early that morning, and he was obviously wondering where she was. Even as that initial realization shot through her mind, she felt the pressure of the gun lessen as the woman jerked in response to the ringing phone. In that split second Toni grabbed her purse and swung it as hard as she could, catching her assailant on the side of the head. The woman groaned and slumped against the back of the pew, momentarily dazed. Instinctively Toni turned and ran, but by the time she'd reached the aisle, a shot rang out behind her.

Praying that the reason the woman had missed was because she was still too dazed to aim accurately, Toni quickly weighed her options. It was a long run to the back of the church, but if she could make it to the front, there was a door beside the stage, which led to the stairway of the choir loft and to a hallway with an outer door at the end. It was twenty steps to the front, compared to a hundred to the back. She made her choice almost before she thought about it, and she was halfway through the door at the front of the sanctuary before she heard the next shot. The bullet hit the top of the doorframe, missing Toni's head by no more than eighteen inches and leaving plaster chips in her hair. She'd hoped to run through the exit and bypass the entrance to the choir loft, continuing down the back hallway to an outside exit that would take her to her car, but she sensed she'd never make it in time.

You are my hiding place; You will protect me from trouble and surround me with songs of deliverance.

Even as the verse popped into her mind, she ducked into the carpeted staircase and scrambled up into the choir loft, wishing for a door to lock behind her but encouraged by the words that suddenly made sense to her.

That's why you gave that verse to April, Toni thought, as she squeezed noiselessly behind the back row of chairs and pressed herself against the far wall of the loft, hoping to make herself as invisible as possible. *I remember now. Just a few weeks ago the pastor was teaching on that very verse. The choir even sang that chorus, and I told Abe I felt as though they were surrounding us with songs of deliverance even as we sat there. Oh, Lord, nothing is an accident with you, is it? You were arranging for my hiding place even then.*

As she silently expressed her gratitude to God, her heart still hammered in her chest as she heard the sound of rushed footsteps in the hallway below. Would the woman continue on to the exit, which was clearly marked at the end of the hallway, assuming Toni had already reached the parking lot and was heading to her car? Would she then limit her search for Toni outside, or, when she didn't find her there, would she come back in and look for her in the building?

Then Toni heard a distant, muffled ringing sound. Her cell phone again! That's when she realized that she must have dropped her purse — with her cell phone still inside — after she'd hit the woman in the head.

Oh, Lord, she prayed, *I don't dare make a run for my phone. I can't call Abe. I can't call anyone! But you can. Please send help, Father. Show me what to do. Hide me, please. Surround me with those songs of deliverance . . .*

CHAPTER 17

Her mending temporarily forgotten, April sat on the couch, trying to focus on praying rather than worrying. Abe had been gone less than ten minutes before he'd called to ask if she'd heard from Toni. She hadn't, and she was disheartened to learn that Abe still hadn't been able to reach her on the cell phone. Yet, she reminded herself, even if Toni was in danger, God was certainly able to take care of her. He'd laid it on April's heart to pray for Toni's protection, and she'd done so all week. Now it all came down to one thing: Did she trust God, or didn't she? Sighing, she scolded herself for her nagging doubts and picked up the piece of mending she'd been working on when Abe arrived.

She'd scarcely sewn a couple of stitches before she was interrupted again.

This time it was Melissa, who burst into the entryway and then headed straight for the living room. "Hi, April," she called, beaming. "Look who's here."

Only slightly more subdued than Melissa, Brad walked in behind her. "Hello, Mrs. Lippincott," he greeted her as the elderly lady rose from the couch and went to welcome them. "It's good to see you again."

"And it's good to see you. Both of you. Especially looking so cheerful." She hugged them. "Oh my," she said, eyeing the white bag Brad was carrying. "What do you have that smells so good?"

"Chinese food," Brad answered. "Melissa didn't eat lunch before she came over after school, so we decided to stop and get some of our favorite takeout and bring it over here."

"Just like old times," Melissa chimed in.

"We have plenty," Brad added. "We hoped you'd join us."

April smiled. "Thank you, my dears, but I've already eaten."

"Come and sit with us anyway," Melissa urged, pulling off her parka and tossing it on the couch. "Is Toni around?"

April hesitated. "No . . . although I expect her soon. She and Abe have a date later." She watched Brad for a reaction to her reference to Abe, but he simply removed his jacket and laid it on the couch beside

Melissa's. If he had reacted, April decided, it was well hidden behind what Toni often referred to as Brad's "courtroom face."

The three of them made their way into the kitchen where Melissa grabbed some paper plates. April joined them as they all sat down and offered thanks for the meal. She was glad that Melissa hadn't pursued the subject of Toni's whereabouts, as she didn't want to worry either of them unnecessarily. She just prayed that Toni would come home or that Abe would call again soon, this time with the good news that he'd found her and everything was all right.

"I love this sweet and sour chicken," Melissa said as she scooped out a large serving and plopped it onto her plate. "In fact, I love everything from this restaurant. I'm really glad you thought of it, Bro."

April smiled to herself at Melissa's use of the familiar term of endearment. It seemed she and Brad had gotten their relationship back on a healthy footing once again. Brad, too, seemed pleased.

"Hey, it's one of my favorite places too," he said. "We'll have to do this more often." He winked at April. "Anything to escape my own cooking. I can barbecue, and I'm not too bad with the microwave. But real cooking? Forget it."

"That's for sure," said Melissa. "I remember one time at your parents' house when your mom and I were busy outside and she asked you to fix the green beans. . . ." She rolled her eyes. "No offense, but they were awful."

April laughed. "Now how could anyone ruin green beans? I think you must be exaggerating, Melissa."

"I'm afraid she's not," Brad said. "I didn't put enough water in them, and they burned. Dad and I had gotten so busy watching one of the first football games of the season, I totally forgot they were on the stove. Mom's the one who came in and discovered them. I hadn't even smelled them burning, but she swore that she and Melissa could smell them clear out in the backyard. From that point on, I was banned from her kitchen. To tell you the truth, that was OK with me because I'd much rather eat her cooking than mine anytime."

"I would imagine so," April said, glad for the lighthearted banter that seemed to brighten the entire house. Things had been so heavy for so long, and they weren't through with their problems yet, she was sure. This was a welcome break — and it helped, at least a little, to keep her mind off Toni.

"So," she said, "how are things in the legal profession? Have you been staying busy?"

"Always," Brad answered, stabbing a piece of chicken. "I've been trying to train myself to take a day off now and then, but it doesn't happen very often, I'm afraid. Something's always going on around the office — and that's good for business, of course — but you wonder at the number of legal cases in a town this size. It's not like ours is the only firm around, and I think they're all just about as busy as we are. I know the court dockets are always full."

Melissa washed down her food with a drink of water. Her voice was quiet. "Speaking of court dockets, Bruce Jensen's trial will be over soon. I have to give my testimony next week. I'll be the last witness for the prosecution." She sighed, then looked at April. "I'll be so glad when that's over. You seemed to get through your testimony OK this week."

April nodded. "Yes, and I know exactly how you feel, but you're going to come through it with flying colors, my dear. You did just fine with the last one, and you'll make it through this one as well — even though I know it's a bit harder. Bruce Jensen was someone you loved and trusted. That makes it so much more difficult."

"He killed my father," Melissa said, "and he was part of the ring that kidnapped me and . . ." She toyed with her food as her voice trailed off. "It's still so hard to believe. Of all people, that he could —"

The wall phone beside the kitchen table jangled, interrupting Melissa. April jumped, her heart pounding as she grabbed the receiver, ignoring Melissa and Brad's surprised looks. She seldom answered the phone when either Toni or Melissa was home, but she was so hoping it was Abe with good news. . . .

Unfortunately, it was a wrong number, and she sighed as she hung up. *Please, God, let me hear something soon. . . .*

"Wrong number," was all she said as she smiled at Brad and Melissa, determined not to let them see her concern. However, the fear in her heart was threatening to overwhelm her confidence that God was in control.

Abe tried Toni's cell phone again as he turned onto the street that led to the church. Still no answer. *Was it possible she'd forgotten to turn it on,* he wondered. It certainly wasn't like her, but maybe she'd just had a lot on her mind after her meeting with Valerie. . . .

Then he saw her car in the parking lot. He breathed a sigh of relief, feeling the tension in his muscles ease as he realized she'd probably turned off her phone so she could spend some time in uninterrupted prayer. That had to be what had happened because Toni's was the only car in the lot, so it was doubtful she'd come to meet with anyone. Besides, Abe remembered Toni's mentioning that the pastor and his secretary were gone on Friday afternoons, so her search for a secluded place of prayer was the only logical explanation. *Maybe she's even sitting in there planning our wedding.* He smiled at the thought even as he scolded himself for overreacting to April's warning. Toni certainly couldn't be in any danger while she was in church.

As he neared the front steps, however, he hesitated. *Hiding place . . . songs of deliverance.* The words echoed in his mind over and over, and he simply couldn't dismiss them. They grew louder as he approached the church's front door. By the time he reached for the door handle, he was wishing he'd brought his gun. It seemed ridiculous even to think of needing a weapon in church, but during his years on the force, he'd developed a keen instinct for trouble. That, combined with the fact that God had called April to pray for Toni's safety, as well as the fact that the words from the psalm were still rolling around in his mind, convinced him to enter the church as quietly as possible, ready for any surprises that might greet him on the other side of the door.

Sophie paced from room to room, wondering why she couldn't stop thinking of Abe. She worked so hard at keeping him from her thoughts, but lately she'd missed him more than ever. She'd even had a dream the night before that Abe and Toni were married and that she was sitting in their living room, holding their firstborn child, a little boy that so reminded Sophie of Abe when he was a newborn. Never having had any children of her own, she'd always considered Abe as the light of her life since the day he'd arrived on this planet. The sweetness of the feel of the baby's soft hair against her lips as she bent to kiss the top of his perfectly round head had lingered even after she awoke. When she realized it had been only a dream and that the chances of her ever holding Abe's child in her arms were almost nonexistent, she'd broken down and cried.

"Sweet little lamb," she remembered crooning to the baby in the dream. "Little lamb of God." How odd, she thought as she paced, trying in vain to erase the memory of the previous night's dream from her mind. It was not a term she'd ever used in connection with Abe, nor did she remember anyone else in the family doing so. The only relevance it evoked for her was the sacrificial lamb of Passover — which, she reminded herself, would soon be upon them. It had always been her favorite holy day, and even though Abe had never celebrated it as an observant Jew, he'd occasionally come to join her for the traditional Seder meal.

That certainly wouldn't be the case this year, she thought — not now that he'd become involved with that *goy* and her Christianity. It was bad enough that her dear sister — Abe's own mother — had turned her back on her faith and married a *goy,* but at least she hadn't embraced the same pagan religion that had persecuted their ancestors. What could her precious *Avraham* be thinking? Could he have been so blinded by love that he'd forgotten his own heritage?

Lamb of God. Lamb of God. Sophie shook her head. Maybe God was trying to tell her that Passover was going to have a special meaning to her this year, despite Abe's defection. She would just have to wait and see.

Toni's heart hammered in her chest as she sat huddled behind the chairs in the loft. She hadn't moved since she'd sequestered herself in the hiding place she felt God had provided for her, but she couldn't help but wonder how he would keep the woman with the gun from discovering the stairway that led to the loft. Could she dare to hope that God might even place an angel there to guard the way?

She'd heard the footsteps as the woman ran past the stairway and toward the exit at the end of the hallway, but she couldn't be sure if she'd gone outside or merely opened the door and looked out. Was she in the building? Toni strained for a sound but heard nothing except the rapid beating of her own heart. If the woman truly had gone outside, how long would she stay there? Long enough for Toni to creep down the stairway and out the front door? Should she try to make a run for it, or was it best to stay in the place where she believed God had directed her to hide?

You are my hiding place; You will protect me from trouble and surround me with songs of deliverance.

As she meditated on the words of the psalmist, it was as if she could hear God saying, "Be still. I will protect you." And so she stayed, listening for the sound of a footfall that would help her pinpoint her adversary's location.

The creak of a door opening was so slight that she thought she might have imagined it. Even the footsteps were almost surreal in their near silence. Imagined or not, they were drawing closer. Of that, she was sure. Her heart raced, and she found herself putting her hand in her pocket to clutch the slip of paper with the reassuring words imprinted upon it. Then she heard another sound . . . this one coming from inside herself.

I am your Father. . . .

How many times had God spoken those very words to her just when she'd most needed to hear them? Reassured once again, she relaxed her grip on the paper, closed her eyes, and waited. Seconds passed. Or was it minutes? She couldn't be sure. She'd lost track of the footsteps she'd heard earlier. Maybe the woman had given up. . . .

Then she felt a hand over her mouth and another one grabbing her arm. Her eyes flew open, and there, staring at her, was the man she loved, crouched down in front of her, his face mirroring the fear she felt inside. Tears sprang to her eyes as he removed his hand from her mouth and pulled her close.

"Don't say a word," he whispered. "When I didn't see you anywhere in the sanctuary, I knew something was wrong — especially when I noticed your purse lying on the floor. When I was at your house earlier, April told me about the Scripture — the one about God being your hiding place and surrounding you with songs of deliverance — and then I remembered that morning in church when the choir was singing that chorus and what you'd said about songs of deliverance. That's how I figured out you might be up here. What is it, sweetheart? What's going on?"

"There's a woman," she whispered back. "She has a gun. She . . . said she was going to kill me. Abe, she . . . she used to be a teacher at the high school. She had an affair with the principal. When he ended it, she used Tom Blevins to get even." She shook her head. "Oh, Abe, it's awful. How could someone be so filled with hatred?"

"Shhh." Abe stroked her hair. "I've got a million questions to ask you about this woman, but we'll talk about it later — after I've gotten you out of here. Do you think she's still in the building? I didn't see or hear any sign of anyone downstairs when I came in."

"I don't know. I heard her run down the hallway toward the exit earlier, but I don't know if she's come back in or not. I thought I'd hear her if she did, but now I don't know. I wasn't even sure if I heard you. . . ."

Abe took his phone from his pocket. "OK, I'm going to call for help. I'm assuming you haven't been able to do that."

Toni shook her head again. "No. My phone is inside my purse, where I dropped it after I hit her."

Abe's eyes opened wide. "You hit her? With your purse?"

"Yes. She had the gun in my side, and I was waiting for a chance to catch her off guard, and then my phone rang. I assume it was you." Abe nodded, and she went on. "The phone distracted her just long enough for me to grab my purse and clobber her on the side of the head. It dazed her and give me a chance to run. I didn't realize I'd dropped my purse until I got up here and heard the phone ringing again. You don't know how much I wanted to run down there and answer it, but God kept telling me to stay here."

He laid a calming hand against her cheek

as she spoke. "You did the right thing," he assured her. His hand then moved to hers to give it a quick squeeze before flipping open the phone. But he'd scarcely thumbed the first number when they heard a voice behind them.

"Put the phone down. You're not calling anybody."

Toni looked up, and there stood the woman with the gun, poised behind Abe and glaring down at them with a smile that made Toni's flesh crawl. Abe set down the phone and pulled back slightly from Toni, turning toward the woman. Toni realized they were at a terrible disadvantage, both of them crouched on the floor and neither of them having a gun. Surely God hadn't brought them this far to die together at the hands of this depraved woman. If they were going to get out of this situation alive, it was obvious that God was going to have to intervene once again.

Ever since praying with the chaplain, Tom's heart had felt lighter. His situation hadn't changed one bit, and prison still loomed on the horizon, as dark and foreboding as ever. Yet he just couldn't stop smiling.

His lawyer had even commented on it at their last meeting. When Tom told him it was because he'd found out that God loved him and that he'd accepted Jesus as his Savior, Harold Barnett blinked and shook his head, making some comment about another jailhouse conversion. Then he'd smiled halfheartedly and said, "Hope it works for you, kid. Nothing else seems to have gone right in your life."

Tom didn't care. He'd even been wondering if he should tell Harold about Vivian — not because he wanted to get her in trouble, but because he now believed it was important for him to tell the whole truth. All this time he'd thought he was proving his love for her by keeping quiet and paying the price alone. Now he knew what real love was, and the price that had been paid to extend that love to anyone who would receive it. Somehow it just seemed right to tell someone the truth of what really happened.

Then he thought of Carrie Bosworth. He'd never answered either one of her letters. Maybe she was just the one who'd understand what he was feeling in his heart right now.

Abe took the woman in with one glance. Fiery red hair piled high on her head, ice-blue eyes, an undoubtedly good figure, visible even under her dark coat, and a heart as hard as a rock. She was dangerous, that much was obvious, even if he didn't know the entire story behind her desire to kill Toni. He only wished he'd had a chance to call for help before she discovered them in the loft.

I thought this was a hiding place for us, God, he prayed silently. *Why did you let her find us? What do you want us to do now?*

"This is perfect," the redhead was saying, her voice heavy with sarcasm. "Not only can I get rid of Miss Toni Matthews, private eye extraordinaire, but it looks like I've found her detective boyfriend as well. Two birds with one stone. Perfect." She smiled again. "I am right, aren't I? You are Detective Abe Matthews of the River View Police — the one whose uncle was killed when you rescued sweet little Melissa from the bad guys?"

Play along with her, Abe told himself. *Keep her talking.*

"That's right," he said slowly, "but I'm afraid I don't know who you are. Have we met?"

The redhead laughed out loud. "Oh, you're good, detective," she cooed. "Cop training 101, right? Keep 'em talking. OK, I'll play along. No, Detective Matthews, we haven't met." She winked and eyed him hungrily. "I sure wish we had though. Bet I could teach that girlfriend of yours a few things about how to treat a *real* man. And something tells me you're quite a man. . . ."

Abe felt Toni tense behind him, but he silently willed her to be still. The longer the cat played with the mice before finishing them off, the better chance the mice had of escaping.

The woman laughed again. "Oh, come on, detective. You're not that much of a prude, are you? I've known a couple of cops in my life, and believe me, they weren't a bit bashful." She paused, and Abe waited, wondering at her next move.

"You must be one of those strong, silent types," she said. "I like that in a man. Less noise and more action." She tilted her head to one side, pouting seductively. "Not interested, detective?" Holding the gun in one hand, she began to slowly unbutton her coat with the other. "Maybe you'd change your mind if you had a better look at the merchandise."

Abe was amazed that she would waste time on something so pointless, but it was also obvious that she was enjoying her sense of control. He realized it was all part of her game, but he watched her closely, wondering just how far she'd go with this ruse and praying she'd make just one mistake along the way. Suddenly they heard the front door of the church open and someone walk in, whistling an old hymn. As the woman jerked her head toward the sound, Abe leaped from his crouching position and threw himself toward her, knocking her down and landing on top of her. Grabbing the gun by the barrel, he forced it up, bending the woman's trigger finger until she screamed in pain and released her hold on the weapon.

"Take the gun," he ordered Toni, securing his hold on the red-haired woman who, by this time, was cursing and screaming at him to get off her.

"Got it," Toni said. "Are you all right?"

"I'm fine. I'll hold her while you call for help."

As Abe listened to Toni making the call, he wondered whom God had sent to rescue them. As it turned out, he didn't have to wait long for his answer. Toni had no sooner gotten off the phone than they heard heavy footsteps climbing the stairs to the loft. Abe looked toward the top of the stairs just as a very tall and somewhat familiar figure came into view, carrying a push broom. It was John King, the church janitor, who'd walked in right on cue.

"What's going on up here?" John asked, his lanky frame one of the most welcome sights Abe had seen in his entire life. John blinked as he looked from one to the other. "Abe? Toni?" His eyes came to rest on the woman pinned beneath Abe. "Is everything OK?"

Abe smiled. "Everything's fine now, John. Thanks to you."

John returned the smile. "Don't know what I did, but I'm glad I could help."

"Believe me," said Toni, "you helped more than you could ever know. In fact, you were an answer to prayer — a real angel of mercy. If you weren't so tall, I'd kiss you!"

Abe chuckled as the almost seven-foot-tall janitor ducked his head in embarrassment, and the redhead let loose with another string of curses. *If John wasn't so tall,* Abe thought, *I think I just might kiss him myself!*

CHAPTER 18

Valentine's Day had arrived, and Toni had just finished putting on the final touches of her makeup before going out for a romantic dinner with Abe. She smiled, fluffing her blonde curls with her fingers and stepping back to view herself in the full-length mirror in her room. The red dress was perfect. Abe would love it, of that she had no doubt. Best of all, she and Melissa had spent the day yesterday picking it out. Though Toni didn't enjoy shopping, Melissa loved it, and Toni had been thrilled that they could once again spend the day doing something together — especially when she realized that up until a couple of days ago their relationship had been rocky, to say the least.

Had it really been only two days since she'd met with Valerie Myers for lunch and then stopped off at the church to pray? So much had happened in the interim that it seemed longer. How grateful she was for the way things had turned out — particularly in light of how tragically the day could have ended.

Thank You, Father. You are so faithful, she prayed silently, remembering the joy and relief she'd felt when she'd opened her eyes and found Abe kneeling in front of her in the church loft. For a split second she'd been sure the red-haired woman, whom she now knew to be a thirty-eight-year-old schoolteacher from Seattle by the name of Vivian Stevens, had found her hiding place. But God had protected her, as he'd promised, and he'd sent help in the most unexpected way.

John King had been the church custodian for several years, but it had never occurred to Toni that he might walk into the sanctuary on a Friday afternoon when both the pastor and his secretary were already gone for the day. And, as John had explained to her and Abe, he usually didn't. Under normal circumstances he waited until the sanctuary was closed to the public at five o'clock before going in to straighten up for the weekend. This particular Friday, however, had been different. It was his thirtieth wedding anniversary, and he and his wife had plans to go out to dinner. Wanting to get through with his work early that evening so he'd have time to pick up some flowers on the way home, he'd decided to do as much cleaning as he could before locking the sanctuary at five. He hadn't bothered to check the church parking lot for cars before entering the church, having parked on the street on the opposite side of the building. When he opened the front door of the sanctuary and saw no one inside, he assumed the place was empty — until he heard voices coming from the choir loft. That's when he'd gone upstairs to see what was going on.

The rest, as they say, is history, Toni mused. Vivian Stevens was in jail, and Tom Blevins had confirmed her story, suddenly becoming very cooperative with the authorities and adding several clarifying details of his own. Jeff Duffield also was being interrogated as to his involvement in the situation. Suddenly Valerie Myers understood why she'd received so many phone calls the previous year from Ms. Stevens, demanding to speak with the principal. *Things aren't always as they seem.* Toni remembered that Valerie had made that observation during one of their conversations in her office. Neither of them had imagined at the time how true that statement would soon prove to be.

In addition, Melissa had said something

the previous day that clicked for Toni — something that had been nagging at her for weeks but that she simply hadn't been able to put together. As the two Matthews sisters had chatted over lunch at the mall, Melissa confessed to Toni that she'd been missing her father so much that her feelings for Brad had become confused. He was an older man, he gave her attention and affection, and she'd misinterpreted her emotions, becoming interested in Brad in an almost romantic way.

As Melissa talked about her mixed-up feelings for Brad, Toni had begun to wonder if Tom's attraction to Vivian, at least in part, had been some sort of transference of his need for his mother's love. Mrs. Blevins loved Tom in her own way, Toni thought, but she obviously had not stood up to her husband and defended her son. The lonely young boy had interpreted her behavior to mean that his own mother simply didn't love him. If that were true, how could he ever expect anyone else to care about him? Tom had apparently come to the conclusion that he was totally unlovable — until Vivian came into his life. No wonder he'd been so vulnerable and receptive to her attentions.

Toni clasped her favorite pendant around

her neck — a diamond star set in gold that Abe had given her for Christmas — and wondered what would happen to Cora Blevins now that her husband was bound to know she'd talked to Toni and Valerie without his permission. Toni had heard that Tom's sister Megan and her husband had once again offered to let her come and live with them, but Cora had opted to stay where she was. It was difficult to understand her decision, and Toni could only pray that Tom's newfound faith would somehow influence his mother in the future.

Stepping out into the hallway from her room, Toni marveled at the change she'd observed in Tom when she'd visited him earlier that day on her way home from church. He said he'd already been to the chapel for Sunday morning service, and he actually smiled when he told her he was going to be baptized as soon as the chaplain could arrange it. She could still see the fear in his eyes when he spoke of the future, but it was tinged with a joy she'd never dreamed she would see on the young man's face. Once again, Toni expressed her silent thanks to God.

April was already letting Abe in when Toni arrived at the front door. After greeting April with a kiss on her cheek, Abe looked past her to Toni. "Wow," he said, a smile enveloping his face, "now that's what I call a dress!"

Toni laughed and went to him, and he wrapped her in his arms as April looked on approvingly. "Do you like it? Melissa and I picked it out yesterday."

Abe held her a few inches away and admired her again. "You know, I wasn't too happy about you and Melissa spending the whole day together yesterday and leaving me out, but if this is the result, then it was worth it."

April laughed in agreement and waved them off as Toni slipped into her coat and then walked hand in hand with Abe out the door and toward his car. The night air was cold, but Toni felt snug and warm as Abe helped her into her seat and closed the door before going around to the driver's side and climbing in beside her. Before starting the car, he turned to her once again.

"You really do look beautiful," he said, his voice husky.

Toni smiled, glad for the streetlight that illuminated the inside of the car. "You don't look so bad yourself, detective. I'm just glad that redhead didn't see you before I did."

"Not my type," Abe said, grinning. "I like my women to be at least a *little* hard to get

— and not quite so tough."

Toni raised her eyebrows. "Oh, so you think I'm not tough, do you?"

Abe laughed. "Believe me, I know you can be tough when you have to be." He touched her cheek. "But in a nice, soft way."

Toni took his hand from her face and pressed it against her lips. "I love you, Abe Matthews."

"I love you too."

Pulling his hand away slowly, he turned the key in the ignition. "We'd better get this defroster going before the windows get fogged up. Ready to go eat?"

"Absolutely."

As he steered the car away from the curb, he said, "I assume things went well with Melissa yesterday."

"It was wonderful. One of the nicest days we've spent together in several months."

"I'm not surprised. When I took you home on Friday afternoon and filled everyone in on what had happened, Melissa was almost hysterical when she realized you could have been killed."

Toni nodded. "She said she'd had quite an emotional day on Friday, even before you brought me home. Apparently she and Brad made up earlier that afternoon. In fact, he'd left just before you and I arrived."

"I know. I was there with April when Melissa called and said she was with him. We were both pretty surprised. I even told April I wondered what you'd think of the two of them making up."

"After talking with Melissa yesterday, I feel very good about it. I think Melissa's got her emotions sorted out again, and she and Brad seem to be back to the big brother–little sister relationship they enjoyed for so many years."

"That's great." Abe glanced over at her. "I mean that, sweetheart. I'm glad they worked it all out."

"Things do seem to be coming together at last, don't they? I'm especially glad that Melissa is doing better before she has to give her testimony this week. Bruce Jensen's trial has been a terrible strain on her, especially with everything else that's happened in the past months." She paused. "You know, I went to see Tom after church today. I was telling Melissa yesterday that I was planning to visit him, and she told me that he'd written a letter to Carrie."

"Really? What sort of letter?"

"It was a response to the two letters she'd written to him, thanking her for telling him about God's love. Seems Carrie's dreams of becoming a missionary are already coming true because the things she said got him thinking, and when the chaplain visited him, Tom prayed with him to receive Jesus as his Savior."

Abe braked at a stop sign and turned to her before driving on. "Toni, that's wonderful. I can only imagine what that must have meant to Carrie."

Toni nodded. "Yes, and it was wonderful to see Tom smiling today — I think that's only the second time I've ever seen a smile on his face. The first was in his baby picture on the wall at the Blevinses' home. So many lost years in between . . ."

Even as they continued down the road, Abe reached over and laid his hand on Toni's. "Don't let yourself get caught up thinking about that. We can't change the past. No one can. We can only change the future — if we're willing."

"You're right," Toni agreed, wrapping her fingers around Abe's. "So let's talk about our future — our wedding, to be precise. Just how soon can we finalize this thing and make it permanent? I'm ready and willing when you are. You name the date and I'll be there."

Even in the muted light of the car's interior, Toni could see the smile spread across Abe's face, and she knew it wouldn't be long before they were standing in front of the altar together. This time Abe didn't wait for a stop sign. He pulled over to the curb and then turned and gave her a kiss that blocked out everything except the joy of being in the arms of the man who would very soon be her husband.

Sophie was horrified. She'd had the dream about holding Abe and Toni's firstborn and calling him "little lamb of God" three times. That wasn't the worst of it though. The dream about the baby had no sooner ceased to confuse her than a new one had taken its place, and just last night she'd had it for the third time. This dream, however, did more than confuse her; it threatened to uproot everything she'd ever been taught and believed in her entire life.

In the dream she was sitting at her dining room table, ready to begin the traditional Seder meal that preceded Passover. Abe was there, as was Toni, and — once again — the baby. Only this time, Sophie wasn't holding the child. Instead she was staring at the empty chair — the one reserved for Elijah the prophet, who would one day come to herald the arrival of the long-awaited Messiah. Then she heard a knock at the front door. Her heart had raced, even in her dream, as she'd hurried to answer it, fully expecting to see Elijah himself standing there. Instead she saw a bruised, beaten man, mutilated almost beyond recognition, reaching out to her with bloody hands. Yet, even in his wounded condition, she'd somehow recognized him. It was Jesus — Yeshua, as Abe called him — the supposed Son of the Christian God.

Sophie had recoiled in horror, but before she could slam the door in the man's face, she'd heard those now familiar words echoing inside her — *Lamb of God, Lamb of God* — and she'd begun to weep, as if in mourning for a lost loved one. She was still crying when she woke up. That had been several hours earlier, yet the tears still threatened to overwhelm her. What did it all mean? Was *Adonai* trying to tell her something? If so, why would he use a figure from a pagan religion to do so? Yet, though she didn't want to admit it, even to herself, her heart had been drawn to this Jesus, so much so that even the thought of him brought a fresh threat of tears.

No, she thought. *I can't allow myself to give in to these feelings. It's just a dream, nothing more.* But Sophie was no stranger to the teaching of the *Tanakh* about God's speaking to people through dreams — particularly

417

when the dreams were repeated three times. Furthermore, she still remembered the strange sense of nostalgia she'd felt when lighting the candles at Hanukkah — especially the tall *shamash* or "servant" candle in the middle of the menorah, the one that bent down to share its light with the others. Was there a deeper connection between the message of Hanukkah and the Passover lamb that she hadn't recognized before? If so, what did it possibly have to do with *Avraham* and his defection to Christianity?

Confused, Sophie raised her hands to the heavens and prayed fervently that with the coming of the Passover season God would clarify his message to her heart.

Saturday morning, March 20, the weekend preceding Easter and Passover, dawned clear and sunny. The church had been the scene of bustling activity since long before noon; but now, at last, the planning and preparations were over, and the main event was about to get underway.

The afternoon sun lent a fiery glow to the stained-glass windows at the front of the sanctuary as the last of the guests were seated by two of the teenaged boys from the youth group who'd offered to serve as ushers. Toni couldn't help but wonder if at least part of their motive for volunteering was to make some points with Melissa, but that was all right. With limited family members available, even a small wedding required some outside assistance.

From the bride's room off to the side of the back section of the sanctuary, Toni was able to peek through the door she'd opened a crack and observe the guests. Most were neighbors and friends from church or the police force, including Officer Ted Malloy, who'd been such a help to them the day of the shooting, and Tom's lawyer, Harold Barnett. Toni was pleasantly surprised to see Brad's parents in attendance, although she certainly understood why Brad wasn't with them. She'd finally come to accept the fact that she'd have to leave the healing of that situation with God. Then Toni spotted Mr. and Mrs. Bosworth, with Carrie sitting in her wheelchair beside them at the end of one of the pews. It seemed as if just about everyone they'd invited had arrived — except Aunt Sophie.

Toni sighed. She'd so hoped . . .

And then she saw Pastor Michael, who was just about to take his place in front of the congregation, underneath the white canopy — or *chuppah* — where she and Abe would exchange their vows. Getting married underneath a *chuppah* was one of the Jewish traditions they'd decided to incorporate into the ceremony, as it symbolized their coming together as one in the sight of God, under his protection, blessing, and authority.

Right behind Pastor Michael came Abe and his best man. Toni's heartbeat quickened when she saw the outline of Abe's broad shoulders in his black tux, his dark eyes already searching the spot where he expected to see her walking toward him at any moment. However, it was the sight of the best man, ducking his head to fit under the *chuppah,* that brought a smile to Toni's face.

John King towered over Abe and Pastor Michael, his face flushed either from the discomfort of his collar, which he kept trying to loosen, or from self-consciousness at standing in front of the sixty or so people who'd gathered to celebrate this happy event. Toni and Abe had agreed it was only fitting that the man God had used to save their lives should also be involved when they committed the remainder of their lives to each other in marriage. It had taken a little persuasion on Abe's part to get John to agree, but there they were, standing side by side, waiting for the ceremony to begin.

"How do I look?" Melissa asked Toni for what seemed the hundredth time.

Toni turned to look at her sister, her long auburn hair swept up off her neck, the soft green dress bringing out the color in her eyes. "You look beautiful," she said, kissing her cheek carefully so as not to smear their makeup. Toni smiled, thinking of how her teenaged sister had matured in the recent weeks and months. Not only was Melissa dealing with her father's death, but she'd also worked through her guilt over Carrie's paralysis and her confused feelings for Brad. Most amazing of all, she'd even found the courage to write a letter of forgiveness to Bruce Jensen, who'd been sentenced to prison for the rest of his life. "Trust me," Toni said. "Everyone will be so busy looking at you, they won't even notice me walking down the aisle."

Melissa laughed. "No way. You're the prettiest bride I've ever seen. I know Abe will think so, too, as soon as he sees you. . . ."

Her voice trailed off as they heard the music that signaled it was time for Melissa to make her appearance. For lack of a flower girl, she'd also carry a basket of rose petals to scatter along the way. "Here I go," she said, her eyes sparkling with excitement as she opened the door and stepped outside.

"And how about you, my dear?" April asked, as she walked beside the bride and took her by the arm. "Are you ready?"

Toni smiled at the woman who'd become so much a part of her life over the last year that she'd asked her to do the honor of giving her away. April looked lovely, wearing a pale blue dress with lace trim and glowing with obvious joy.

"I'm ready," Toni answered. "Very, very ready."

The first strains of the wedding march reached them then, and they smiled at each other, took a deep breath, and began the last walk Toni would take as a single woman. The closer they drew to Abe, the more her heart pounded in response to the smile that lit up his face. She was so grateful to have April walking beside her, and yet her heart yearned for her father's presence on this special occasion. She was thinking a lot about her mother, too, as she made her way down the aisle in the white silk gown her mother had worn the day she married Toni's father. If only they were here. . . .

I am your Father . . . and I am here.

The silent voice brought a smile to Toni's lips, as April, in response to the pastor's question, transferred Toni's hand from her arm to Abe's. Then she was standing beside him under the *chuppah,* ready to take their vows.

As a hush fell over the congregation, the sound of the back door creaking open caught everyone's attention. Reflexively, Abe and Toni turned to identify the late-comer, as did many of the guests. It was Aunt Sophie, already dabbing at tears with a white handkerchief and trying — unsuccessfully — to make her way to a seat without being noticed. Toni felt Abe squeeze her hand, and they turned back toward the pastor, who then welcomed and thanked everyone for coming to share in this holy and wondrous occasion. When he invited them all to join him in an opening prayer of blessing, Abe and Toni, their hands clasped together, bowed their heads.

"We welcome you, Lord," Pastor Michael said, "to this most sacred ceremony, made holy by your presence and by your institution of the lifelong covenant of marriage. Together we celebrate the love that has brought us here today, and we thank you for the price you paid when you sent your Son, Jesus, the Lamb of God who takes away the sins of the world, so that we, too, might experience that love and have eternal life. For your love, God, is indeed the greatest love of all. We can do nothing to earn it, but we gladly receive it now, and we thank you and bless you for giving us such an awesome gift. May that love rest upon us today, and especially upon this young couple who stands before you at this moment, about to pledge their lives and their love to each other — and to you — for all eternity. In the name of Jesus we ask it. Amen."

Already Toni was fighting tears, wondering how long she'd be able to hold them back before they spilled over and smudged her mascara. Still so many questions about the future. . . . Abe was back on active duty with the police department, and she was still subbing for the school district. Yet they were both sensing a growing desire to keep the detective agency open. It was a decision they would have to make soon, she knew, but not before they'd had a chance to get away for a two-week honeymoon in Hawaii. She smiled to herself at the thought of the warm, sunny beaches and the soft, romantic nights.

As Toni turned toward her beloved and looked up into his handsome face, the thought of all the pain and loss they'd endured to get to where they were today came flooding back. However, she knew, even as she gazed into Abe's eyes, that she'd do it all again if need be. For she'd learned, through it all, that there was no price too great to pay for love — and she knew Abe felt exactly the same way.

I am your Father. . . .

Yes, she answered silently. *You are. And I am your grateful daughter.*

ABOUT THE AUTHOR

Kathi Mills-Macias is an award-winning writer whose love of the written word was birthed as a young child when she was quite ill and often unable to attend school or participate in normal childhood activities. As a result, she became an avid reader and developed a passion for books that continued on, long after her health improved.

At the age of eight, Kathi wrote a short shory for a school assignment. The teacher liked the story so much that it was turned into a play and performed at a PTA meeting. From that point on, Kathi had no career aspirations other than becoming a published author. In fact, her husband and high school sweetheart, Al, remembers the day he and Kathi were walking home from school and she announced to him that she would someday be a writer.

Although Kathi's career was sidetraked for a time when she became a wife and mother almost immediately after graduating from high school, she continued to pursue her dream, publishing poetry, articles, and short shories, as well as writing for newspapers and editing church newsletters. She finally had her first book published in 1989 — twenty-three years after her high school graduation.

A mother and grandmother, Kathi now lives in Lemon Grove, California, with her husband, Al, and her mother, Mary.